# DEEP ROOTS

## THE DEEP SERIES - BOOK THREE

# NICK SULLIVAN

Cover design by Shayne Rutherford of Wicked Good Book Covers
Cover photo of the New River near Lamanai by Duarte Dellarole/Shutterstock.com
Copy editing by Marsha Zinberg of The Write Touch
Proofreading by Gretchen Tannert Douglas and Forest Olivier
Interior Design and Typesetting by Colleen Sheehan of Ampersand Book Interiors
Original map of Belize by Rainer Lesniewski/Shutterstock.com
Original map of Caye Caulker by Kristie Dale Sanders

ISBN: 978-0-9978132-5-8

Published by Wild Yonder Press
www.WildYonderPress.com

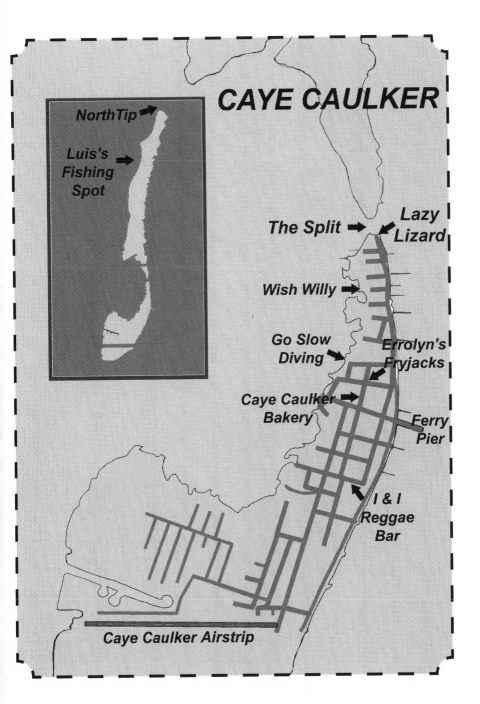

# CAYE CAULKER

NorthTip

Luis's Fishing Spot

The Split → ← Lazy Lizard

Wish Willy →

Go Slow Diving →

Errolyn's Fryjacks

Caye Caulker Bakery →

← Ferry Pier

I & I Reggae Bar

Caye Caulker Airstrip

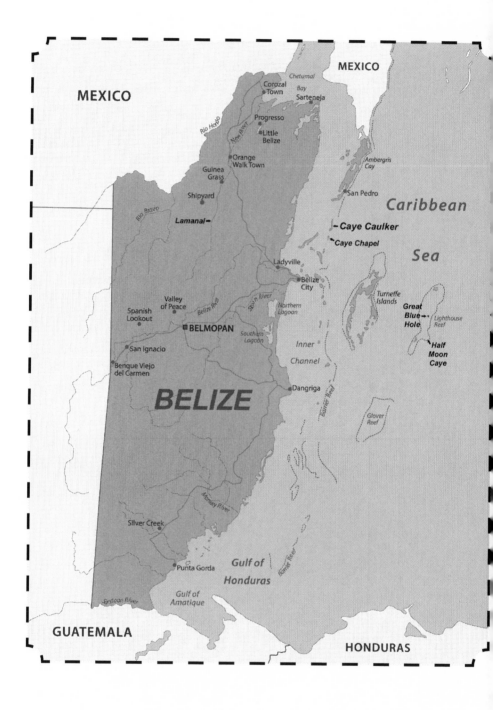

*To the memory of Clive Cussler:*
*Ocean–based action adventure*
*owes the world to you.*

*Belizean Creole Proverb:*

*"When trouble ketch yuh, pickney shut fit yuh."*
*(When trouble catches you, you*
*will fit into a child's shirt.)*

*Meaning:*
*When you find yourself in trouble, you will*
*try to get out of it in impossible ways.*

"Ohmigod... is that...?"

"Yeah."

The small boat coasted to a stop, the port bow gently thumping against a cluster of mangrove roots. Ahead, an object floated facedown. A body. And it had company.

Emily Durand leaned over the bow, lifting her sunglasses to squint at the shapes on the surface of the water ten yards ahead. "And... is that...?"

"A crocodile... yeah..." Boone Fischer hefted the boat hook they'd been using to gaff trash out of the water and stepped over the bags of garbage in the bilge.

"Dat's a big 'un," their skipper said, his voice low with reverent admiration. "Dey don't usually get like dat, with all da boat strikes and poaching." Ras Brook pushed a cluster of dreadlocks aside while gently urging his little boat around the exposed mangrove roots with short pulses from the outboard.

Boone moved to the bow alongside Emily and looked at the body floating against the roots. A diver, from the looks of it. If the tank on its back wasn't clue enough, one of the feet still had a fin on it. Its counterpart may once have had a fin, but that limb was currently in the toothy maw of an American Crocodile. An impressive specimen, this one appeared to be over twelve feet in length. Belize had two species of crocs, and Boone had seen a few juveniles and young adults on the lagoon side of Caye Caulker, but up here on the undeveloped north side, they must grow them large. The crocodile adjusted its toothy grip and spun into a death roll. The pop of a leg joint was audible across the ten yards.

"Crikey Moses..." Emily hissed and turned away, looking quite pale.

Boone placed a hand on her shoulder and gently tightened his long fingers on the lime-green spandex of her rash guard. "Ras!" he shouted. "Bring us in close."

The Belizean sucked his teeth. "Whoever dey were, dey ain't feelin' nut'ing now, Boone."

"Ras!"

"Don't want da croc swamping me boat, hear?"

"We'll be fine," Boone said, hoping his confidence was warranted. Ras Brook's vessel was a shallow fisherman's boat with a single outboard, but she seemed fairly stable. He eyed the large crocodile as they coasted closer. After a moment's thought, he dropped the plastic hook and grabbed his scuba gear, rapidly detaching the tank from his regulator and BCD vest.

Emily watched him for only an instant before figuring out what he was doing. She snatched up the boat hook Boone had dropped and settled in to the right of the bow, snugging her petite frame against the gunwale. "Go for the eyes, yeah?"

8

"That's the plan," Boone said, moving alongside her with the aluminum tank in his hands. For the past month they'd been volunteering for a weekly mangrove cleanup. After the first afternoon, Boone had started bringing a scuba rig aboard in case they spotted any miscellaneous trash on the bottom.

"All right Booney... you blast, I'll hook." Emily leaned forward.

"Boone, keep yo empress back, hear? She be a morsel to dat t'ing!"

"Ras, I'm right here, y'know," Emily said with a tinge of annoyance in her voice. Then she looked back over her shoulder, the smirk on her lips bringing an impish dimple to the surface. "Did you just call me royalty?"

Ras flashed a brilliant smile. "Oh, you mean 'empress'?" He pulsed the motor a couple more times, gently sending the boat toward corpse and croc. "It's how we Rastafari say 'girlfriend.'"

"I like it," Emily mused. She returned her attention to the water ahead of the bow, knuckles white on the shaft of the boat hook, bracing herself as the boat glided toward the scene of carnage. She let out a shaky breath. "Boone, your empress commands you to be ready." The levity of her statement was undercut by a tremor in her voice.

"Your Majesty..." Boone said absently, pressing the sole of a bare foot onto the bow and hefting the pressurized tank. The remaining inches of distance were eaten up as the crocodile completed its roll, gulping down a chunk it had torn loose. Boone leaned forward, his long arms extending the top of the tank toward the reptile. With a quick twist of the valve knob, Boone released a blast of pressurized air into the left eye of the crocodile. Startled, it whipped its head away from the unexpected stimulus.

"Brilliant!" Emily shouted, thrusting the hook forward and snagging an edge of the BCD vest, quickly pulling the body against the side of the boat.

Boone closed the tank and dropped it on top of the bags of trash. Leaning over the gunwale, he grasped the base of the valve at the top of the corpse's scuba tank. Lean muscles cording, he lifted the body out of the water and partway into the boat. The body was male, a dive mask still secured to the face. The small boat wobbled in the water as Boone struggled to get a better grip on the man's gear.

The crocodile turned, darting forward with a slash of the tail. Its charge was suddenly arrested by a sharp whack on the tip of its nose.

"Bad croc!" Em shouted, whipping the boat hook against the tip of the croc's toothy snout a second time as Boone hauled the body the rest of the way into the boat. Disgruntled, the croc submerged, its silhouette moving through the shallow water into the mangroves.

While Ras Brook made a call to the Caye Caulker police on his cell, Boone removed the BCD and tank from the man's body.

"He's dead, yeah?" Emily said softly.

"Very." Boone replied, gently rolling the corpse faceup. The man's face was deathly pale but didn't show any signs of bloating. Boone figured he couldn't have been dead that long. *On the other hand, everything I know about forensics comes from television,* he thought. Glancing at the leg where the croc had torn loose a patch of flesh, he noted that the wound was oozing but that there wasn't a great deal of bleeding. Then something else caught his eye. He frowned. "No weight belt."

"Probably came loose when that crocodile starting chomping," Emily suggested.

"Babylon say to bring da body up to San Pedro," Ras interrupted. He settled in at the outboard and spun the boat around to the north.

Boone had heard some in the Rastafarian community on Caye Caulker refer to the police as "Babylon" and took the slang in stride. He wasn't surprised by the request—the little island had seen a population boom in recent years, but that "boom" had only brought the population up to about 2,000 souls. Popular with backpackers—and once a stop for hippies on the "Gringo Trail" in the 70s—Caye Caulker was still one of the quietest locations in Belize, her motto being "Go Slow." Her police force was quite small, and many of her policing needs were handled on the larger island to the north, Ambergris Caye—specifically the police station in that island's primary town of San Pedro.

"At least they're not asking us to go down to Belize City," Boone shouted, as he and Emily settled into the bottom of the boat for the crossing. The water taxi ferry to Ambergris normally took half an hour, but the mangroves where they'd been working, on the tip of the largely uninhabited northern half of Caye Caulker, were only nine miles away from San Pedro's ferry terminal. Besides, Ras wasn't going to make this a leisurely cruise. The boat's bow rose as the outboard launched the boat across the turquoise waters.

Emily leaned in to Boone's ear. "What's a diver doing up in the mangroves?" she asked above the roar of the outboard. "There aren't any reefs around here."

"Diving with the manatees, maybe? Supposed to just snorkel with them, but... who knows?"

"I haven't heard of any divers going missing, have you?"

"No," Boone replied. "Ras... you?"

"No, mon," their skipper shouted from alongside the engine. "Been quiet."

Boone and Emily had been in Belize for nearly eight months and in that time they'd gotten to know many of the other dive ops. If a diver had gone missing, they'd have heard. And not just from the Caulker dive ops—they would have learned of any incidents on Ambergris too, because they worked for Go Slow Dives. Unique among the offshore dive ops, Go Slow had a shop in San Pedro *and* one on the lagoon side of Caye Caulker.

"No dive shop markings on his tank," Boone remarked, frowning. It would be unusual for a diver to have his own tank on this remote island, particularly with the weight allowances on the little puddle jumpers that serviced the small, sandy airstrip on the southern tip. "He's got a wrist-mounted dive light." He patted the side-pockets of the man's buoyancy compensator. "Feels like a spare in there, too."

Ahead, the island of Ambergris Caye came into view. Her southern coast was mostly mangrove, a mirror to Caye Caulker's northern half. Beyond, the town of San Pedro was visible. While most of Caye Caulker's single mile of inhabited streets was composed of one and two-story buildings, with a few taller ones popping up in recent years, very few were over three stories in height. San Pedro, on the other hand, was much more developed. Immortalized in song by Madonna, "La Isla Bonita" was still laid-back compared to Mexican tourist destinations like Cancun or Cozumel to the north, but there was quite a bit more bustle on Ambergris Caye compared to her smaller sister caye to the south.

A year ago, Boone and Emily had been working 1,600 miles away on the mountainous island of Saba, but the arrival of Hurricane Irma had ended their jobs at the fledgling dive op they'd been working for. Fortunately, a Dutch divemaster they'd befriended in Saba knew a former schoolmate who was divemastering in Belize. She had shared Go Slow Diving's plans to expand from their little shop in Caye Caulker. The owner, a Caulker native named Ignacio, was looking to open a branch in San Pedro, building a new staff from the ground up. He'd quickly snatched Boone and Emily up. The young couple soon learned that the diving here was spectacular: the reef system bordering Belize was part of the second largest barrier reef in the world, stretching from Cozumel in the north all the way to the Bay Islands of Honduras to the southeast.

Ras slowed the boat as they neared San Pedro, due to its heavier boat traffic. "Dey say to bring da body to da pier by dat new hotel construction south of Ramon's—don' want to scare da tourists."

"Understandable," Emily said, peeling a trash bag off a roll they kept for the cleanup.

Boone saw what she was planning and stripped several weights from his weight belt, helping her to cover the corpse's face with the flattened garbage bag and securing the corners to keep it from flying off into the sea. Satisfied, he raised his eyes to the horizon.

"Weird..." Emily said absently. "Such a beautiful day. Sun shining in a cloudless, blue sky... turquoise water sparkling. It's paradise... and we've got a dead body next to us."

Boone didn't reply. Something was scratching at the back of his brain, like a dog wanting to be let in from the yard. He looked down at the black plastic. *Something... what was it...?*

"Boone?"

Boone stared at the shape under the improvised shroud. After a moment, he removed the two weights on either side of the deceased man's head, folding back the trash bag. The face was covered in muck and leaves from the mangroves. "Em, would you get me my water bottle?"

Emily dug in his gear bag and handed him the insulated, stainless-steel bottle, watching him closely. "What is it?"

Boone unscrewed the top. "Don't know, I just…" He splashed water on the face, rinsing it off. Leaves, sand, and silt sluiced away. The dive mask was askew, and Boone gently shifted it down a quarter inch.

"Oh my God…" Emily murmured.

"Well… now we know the cause of death probably wasn't drowning."

Above the mask, centered neatly over the man's eyebrows, was a bullet hole.

**2**

"There's a police boat tied up," Boone said as they neared the location where they'd been asked to dock. "Fair amount of police on the pier."

"Guess I have to cancel me date tonight," Ras lamented with a sigh.

"What, with *your* empress?" Emily asked, tipping her ever-present sunglasses down on the tip of her turned-up nose. "Now, would this be empress #1, empress #2, or..."

Ras laughed. "Not put a crown on any one of dem as yet, ya tricksy gyul."

Emily laughed, but her mirth abruptly died as she remembered the body at her feet. Blowing out a breath, she gathered up the stern line while Boone moved to the bow. In moments they were alongside the pier. It was intended for bigger boats, but Boone stepped up, his tall frame and long limbs bridging the gap easily. Emily remained behind and tossed the stern line to Boone once he had affixed the bow. Ras killed the engine.

"Ras Brook," an older man in a crisp, khaki uniform called down. Under his arm he had some sort of baton. "You find the body?"

"Yes suh, Superintendent. North tip of Caulker, in da mangroves. 'Boonemily' and I were doing cleanup for da Conservation Society."

Boone reached down and grabbed hold of Emily's hand. She placed a bare foot on the side of a column and hopped as he lifted. With practiced ease, Boone lofted her tiny frame onto the pier beside him. Two officers lowered themselves down into the boat to begin the process of bringing the body up. Now that Boone was alongside the superintendent, he could see that the baton was actually a military swagger stick. He didn't think he'd actually seen one of those outside of old war movies or *Monty Python*.

"You two were with Ras?" the superintendent asked.

"Yes, sir. Name's Boone Fischer… and this is Emily Durand. We work for Go Slow Diving."

"Oh yes, Ignacio's outfit. He's a good man, I know his family. I am Superintendent Flores. Do you have any idea who this person was?"

"No, sir," Boone replied. "The body is male. There's a small bullet hole in the forehead above the mask. I didn't notice any damage to the back of the head when we brought him up, but…"

One of the men below overheard this and lifted the makeshift shroud from the body. "Looks like a .22 caliber. Those don't always go through."

"Bring him up," ordered the superintendent. "We need to take him to Belize City. And I must ask you three to go, too—we'll need statements."

An audible groan rose from the boat.

"Don't worry, Ras… we'll bring you back on the last Tropic Air flight," Flores assured him. "Your boat will be safe here until then."

As the officers brought the body up, Boone dropped down to grab their dry bags and hand them up to Emily. "Give Ignacio a call, let him know we won't be around to close up shop."

"Right-o," Em responded, digging her phone out and placing the call. "Iggy… so… spot of bother popped up, yeah?"

Boone was about to haul himself back up to the pier when a thump sounded from the bottom of the boat. The police had just lifted the deceased man's scuba rig up to the pier and Boone noticed one of the Velcro side pockets on the BCD was partly open, a hefty dive light poking out. He let go of the pier and dropped back into the boat, his eyes scanning the bags of trash at the bottom.

*Something fell out of that pocket when they lifted the gear… dive light probably pushed it out.*

Boone's eyes fell upon a flash of green, peeping out from a narrow rivulet of blood. *There you are,* he thought, reaching between two of the trash bags to retrieve the object and hold it up to the late afternoon sun. It looked like a little stone statue, a figure reclining with a tiny bowl on its belly, its head sporting a headdress and its face turned ninety degrees to the side. It was exquisitely carved, and the eye sockets were quite deep, with a single small stone imbedded in one orbit. He grabbed his water bottle and rinsed the small amount of blood that clung to it.

"That looks like jade." Emily was crouched on the pier, peering down at the tiny sculpture.

"The shape… it looks familiar," Boone said.

"Hold it up, yeah?" Em leaned over from the pier and took several photos on her smartphone as Boone held it up to her.

"Come on, we're ready to go!" the superintendent shouted from above, rapping the side of the police boat with his swagger stick.

Boone pocketed the little item in his swim trunks and pulled himself up onto the pier, joining Ras and Emily aboard the small police patrol craft. The superintendent gave last minute instructions to his officers before stepping into the boat alongside their grisly cargo.

——◆ ◆ ◆——

The trip from Ambergris Caye to the mainland was a long one, even at the twenty knots the police skipper managed to coax out of the vessel. An hour and a half later they reached the mouth of Haulover Creek and the docks of Belize City. Although the largest city in Belize, it was no longer the capital, that distinction going to the little town of Belmopan in the interior. After Hurricane Hattie had nearly destroyed Belize City in 1961, a decision was made to shift the government away from the coast. Nevertheless, much of the police infrastructure remained in Belize City—in no small part to deal with rampant gang activity in the southern neighborhoods of the city.

Arriving at the dock, the local police began offloading the body and its scuba gear, triggering Boone's memory.

"Superintendent Flores," he said, retrieving the green statue from his trunks. "This fell out of the buoyancy vest when your men lifted it out of the boat back on San Pedro."

Flores tucked his swagger stick under his arm and took the object, turning it over in his hands. "This looks Mayan. I took my wife to Chichén Itzá in Mexico last year and there is a statue like this in one of the temples there, I think. Where did he get it?"

Boone noticed a young policeman looking intently at the little artifact, before turning away to speak to another officer. Boone returned his attention to the superintendent. "Truthfully… I'm guessing he found it while diving. No one would put a valuable object into a BCD pocket and then jump into the water."

"Assuming it *is* valuable," Emily said. "It might just be a souvenir."

Flores grunted. "I've not seen any of these in the San Pedro gift shops… but you might be right. Maybe it came from Chetumal, the Mexican city across the border. I'll have one of my men run it over to the Museum of Belize."

The next hour was filled with questions, paperwork, and sub-standard coffee. Just before sundown, the Belize City police department drove Emily, Boone, and Ras to the Municipal Airport and put them aboard a Tropic Air puddle jumper bound for San Pedro.

"Pity you missed da last flight to Caye Caulker, but I can run ya back on my boat," Ras said, as he settled into his seat at the back of the little plane.

"Gonna be dark," Em commented, as she made her way toward the front of the cabin.

"Won't be da first time I went across in da dark," Ras assured her. "I got a mean spotlight, no worries."

Emily settled into a window seat, Boone taking the aisle beside her. "We could stay over, Boone. We've got that Blue Hole/Lighthouse Reef charter in the morning and it'll be Ignacio's big Ambergris boat. Divers from both islands on it. Could hitch a ride down in the morning, grab our stuff…"

Boone shook his head. "Tomorrow's dive trip is an overnighter… I don't want us to have to rush and hold everybody up while we gather our gear. They're gonna want the Caulker stop to be a grab 'n go." Boone turned in his seat and called out over the idling engines, "Ras, you going back anyway?"

"Ya, mon."

"All right, then," Emily said as the turboprops rose to a buzzing roar. "I admit, I'm pretty knackered. Be good to get a nice long kip in our own bed, yeah?"

Boone smiled down at Emily. "Kip means sleep, right? It doesn't have any other hidden connotations?"

Emily's eyebrows rose from behind her lime-green sunglasses. "Why, Mr. Fischer... whatever could you be insinuating?" She bit her lower lip, stifling a grin.

Boone plucked the sunglasses from her face and tucked them into the neckline of the dive shop T-shirt she'd changed into. "It's sundown... I get to see your eyes now."

Emily smiled and leaned against the window. "Not if I kip," she said, closing her eyes with a smirk on her lips. Outside the window, the runway began to blur as the Tropic Air flight took off for the fifteen-minute hop.

"Excuse me," came a voice from across the aisle. "I didn't mean to eavesdrop, but I assume from your conversation that you work for a dive shop?"

"Yes. Go Slow Diving in Caye Caulker."

"Ah yes, named for the motto there," the man said. He had a light accent and looked to be of Mestizo heritage, the Spanish/Mayan blend being a common ethnic group in Belize. All the same, he carried none of the Creole or Caribbean sound that colored the speech of many Belizeans.

Boone smiled and held out a hand. "Boone Fischer."

The man shook it. "Manuel Rojas. You are American?"

"Mostly. Got some Dutch hiding in there on my dad's side. I'm going out on a limb that you're not from Belize, are you?"

"No, no... Mexico City. But I've been in Belize for several years."

Boone tossed a thumb over his shoulder. "Well, sleeping beauty here is—"

"Emily Durand," Em said quickly, popping up from her counterfeit nap and reaching across Boone. "Very pleased to make your acquaintance, Mr. Rojas."

"Doctor, actually." He smiled. "You are… Australian?"

Boone snickered quietly and Emily smacked his arm. "What, the accent? Um, no, just a Southie from London."

"My apologies," Manuel said.

"She gets that a lot," Boone assured him. "So, what do you do in Belize, Dr. Rojas?"

"I'm an archaeologist, specializing in Mayan ruins. I have been on assignment from The National Museum of Anthropology in Mexico City, and am currently working at the Marco Gonzalez site on the southern tip of Ambergris Caye."

"Is that the Mayan site in the mangroves?" Boone asked.

"Yes, although the site itself is somewhat higher than sea level. Not a temple site like the famous tourist sites on the mainland; this one was probably a trading settlement."

"Wait… Em…?"

"Way ahead of ya, Booney-boy," Em said, already retrieving her phone and opening the photos. She handed it to Boone, who passed it to Manuel.

"Ever find anything like that?" Boone asked.

"Ah… a chacmool."

"Chac-who-za-what?" Emily asked.

"Chacmool… from the Mayan words for 'thundering paw.' There is a famous one at the Chichén Itzá site in the Yucatán. It was found under the Platform of Eagles and Jaguars. This reclining figure with the bowl on its chest, resting on its elbows, knees raised, facing to the side… it is actually quite common in Mesoamerican areas. Chacmools have been found from Aztec sites in Mexico in the north, to Mayan and pre-Mayan sites as far south as El Salvador and Costa Rica."

"Emily thought it might be made of jade," Boone remarked.

Manuel humored them with a patient smile. "Possible, but not likely. Actual chacmools are quite large, usually made of various types of stone. A little one like this, it's almost certainly a souvenir. Probably white onyx, dyed green. The stone in this one eye is probably glass." He zoomed in on the image. "Although I must say, the detail is surprisingly good. Where did you find this?"

Emily started to speak but stopped and looked at Boone.

"Snorkeling in the mangroves on the north tip of Caye Caulker," he supplied.

"Ah, well… definitely a souvenir." He handed the phone back. "Probably dropped by a tourist on a tour boat. They do snorkeling tours with manatees up there, do they not?"

"Yeah," Boone said. "We had quite a few this year."

"I would like to do that sometime… but also, I want to learn to dive. I've been here for some time and it seems heresy not to enjoy the beauty of the reef. This is why I asked if you worked for a dive shop. Do you teach?"

"Sure. Emily and I teach courses on Caye Caulker, but we could set you up. Our dive shop has a branch in Ambergris."

"Excellent," Manuel said, fishing a card from his wallet. "I am staying at the Spindrift Hotel in downtown San Pedro. My email is on there, if you'd be so kind as to send me a list of what I need to get started."

"You got it," Boone said. The plane began its descent. "We'll be out at sea for a couple days, but I'll be sure to drop you a line."

———— ✦ • ✦ ————

A quick golf cart taxi ride later, Boone and Emily were back on the water as Ras Brook motored slowly into the moonlit night. His boat had a pair of battery-operated running lights affixed to the bow and he hefted a pistol-grip spotlight from a storage box beside the outboard. "Won't need dis just yet, with da lights from Pedro, but we might want it for da crossing. Although…" He pointed skyward. "Jah has provided us wit' his own spotlight."

Above, the waxing moon was nearing full, shining down in a pearlescent road across the water ahead. As they left the glow of San Pedro, the Milky Way bloomed in the sky all around. The water itself offered up its own illumination as tiny, bioluminescent organisms glowed in the boat's wake.

Emily let out a wordless sound, mingling awe and contentment.

Ras laughed. "Ya got dat right, sistuh. Everyt'ing irie dis night."

———— ✦ • ✦ ————

The pounding music subsided as the man took his phone away from the din of the night club, and asked the caller to repeat what he'd just said.

"I said they found the body. That rookie in the Belize City police said they just brought it in by boat. The triple-weighted belt must have come loose. Two divemasters and a guide were cleaning trash in the mangroves and called it in. And get this— one of them had another of those jade statues."

"How did you miss it?"

"I dunno. I thought the two he gave us were it. Musta been stuck in his gear somewhere."

The man unceremoniously ended the call and viciously kicked the wheel of a golf cart parked alongside the club. Taking a calming breath, he pushed the rage aside and did what he always did— sought opportunity in adversity. After a moment, he raised the phone and sent a text to the number that had just called him.

*The divemasters. What were their names?*

"Rise and shine, my empress."

"Sod off, peasant."

Boone laughed, silencing the alarm on his cell phone and pulling on a pair of shorts.

Emily groaned and rose from the bed, shoving Boone aside on her way to the bathroom, her bare feet slapping softly on the tile. "Quit looking at my ass," she said through a yawn, not even glancing back.

"Busted," Boone said with a grin.

"Eh... you're only human," Emily countered, turning her nude form to face him before closing the door in slow motion, her smile growing by the minute.

Boone blew out a breath of air and adjusted his shorts before heading to the kitchen. Grabbing a coffee pot, he filled it from the water cooler. Much of the fresh water on Caye Caulker was cistern water, just like on Saba... but here it really wasn't a good idea to drink it. Besides, you could get a five-gallon bottle of purified water for just five Belizean dollars, or $2.50 US. He brewed a strong pot of coffee, once again thanking his lucky stars that Emily wasn't a Brit of the tea-sipping persuasion. If anything, she liked her coffee stronger than he did.

"Six in the morning," Em said as she padded into the kitchen. "So much more civilized than the four a.m. days."

"Hey, that's my T-shirt," Boone said.

Emily looked down at the XLT T-shirt: on her four-foot-eleven frame, it hung past her knees. "I couldn't find mine." She spun around and modeled it, showing off the logo on the back: *I Climbed Mount Scenery.* Last year, they had survived a run-in with a psychotic killer atop Saba's highest peak, followed by a harrowing night of record-breaking hurricane winds. When Emily spotted the T-shirts in the Saban gift shop "Everyt'ings," she didn't hesitate to buy a matching pair.

"How about your *I Survived the Saba Landing* shirt, you still have that?" Boone asked, filling a mug for Emily.

"You better believe I still have it—first thing you ever bought me."

"I bought you stuff before that!"

"Drinks don't count."

"Hey, some of those drinks from Captain Don's came with little painted birds and fish, so… *technically*… I bought you works of art."

"Gimme my coffee, you berk."

He handed over the brew and watched as she inhaled the strong aroma, then took a sip and sighed. "Cor, that's good. I think I'll keep you." She walked to the kitchen window, where a line of tiny, wooden animals sat along the sill. "For the record, I cherish your works of art… and the memories attached to them." She touched each colorfully painted carving in turn: a parrot, an angelfish, a sea turtle. "Piña colada… rum runner… margarita."

Boone frowned, pointing at a pink flamingo, the national bird of Bonaire, the island where they'd met. "What about the flamingo?"

Emily gently lifted the bird from the sill. "What, Flamingee?" She raised her eyebrows, an impish look creeping onto her face.

"I don't remember that one."

"No? Well… not surprising. You weren't the only one in Bonaire who bought me drinks." She gave the wooden beak a playful smooch. "Oh Flamingee, you tease… I'm taking you back to the bedroom…" She padded out of the kitchen, throwing a meaningful look over her shoulder.

Boone checked the clock on the stove… made a quick calculation… and followed.

⬩ ⬩ ⬩

Forty minutes later they left their apartment on Middle Street and were greeted by tantalizing aromas wafting from their neighbor, the Caye Caulker Bakery. Unfortunately, it wasn't open yet, so Boone and Emily hustled over to the Go Slow Divers shop on Pasero Street, personal gear in tow. Ignacio was already there, loading rental gear into a golf cart. Since these overnighter charters originated in San Pedro, the tanks would already be aboard the forty-footer that was based over there.

"There you are!" the owner called out. A bit on the heavy side, Ignacio was a native-born Caye Caulkerite, a "Corker". In his mid-fifties, he was also a member of the Village Council, the local equivalent to a city councilman.

"Sorry we're a little late," Emily said.

"No, no, we're fine. The *Leeward to Seaward* hasn't even left San Pedro yet. She'll be at the dock on the reef side just after eight. Emily, can you get the list of our Caulker divers and head over there? I'll follow with the rental gear. Boone, could you run up to Belize Diving Services and borrow some three-pounders? See if they can spare ten. And maybe a few fours and a couple fives. A bunch of our weights went missing the other day. Just go straight to the dock with them."

"Sure," Boone said.

"*Gracias.*"

"*De nada.*" He grabbed a heavy-duty mesh bag. "See you over there, Em."

She snagged his T-shirt as he turned to go. "If you happen to find yourself in the vicinity of the bakery on your way over..."

Boone grinned. "Pineapple Danish, right?"

"And a ham and cheese roll for you... ohmigod, are we in a predictable rut?"

"No one I'd rather be rutting with."

Emily's mouth dropped open in amused shock before snapping back shut. "Okay, that was a good one. Off with you."

Boone headed past the P.A.W. pet sanctuary and turned north. *Missing weights. Weird.* Petty theft wasn't unusual on the island, but old dive weights were an odd thing to take. As Boone walked along the lagoon shoreline, he noted the Belize Diving Services boat was at the dock, ready to be loaded. As one of the most venerable shops on the island, BDS was known to have an excellent stock of gear. Boone himself had bought a few items from them. In fact, he and Emily had taken a break from their own dive instructoring to take a class from Belize Diving Services; specifically, their fifteen-day cave diving course.

Shortly after they'd arrived in Caye Caulker, Boone had been shocked to learn that the tiny island sat atop what might be one of the largest underwater cave systems in the world. The entrance to Giant Cave lay just fifty yards from Belize Diving Services, the narrow squeeze of an entrance frequented by schools of huge tarpon. The cave was only discovered in the 1980s, but after early explorations resulted in several deaths, cave diving largely stopped for quite a while. Then, in 2012, the new owner of Belize Diving Services, a cave diving specialist himself, had begun a series of careful, methodical mapping expeditions and the true scale of the cave system began to unfold.

"Hi, Boone!"

A young woman in a BDS T-shirt was coming around the side of the dive shop. She was a new hire from Florida, and it took Boone a second to remember her name, having only just met her a few days ago.

"Loretta, good to see you! How are you enjoying Belize?"

"I miss the Keys, but hey... I guess I'm still in some Cayes... they just spell it differently." She cocked her head. "Isn't today Go Slow's day for the overnight camping trip?"

"Yeah... I'm headed reefside, but actually, I'm here to 'borrow a cup of sugar,' as my mom would say. Ignacio had a buncha weights go missing and asked me to come by, see if you could spare a few."

"Sure, how many?"

"Ten threes, a few fours, and a couple fives?"

"That's a lotta sugar, but not a problem. Come around back." As Boone followed, Loretta looked back at him. "Hey, you did the cave diving course, right?"

"Yeah," Boone confirmed. He squatted and scooped up several of the rectangular weights, dropping them into the bag with dull clinks. "It was intense."

"I knew some guys back in Florida who did some cave diving. I want to try it, but... well... is it scary?"

Boone looked up at Loretta. "Yep. Exhilarating, too. But make no mistake, it's not something you go into casually."

"Oh, I know. My boss stresses that to everyone."

"Well, listen to him… he's one of the best." He stood and hefted the bag of weights. "You find a place to live yet?"

"No, I'm still at a hostel on Crocodile Street. It's close and it's clean. I just didn't feel the need to rush around, apartment hunting."

Boone smiled. "Goin' slow. You're in the right place for that."

◆ ◆ ◆

After a quick side trip to the bakery, Boone headed for the windward side of the island, passing by white picket fences and numerous little buildings painted in a riot of color. The ever-present signs for Belikin Beer, the national beer of Belize, punctuated every other establishment. Ubiquitous chalkboard menus with the day's offerings stood outside many a door. This journey was not a long one; most of the inhabited part of Caye Caulker was only a thousand feet from the lagoon side to the reef side.

When first arriving in Belize, Boone and Emily had started their work in Go Slow Diving's newer Ambergris Caye dive shop. In practice, each shop's boats would operate out of their respective islands, but for the popular atoll dives, groups from both shops would combine for the lengthy trip to the impressive offshore sites. This was a brilliant ploy of Ignacio's; oftentimes dive shops had to cancel trips due to a lack of divers. The long voyage took a lot of fuel, and half-empty boats would lose money. Having two different islands to fill charters from meant Go Slow rarely had to cancel, even now in the low season.

After a couple of months working out of both shops, Boone and Emily had elected to make their home in Caye Caulker. The little island was quiet, and the overall vibe was so much more relaxed. After the events of the last year, the young couple was more than ready to "go slow" for a while.

Nearing the pier in front of Yuma's, Boone noted the *Leeward to Seaward* from the Ambergris shop was just tying up and Emily was wrangling the divers from Caye Caulker onto the dock. As he approached, Boone held the bakery bag aloft and waved it back and forth. Salvador, the charter skipper, pointed at him from the flybridge. He killed the engines and climbed down to greet Boone, a huge smile on his face.

"That's the *big* bag! No little bakery bag this time, that's the big bag!"

"Sure is," Boone said, setting down the weights with a thunk.

"Oh good, you got the weights," Emily said, turning back to call out: "Everybody who needed some three-pounders, come and get 'em!" She turned back to Boone and nodded a head toward the bakery bag. "Better be a pineapple Danish in there."

"There is... annnnnd..." He opened the bag for Salvador to see. Inside was a veritable sea of blue-frosted donuts.

"Da Blue Holenuts! *Excellente!* You bring enough for everyone?"

"I bought 'em out."

Emily looked at the bag of bright blue donuts, then back at their divers. "Oh boy... umm..." She stepped forward, raising her voice. "So, everybody... remember that the trip to the Blue Hole takes two and a half hours from here and it can be quite choppy, so if you have any Dramamine and haven't taken it yet, take it now, yeah? All right... roll call!"

While Emily starting rattling off names from a clipboard, Boone handed the skipper the pastry bag and stepped across to be ready to help the Caulker divers aboard. "How's *Leeward to Seaward* holding up, Salvador?"

"She's very good! Had a tune-up last week."

"Who do we have with us?"

"Just Augusto. We have twelve divers, so not too bad." Salvador looked around before leaning in. "Hey, I hear you and Emily found a body?"

"Yeah… I'll tell you about it later, okay?"

"Sure, sure…"

"All right, lads 'n ladies," Emily called out. "All the Corker divers are accounted for. Augusto! You got all your Ambergreasies?"

The Belizean divemaster from the San Pedro shop grinned. "All here!"

"Right-o! All aboard for the giant hole in the ocean!" Em called out.

Boone stepped to the gunwale and assisted Emily with gear and divers.

"Excuse me…" One diver, an American woman in her forties handing her gear bag across, addressed Emily. "Just curious… you said 'Corker.' I thought it was Caye 'Caulker,' but I heard a nice, Rastafarian gentlemen say 'Corker' the other day, and… well, it took me long enough to learn the first part is 'Key' not 'Kay'… I just like to say things right."

"Blimey, I know just how you feel!" Em said. "Same thing happened when I came here. Tell you what, I'll tell you all about it during the long boat ride, yeah?"

"Or *I'll* tell you about it, if you can't understand Emily's accent," Boone said, deadpan.

Emily turned to glare at him, but the woman laughed. "Oh, no, don't be silly. One of my neighbors is an Australian, I can understand this young lady just fine." With that, she stepped across into the boat.

Boone snickered and started to say something, but the tip of Emily's index finger pressing against his mouth prevented any speech.

"Don't... say... anything..." Emily muttered, turning to gather up the remaining divers on the pier.

**4**

An hour and a half into the ride, Emily settled in next to the American woman who had asked about "Corker." Her name was Mia, and she and her husband Thomas were sitting in the shade of the flybridge overhead.

"All righty, I promised you an explanation, right? First off, where are you two from, eh? Wait, I'm gonna guess... Minnesota!"

"Close," Thomas said. "Wisconsin."

"That's right next door, yeah?"

"It sure is," Mia said. "And where in Australia are *you* from?"

*Ohmigod, just because I don't sound like the Queen... thank goodness Boone's up top.* But Boone was right... she did get this a lot. Emily smiled broadly. "Actually, I'm from London. South London, specifically. Border of Greenwich and Deptford. We ain't too posh in how we talk, but I like to think we're a bit more 'salt-of-the-earth' than those blokes on the BBC."

"Oh, my goodness, I just assumed...."

"S'alright... I thought *you* were from Minnesota." Emily winked at them—a wasted effort, as her eyes were ensconced behind her lime-green sunglasses. "Anyhoo, 'Caye Caulker.' First, the 'Caye'... some folks say 'key' and some say 'kay'... doesn't matter. Now, that's just a word for a low island, usually a lotta sand, maybe a buncha mangroves. Low-lying, no mountains. Sometimes spelled K-E-Y like in Florida... down here, where there's a lot of Spanish influence, it's C-A-Y-E... in the Bahamas, they drop the 'E' cuz... y'know, I have no idea, not important. Moving on. So... in some old British maps it was Caye 'Corker'. Some said ships would come here to get water from a little fresh-water hole and they'd 'cork' their bottles."

"Oh, well, that makes sense..." Thomas said.

"Hold on a tick, cuz there are also stories that ships would go into the lagoon side and get their bottoms... 'caulked.' See? So... that's where those come from. The official name is Caulker, but some folks like to have a little fun."

"Thank you for the lesson," Mia said.

"My pleasure! Now if you'll excuse me," Emily said, rising and lapsing into an atrocious Australian accent, "I gotta go put some shrimp on the barbie!"

Thomas laughed. "Oh, *you're* a corker!"

Emily beamed. "Nice one, Thomas! Topical wordplay folded into conversation... you Wisconsinites got a lot going for ya besides the cheese, yeah?"

She carefully made her way forward—the dive boat was up on plane and in open ocean, so Emily kept a wide stance as they bounced across the waves. Grabbing her reusable water bottle from the cooler, she took a long drink. As she replaced it, she glanced toward the stern and saw another diver, a young college girl—Hannah if she remembered correctly—leaning against the gunwale and looking a bit green around the gills. Her dive buddy, another young woman, was rubbing her back. The passage was a rough one, and there was always someone who got nauseous. Emily started to go aft but Boone was already stepping down from the flybridge ladder, making his way to the seasick passenger.

*He just knows,* Emily thought. *Sure, maybe he saw the girl looking sick… but dollars to blue donuts, I bet he just felt it.* She moved closer, ready to assist if he needed her.

"Hey… Hannah?" Boone sat down beside the girl. "Feeling a bit queasy?"

Hannah turned a pair of miserable eyes to Boone. She just nodded, looking afraid that any attempt to speak might trigger a bout of vomiting.

"It's okay… we've all been there. Tell you what, I may be able to help." He leaned toward Emily and said, "Ice in a rag," then returned his focus to Hannah.

Emily grabbed a rag she used to clean the whiteboard and filled it with a handful of ice from the cooler. She brought it to Boone, who was mid-sentence, speaking softly.

"…trick a fisherman in Bonaire taught me, okay? But this will take all three of us. Emily, please hand the ice to… Gretchen, is it?"

Hannah's friend nodded, taking the wad of ice from Emily, who stepped back, watching intently. Poor Hannah looked like she was about ready to feed the fishes.

"Okay… Hannah, I want you to pick a point over my shoulder and look at the horizon. Good. Keep your eyes there. Gretchen, hold the ice against Hannah's neck, okay? Don't press it hard or anything, just put some cold back there."

"Like this?" She placed the ice on her friend's neck and Hannah shivered for an instant.

"Perfect. Now…" He took Hannah's arm and turned it palm up, holding it gently in one hand. "This is a little pressure point trick. I'm going to go three finger-widths down from your wrist… and press my thumb tip between the tendons… here." Boone pressed the pad of his thumb into that point on her arm and gently moved it in little circles, massaging the spot. "Keep your eyes on the horizon… and now you've got something else to do… I want you to take slow, deep breaths in, and as you let them out, I want you to count to five in your head before you breathe in again. Okay?"

Hannah nodded and took a deep breath before slowly letting it out.

Emily watched as Boone continued to massage the spot on Hannah's inner forearm. Her friend held the ice to her neck and Emily could just hear Boone say, "Eyes on the horizon," in a soft voice. She watched as Hannah's body visibly relaxed and, while her eyes looked out to sea, Emily saw her eyelids flutter. *He's hypnotizing her. Well… kinda-sorta.*

After several minutes, Boone caught Gretchen's eyes and she removed the ice just as Boone gently laid Hannah's arm on her thigh and released his grip. Hannah blinked, coming out of the trance.

"How do you feel?" Boone asked.

Hannah looked confused for a second. "Good. Really good. How did you do that?"

Boone smiled. "*You* did it. I just helped." He rose from the stern and headed forward to get some water.

Emily grabbed his arm as he passed. "Oh, no, no, no… none of that Obi Wan Yoga Guru shite, how *did* you do that?"

"It's not 'shite.' I gave her a bunch of different things to focus on other than her stomach… the ice, the horizon, the breath, the

38

counting, the circular motion of my thumb. Enough stimuli for her to move past her nausea. Sort of...*forget* the nausea."

"But it looked like you zonked her out or something."

"Well, it was a form of meditation, I guess... and that spot on the arm *is* an actual acupressure point for nausea or dizziness." He took a long drink from his water bottle and tossed it back into the cooler. "Actually... on Saba... didn't Sophie teach you about pressure points when she was giving you Krav Maga lessons?"

Emily nodded, a little smile at the corner of her mouth as she remembered her lessons in the Israeli martial art. "Yeah, she did. Though some of 'em would more likely *make* you vomit than stop you from it. I only had a few days with her before Hurricane Irma, but during the weeks we were helping with the cleanup, she taught me quite a bit."

"Same principle," Boone said.

"Hey, have you found a capoeira sparring partner yet?" Emily had watched Boone practicing alone on the beach a few times since they'd come to Belize. He was a master of the Brazilian martial art, its flashy tumbles and kicks as much a dance as a fighting form.

"No... but I know there's a Brazilian jiu-jitsu dojo in Belize City. At least I can brush up on that."

The boat slowed and Augusto's head appeared at the top of the flybridge, peering down at them. "Almost there. Crossing into the atoll."

"Right, I'm on reef duty," Boone said, stepping onto the gunwale to head around the partially enclosed cabin to the bow. "You start the briefing."

"Right-o." Emily went up the ladder and popped her head into the flybridge. "All you sunbathers, come on down here a sec. Grab a seat while we cross into the lagoon." Several divers who'd been lounging up top headed for the ladder as she dropped back down to the deck, gathering up her dry-erase markers and going to the whiteboard. In bright blue she wrote "The Blue Hole," then drew a big blue circle underneath it. Then, below that she added: "Not to scale."

Peering through the cabin window, she could see Boone at the bow, directing Salvador as the fringing reef of the Lighthouse Reef atoll came into view. The boat angled slightly to starboard, as Salvador followed hand gestures from Boone. Once everyone was below, Emily called up to Salvador and the *Leeward to Seaward* increased speed, aiming for the gap Boone had indicated.

"Do we gear up now?" Hannah asked. Her color was good, and she seemed to be completely recovered from her bout of seasickness.

"No, not yet… but the good news is, we'll be done with all the bouncing and jouncing right about—" Emily held up a finger, pausing as the boat rose over the breakers and glided down into the calm waters beyond. "—now! We're inside the atoll, ladies 'n lads. Welcome to Lighthouse Reef! One of Belize's three offshore atolls… the others being Turneffe and Glover's. Lighthouse Reef is twenty-two miles long, five miles wide… and most of it is a sandy bottom with a depth between six feet and twenty feet. Nice and shallow, crystal clear waters… so, if you like, we can forget about that silly old Blue Hole and just go snorkeling instead, yeah?"

Emily looked around at the bemused and amused reactions. Beside her, a familiar laugh signaled Boone's return. He spun a finger, signaling her to continue as he stepped past her to grab the whiteboard. Emily adopted a contemplative expression, stroking her delicate chin.

"I am sensing that some of you would perhaps prefer that we do the Blue Hole after all... are you sure?" A chorus of affirmatives, and Emily threw up her hands. "Well, all right then!" She turned to the whiteboard, which Boone had affixed to the ladder. He handed her a black marker.

"Now... I told you some of this lagoon is just six feet deep, yeah? So... anyone want to venture a guess how deep *this* is?" She rapped a knuckle on the blue circle on the board.

A youngish teen raised his hand. "Four hundred feet!"

"Very good! Just a little over, in fact..." She wrote "410 feet" inside the circle. "How'd you get so smart?"

"Wikipedia," the boy said proudly. His father laughed and tousled his son's hair.

Emily addressed the group. "The extreme depth is why the hole is such a deep blue, while all the shallow water around it is a lighter turquoise. Actually, later this year, Sir Richard Branson and Jacques Cousteau's grandson, Fabien Cousteau, are supposed to mount an expedition with submarines and sonar—they plan to completely map the Great Blue Hole. Maybe find out if Godzilla's hanging out down there."

"How deep are we going to go?" the teen asked.

"Well, I'm guessing you've got your Advanced Certification?" she asked, her eyes querying the parents. When the father nodded, she continued. "So... you tell me. How deep *can* you go?"

The boy thought a moment. "One hundred thirty feet."

"Again, you amaze me, young sir! Yes! One-thirty is indeed the sport-diving limit for PADI... *but*... guess what? On this dive, we're going to have to cheat. Just a little. Boone, take over while I make a pretty picture." She erased the circle and began a side-on, three-dimensional map of the dive while Boone continued the briefing.

"The Great Blue Hole is the largest marine sinkhole in the world. Not the deepest, but the biggest—a thousand feet across. It used to be a limestone cave, most of it above sea level. The reason we know that? The stalactites that surround the rim. Those can only form above water. At some point, the roof collapsed and the sinkhole filled with sea water. Anyone heard of the cenotes you can dive in Mexico?" As a couple of hands rose, Boone continued. "Same thing... only this one's in the middle of the ocean instead of a jungle. Now, Emily here mentioned 'cheating.'"

As he joined Emily at the whiteboard, she tapped a series of jagged features she'd drawn on the side of the three-dimensional picture. "In order to get under the lip of this overhang of stalactites, we're going to briefly drop to one hundred forty feet," she said. "We are not going to hang out and have a party at one-forty; we are going to transition back up into the stalactites and enjoy the view. Come a bit shallower if the topography allows, yeah?"

"Total bottom time on this dive is twenty-five minutes," Boone said. "This is a *deep* dive, so watch your computers. As you know, our dive op doesn't allow nitrox on this dive due to the dangers of oxygen toxicity at this depth, so you're all on air. Anyone know what nitrogen narcosis is?"

Hannah spoke up. "That's where you get... giggly?"

"It can be. Everyone is different. Some divers can feel euphoria or get light-headed or giddy... some don't get it at all. But at this depth, it may happen. If you feel confused or anxious, don't be alarmed, just signal one of us and do this..." He tilted his fingers by his face a couple of times, as if he were drinking something.

"What does that mean?" Gretchen asked.

"It's a martini," Emily said. "From 'Martini's Law'... bit of a joke name, that. The saying goes that below sixty-six feet, every additional thirty-three feet is like drinking a martini... so this'll be a two-and-a-half martini dive. It's a bit of an oversimplification really, but for some people, getting narced can feel a bit like being drunk."

"Don't worry, you'll be fine," Boone reassured them. "We'll have a close watch on all of you. Emily will be leading the group, I'll be in the middle, and Augusto will be bringing up the rear. We're almost there, so gear up… then we'll go over the exact dive plan."

Ahead, a dark-blue expanse of water came into view.

**5**

"**E**verybody, keep an eye on your buddy and stick close together," Boone called out. "You're supposed to do that on every dive, but for this one you *really* need to do it, okay?" He gestured across the water. "One of the reasons I like these overnight trips… a late start means the other boats are gone! You have the place all to yourselves. Enjoy it."

Emily stepped by him, pulling on her lime-green fins at the swim platform. "All right, pool's open!" She went in first while Boone and Augusto stayed behind to assist the divers.

"Hey, uh… you guys do that shark feedin' thang? Chum the water?" a beefy diver from Texas asked. "I heard some boats do that…"

"No, we don't. Nobody's supposed to do that anymore." *Although several of the ops still do,* Boone thought. *A foolish practice on such a deep dive, where you've already got enough to think about.*

"Aw, shoot."

"There are some big sharks in there, though," Augusto said. "You may see them. I think they still remember they used to get fed, so they may come. Mostly reef sharks, but we get tigers, bulls… even a hammerhead once in a while."

The man's face brightened. "Well, all right, then! I'll keep an eye out!"

"Keep an eye on your computer, too," Boone chided, assisting the man as he stood, noting a camera in an underwater housing held firmly in one hand. "That camera… is it rated for this depth?" Many a camera had met its doom in the Great Blue Hole, the pressure of nearly five-and-a-half atmospheres overwhelming the waterproof seal of the housing. Boone always asked, and not just for the sake of the camera. Having an expensive camera flood was a distraction, and he wanted his divers focused.

"Yeah, yeah, all good. It's rated to three hundred." He popped his regulator into his mouth and took a giant stride off the swim platform.

Minutes later, the group descended to the sandy lip of the hole and dropped into the abyss. Boone still remembered the first time he'd done this dive: that endless blue—almost purple—void stretching below had taken his breath away. Disorienting… even a little disconcerting. Many found this dive a bit dull, as there wasn't a lot of life to see, especially if the sharks didn't come. Still, this was a "bucket list" dive for many—no other dive was quite like it.

Below, Emily started her turn, taking the group along the wall of the hole, angling steeply down. In seconds, her fins lost their greenish hue as the deep waters did their trick, sucking the color out of the visible spectrum. She looked back over her shoulder. Boone caught her eyes and raised an *OK* sign. He watched her scan the divers behind her and raise her own *OK* in return.

Boone looked back at Augusto, who was bringing up the rear. He signaled all was well, too. Boone returned his gaze to the group, watching the divers for any sign of buoyancy issues. Sinking like a stone in a four-hundred-foot hole was something to avoid. In a similar vein, popping up uncontrollably once they got into the stalactites would also be a no-no. Some of those formations were likely millions of years old, from when the cave was above water, and may have taken two hundred years to grow a single inch.

Ahead, Emily's mask shot to the left. She stopped kicking and floated, then raised her flattened palm to the top of her head like a fin. *Shark.* Then she pointed into the blue, looking back at the group, making sure they all got a look. Boone could barely make out the tail fin of a blacktip as the creature swam away from the group, vanishing into the gloom.

Soon they neared their maximum depth and the jaw-dropping spectacle of stalactites came into view. As Emily scooted under the formation to lead the group into the grotto, Boone kicked himself down to one hundred forty feet and took up station near the preferred entry point, watching each diver carefully. He noted Augusto looking down, then raising a hand to his head. *Shark.* Boone could see this one clearly. A massive body, blunt head. *That might be a tiger,* he thought. *But it's too deep to go check it out. Probably at two hundred.*

Boone caught Augusto's eyes, shaking his head, letting the Belizean know he didn't want to call attention to it. This was the deep point of the dive, and Boone wanted everyone to stay focused on getting up under the overhang.

One of the last in the chain of divers spotted the shark and was going down, camera extended. The Texan. He'd hit one fifty in a moment. Boone signaled to Augusto that he'd take care of it and finned down toward the diver, who was completely engrossed in the viewscreen of his camera. Boone quickly unclipped a stain-less-steel carabiner he kept handy and tapped the back of his tank. The man looked around, then up, spotted Boone, then looked down at his computer. *Yeah, you just realized you're way too deep, didn't you?*

The man looked back at Boone and the young divemaster jerked a thumb up, signaling the man to ascend. Fortunately, the Texan needed no urging and left the shark alone to continue its journey into the depths of the Hole.

By now their bottom time was half over and Boone returned to the stalactites. He spotted Gretchen coming out from under the overhang, not following the group. He could see Hannah up ahead, looking back at her dive buddy. Boone kicked toward Gretchen, flashing the *OK* sign to ask if she was all right.

She waggled a flattened palm. *So-so.* Then she tipped the martini glass.

Boone nodded, pulling out his underwater slate as he finned up next to her. He quickly scrawled the equation *"12+5="* and held the stylus out to her. She took it, and Boone could see her brows knitting behind her mask. After several seconds she scrawled an eight… and then a question mark. Boone slid the slate back into his vest, signaling *OK*. Then pointed to her, then himself, then gave a thumbs up. *You. Me. Ascend.*

She nodded and started up slowly… and calmly, Boone was glad to see. He caught both Emily and Hannah's eyes, flashed the *OK* sign and signaled his intent. Emily signaled she understood and led the group through the last portion of the dive. Augusto, who had been watching all of this, moved in to reassure Hannah and guide her back to the group.

Boone checked in with Gretchen and she seemed clearer now, the shallower depth having lifted the narcosis. The dive was almost over, so he continued to take her toward the safety stop. On the way, several shapes swam into view. Caribbean reef sharks. Gretchen pointed excitedly and Boone nodded. They were the most common shark here in the Blue Hole and it wasn't unusual to see them, even after the chumming had been discouraged. One angled toward them, probably just curious—nothing out of the ordinary, nothing alarming, and yet there was something about how it rapidly changed direction that triggered a memory in Boone's mind.

All of a sudden, he was back in Saba, when a lionfish hunt had gone awry and Boone had freedived down to save a diver from a reef shark feeding frenzy, nearly drowning himself from a shallow water blackout. To Boone's recollection, he had remained entirely calm during those harrowing moments. A calm and focused mind was something he prided himself on, but in *this* moment, Boone felt something he was unaccustomed to: *fear.* Well, maybe not fear exactly, but a sudden tightening in his chest, his heart hammering away. *Am I having an anxiety attack?* The shark lost interest and swam away, but the feeling remained. *Focus on the task at hand. Head for the sand.*

Below, the divers were ascending, Emily in the lead, Augusto out of sight at the rear. Boone reached the sand in sight of the boat and signaled Gretchen to join him at a spot on the sandy slope and level off, tapping his watch and flashing the number five twice to tell her to remain at that fifteen-foot depth for an extended ten-minute safety stop. On most dives, safety stops were just three minutes, but Boone preferred a longer one for this deep dive. He might go as high as fifteen minutes for the stragglers, with their greater time at depth.

Gretchen leveled off in the sand, then mimed writing and pointed at his slate. He showed it to her. Her eyes went wide when she saw her answer to the simple math equation. She smacked her palm against her head, and Boone took the signal to mean "what was I thinking?"

Boone waved his hand and shook his head, then capped it with an *OK* sign. *No big deal. All's well.* He took a moment to assess his breathing. The anxious feeling was still there, but it was ebbing. He turned and found Emily looking at him.

She cocked her head. Signaled *OK?* and watched him closely.

He waggled his hand: *So-so.* When he saw the concern in her eyes, he quickly pumped an *OK* sign. Whatever had happened, it wasn't important enough for her to worry about right now—she needed to focus on the divers. *And so do I,* he thought.

◆ ◆ ◆

After everyone was aboard, the *Leeward to Seaward* headed south toward the Half Moon Caye National Monument for a lunch break. After such a deep dive, the group would need time to get some of the nitrogen out of their systems. On the way, they passed the rusted remains of a ship, the site having been named "Harrier Wreck", for the jump-jet fighter the Royal Air Force had used when bombing it for target practice. Before Belize had gained its independence, the little country had been known as British Honduras, and the United Kingdom still kept a military presence there.

Boone was sitting alone at the bow, enjoying the breeze, the sun warming his bare skin. He didn't like to overuse sunscreen, so he wasn't the sort to run around shirtless all day; still, some days you just had to soak up the vitamin D. Closing his eyes, he reached up to the Statian Blue Bead that he wore on a thong at his neck. The five sides of cobalt blue were smooth as sea glass, and Boone found it comforting to use it like meditation beads. A soft thump heralded Emily's arrival as she sat down beside him. She didn't say anything, just put a hand on his knee and gave a squeeze. He looked down at her, catching his reflection in her oversized shades.

She said nothing. Waiting.

Boone placed his hand over hers. "So… umm… I *might* have had a panic attack. I say 'might,' cuz I've never had one before and… well… no frame of reference, I guess, so…"

"You don't exactly strike me as the panicky type," Em said, turning her hand palm up and grasping his in a firm grip. "Tell me what happened."

Boone did, describing the sensations and what he thought had triggered them. The incident seemed distant as he recalled it, something clinical to be examined. Ahead, the beautiful little island of Half Moon Caye grew larger, a dollop of green in a sea of turquoise. The sight of it, the breeze on his face, the girl at his side… everything combined to fill Boone with contentment. He stopped speaking.

"How do you feel now?" Emily asked.

He replied with a kiss, following it up with a smile. "Like it never happened."

She smiled back, but the smile only reached half-mast. "But it did."

Boone felt a gentle touch on his ribs and looked down. Emily's fingertips traced the shiny scar there, a souvenir from a near-fatal encounter with a machete-wielding madman on the island of Saba.

"We've both been through a lot, Boone." She removed her sunglasses, an uncommon move for Emily under a tropical, noonday sun. "Look, this might not be your cuppa tea, but… if you need to talk to someone about this, let me know. "

"I've got *you*."

Emily squeezed his hand. "You and me can always do a little chin wag, yeah… but I mean someone… professional. I can set it up. If you need it."

Boone shrugged and gave her a brief kiss. "Thanks. But I'm okay." He rose, preparing to tie the boat up as it coasted into the shallows by the dock.

Emily remained behind, looking across the shallow waters ahead.

After lunch, the dive boat traveled to two of the most popular dives, Aquarium and Half Moon Caye Wall. Any diver who might have been disappointed at the lack of coral and marine life in the Blue Hole would come away fully satisfied after these dives. They were in luck today, with visibility exceeding a hundred feet, schools of colorful fish filling the reefs, and multiple eagle rays greeting them along the wall during the second dive. Satisfied, the divers were all abuzz as they approached Half Moon Caye again, this time for their overnight stay and a sunset barbecue.

"Another boat's here," Salvador commented.

Beside him on the flybridge, Boone raised the small pair of binoculars he'd brought. Having spotted sperm whales a few times during the passage to and from the atolls, he liked to keep the binos handy. He glassed the pier. "What the heck is *that* doing here? We're the only charter scheduled for today."

"Maybe someone bringing in supplies," Salvador suggested.

"Not in *that*. It's a Sea Ray Sundancer... looks like the 400 model. Saw one in the Harbour Village Marina in Bonaire. That is an *expensive* boat. High-speed cruiser."

Emily was at the bow, readying a line as they approached the pier. "Check out the posh yacht!" she called up excitedly.

While not a true yacht, the word didn't seem entirely out of place—the graceful lines and gleaming white surfaces screamed *money*. As they slowed and sidled up to the pier opposite the flashy visitor, Boone climbed down the ladder to toss the fenders over the side. Stepping across as Emily and Augusto lassoed the cleats, Boone quickly secured the lines.

"Ha! That's a good one." Em pointed across to the Sundancer.

Boone glanced over his shoulder at the name along the bow: *Liquid Asset*.

＊ ◆ ◆

After everyone disembarked and headed for the shade of the palm trees, Boone and Emily remained behind to rinse the gear with the freshwater hose aboard the *Leeward to Seaward*. Overhead, Magnificent Frigatebirds glided through the blue sky, and an occasional Red-Footed Booby joined them. The western part of the island was a protected nesting site for the red-footed birds, their squawks audible even out here on the boat. Down a sandy trail, a wooden viewing platform sat amongst the trees, allowing birders to climb up and take photographs.

Half Moon Caye was a tiny island at the southeastern corner of Lighthouse Reef, less than a mile across and only 750 feet wide. The western half was dense, green vegetation while the eastern half was primarily sandy beach and copious palm trees. In amongst these palms sat a few one-room buildings, restrooms, and a bank of square, white tents. The largest structure was a simple, canvas-walled platform that served as a dining area during rainy weather. Near the little camp, the rusting remains of an old lighthouse stood beside the shore, its metal framework creaking in the tropical breeze.

"What's for grub tonight?" Emily asked, shutting off the hose.

"Salvador got some kingfish and snapper from a fisherman while we were blowing bubbles at Aquarium," Boone said.

"Scrummy!" Em exclaimed. "I see Augusto firing up the grill. Multi-talented, that one. Let's go give him a hand." She stripped off her long-sleeved T-shirt and tied it at her waist, revealing a lime-green bikini top, its bright hue in stark contrast to her lightly tanned skin. "An hour 'til sunset. Might as well enjoy a little no-shirt time before the mosquitos get bitey."

"Pretty stiff sea breeze—I think we'll be skeeter free." Boone pulled his T-shirt over his head and stuffed it against his dry bag just inside the cabin.

They strolled up the pier to the beach and headed toward the cooking area. Hammocks, Adirondack chairs, and benches dotted the sand amongst the palm trees. The dive group was spread out, relaxing and enjoying the tranquility of the island.

"Señorita!"

"Esteban!" Emily called out, flashing a brilliant smile.

The old caretaker returned her smile with his own, though his was one tooth shy on the top row. He was at his usual perch, a bench next to a pile of coconuts, a machete sticking out of a nearby palm stump. Heading toward the grill, Boone spotted his skipper and gave Salvador a fist bump, momentarily coveting the Belikin beer in the man's hand. *Three dives tomorrow. No brew for me.*

"Boone!" Augusto waved them over. "You're just in time to help with the fish!" He snapped a pair of tongs in the air and held them out to Boone.

"You got it, 'Gusto." He took the tongs and nudged some of the hot coals together. "Kingfish and snapper, right?"

"Yes, but also..." He reached down and came up with a medium-sized cooler.

Boone lifted the lid. "Lobster?" Inside, packed in ice, were a number of Caribbean spiny lobster.

"What? I love lobster!" Emily gushed. "Where'd you get those?"

"From Mr. Price," Augusto said.

"Please, Augusto... it's just Oliver," said a voice from a nearby Adirondack chair. The owner of the voice stood.

"Well... hello, hello, hello..." Emily said under her breath.

Boone immediately knew that this was the owner of the Sundancer. Oliver Price's lightweight attire—a white, button-down shirt and chinos—looked as if it'd been spun from silk and tailored. Boone figured the polarized sunglasses alone probably cost more than he earned all week. Nearly as tall as Boone, his skin was perfectly tanned, and from the way his form filled out his expensive clothing, he clearly had money left over for a personal trainer and gym membership. Though dressed in tropical splendor, his sleeves and pant legs were rolled up, feet bare, and shirt unbuttoned to the sternum.

"I hope you don't think I'm crashing your shindig," the man said, speaking with impeccable diction that would have been at home in an episode of *Downton Abbey*. "I'm a staunch supporter of the Belize Audubon Society and I was here to donate a new solar panel unit and a water purifier to the visitor center." He gestured to one of the buildings. "And, of course, some cases of Belikin for the staff, and a bottle of One Barrel Rum for Esteban."

"*Gracias*, Señor Price!" the old caretaker said as he walked by them, angling toward a pair of divers, two opened coconuts in his hands.

"*De nada*," Oliver replied. "And as for the lobsters, I realize we're outside of the season, but I picked those up in the Bay Islands and, well… I hope you don't mind."

Emily snorted. "Mind? There are few things I like more than lobsters, hand-delivered by a handsome Englishman. Especially ones that ride around in a boat like that!"

Oliver smiled, appearing to blush, although it was difficult to tell through his tan. "Thank you, m'lady. You're English too, if I'm not mistaken. South London?"

"*Thank* you!" Emily gave Boone a look that said: *See?* She recovered herself and beamed at Oliver. "I mean… thank you for recognizing where I'm from." She held out a hand. "I'm Emily Durand."

"Charmed." He took her hand.

*He's actually going to kiss it,* Boone thought, and sure enough the man began to lean in but then caught Boone's eye. Suddenly looking sheepish, Oliver instead placed his other hand over Emily's, giving her an awkward handclasp-shake.

"Oliver Price." He released Emily and extended a hand to Boone, who took it.

"Boone Fischer." He gave the man a firm shake but was pleased to see Oliver wasn't an alpha-male knuckle-crusher. "The *Liquid Asset* is beautiful. Sundancer 400?"

"Oh, you know boats? Yes, thank you, I rather like her myself. If you wish, you're welcome to come aboard." He turned to Emily. "I'll give you the ha'penny tour."

"I promised Augusto I'd help with the grill," Boone said.

"I'll go!" Emily said, and headed toward the pier. "Don't burn my lobster, Boone!" she tossed over her shoulder. Oliver followed.

"I can handle the fire, no problem," Augusto said. "You better go, or he might drive off with your *mamacita.*"

Boone relinquished the tongs and trotted across the beach, joining Emily and Oliver alongside the Sundancer. Looking at the gleaming decks, he instinctively began brushing sand off the soles of his bare feet. Emily followed suit.

"No, no—none of that." Oliver stepped across without cleaning his feet. "Wilson? Why don't you go ashore, see if Esteban needs any help."

Inside the salon, a broad-shouldered black man rose from the captain's seat, his white polo shirt straining to contain his musculature. He gave Boone and Emily a courteous nod of his gleaming bald head as he brushed by them and crossed to the pier. He made his way toward the camp, shaking loose a cigarette from a pack as he went.

"Wilson skippers for me when I'm not driving the boat myself and... well, with a boat like this... he's a bodyguard as well."

"Piracy?" Emily asked.

Oliver sighed. "It happens. Can't be too careful."

"You have any run-ins?" Boone asked.

Something passed over Oliver's face and Boone saw it, but it was gone in an instant and the Englishman was shaking his head, waving a hand. "I brought you here for a tour," he said, beaming. "In all sincerity, I enjoy showing off my toys. I supposed that's some narcissistic failing on my part, but... sod it all, I *love* this boat! This aft deck is my favorite spot aboard, if I'm honest." He gestured to a sectional seating area with a little table. A swing-gate alongside the seating led to the swim platform. "We'll return here shortly. Let's start in the salon."

For the next few minutes, Oliver showed them the impeccable interior of the boat, gleaming surfaces, rich materials, and polished wood—or an excellent facsimile. The salon was surprisingly roomy, with a kitchen flanking the captain's station, and ample seating surrounding a small, high-def television. Below, two full staterooms stretched along the beam. The one in the bow sported a king-size bed, the one aft containing two twins. A well-appointed head with a standing shower rounded out the tour.

"Can I get you two a drink?" Oliver asked from the galley, as Boone and Emily settled into the aft seating area. To the west, the sun was a half hour from kissing the horizon. "I've got a Don Omario 15-year rum," he said, lifting a square bottle. "Belize's top distiller re-released this for Prince Harry's visit in 2012."

"We've got a full day of dives tomorrow," Emily said. "Just some water for me, thanks."

"Same," Boone said. "But we appreciate the offer."

"Of course, silly me. You're the divemasters for this outing, yes? Well, *I'm* not diving." He poured himself two fingers of the vintage rum into a solid-looking rocks glass and tossed a single cube of ice into it. Coming aft, he handed them each a bottle of water. "I recycle those, so leave them with me and I'll put them in my blue bin." He settled into a solo portside seat, took a sip, and sighed. "Can't beat a good sipping rum."

"Expensive?" Boone asked.

"No, not really. Same chaps that make One Barrel. What shop do you work at? I'll send you over a bottle."

Boone thought that was oddly generous, given that he'd just met them. "That's not necessary, but thank you all the same. We're with Go Slow Divers in Caye Caulker."

"Oh, we're neighbors! I have a place on Caye Chapel."

*The exclusive little island to the south of Caulker,* Boone thought. They regularly drove by it on the way to the atolls and he'd spied some impressive-looking properties, but he didn't know much about it other than what he'd been told. A fraction of the size of Caulker, Chapel was a private island with its own eighteen-hole golf course and airstrip.

Oliver took another sip. "So… these overnight camping trips. Six dives over two days, yes?"

Boone nodded. "It's my favorite outing. We don't do it very often, a couple times a month. Frenchie's Diving came up with the idea, so we never go if they've got a trip planned. Frenchie's is one of the oldest ops on Caulker."

Emily was snickering. When Oliver raised an eyebrow, she explained. "Our dive shop back in Bonaire… the owner, we called him Frenchy the Belgian. But that wasn't his name and he wasn't French. And then we come here and find another non-French Frenchie. The world's a funny place, so say I."

"I'll drink to that," Oliver tipped his glass toward Emily, then back to himself for a sip. "Your Frenchy the Belgian… he was Belgian, at least?"

"Oh yes," Boone said somberly. "Walloon Belgian. God forbid you suggested he was Flemish."

Oliver laughed, then swirled his rum, looking at them. "Bonaire is a long way from Belize."

Boone didn't want to get into their life story with Oliver. True, the man was well-spoken and charming, seemed to be eco-conscious and a bit of a philanthropist—and handing out free lobsters and expensive rum were marks in his favor—but the events Boone and Emily had gone through in Bonaire and Saba were still raw. As Emily had suggested earlier in the day, they were still sorting through it all. Besides, if they explained how they'd come from there to here, they'd miss the cookout. "We're sorta… diving nomads, I guess you could say." He turned to Emily to give her a smile and a microscopic shake of the head.

"Oh, yeah, we like to change it up," Emily said quickly. She probably didn't care to go into their story either. "We've been in Belize for about eight months, though. Really loving the diving here!"

"Oh… speaking of diving, do either of you cave dive?" Oliver sat forward, setting his half-finished rum on the little table in front of Boone and Emily. "I've heard that Caye Caulker is criss-crossed with limestone caves."

"Yeah, Giant Cave. Emily and I dived it several times. We got certified last year. Took the course at Belize Diving Services."

"You've actually got a cave over by you," Emily said. "Winter Wonderland."

"Really! You don't say."

"I *do* say. The entrance is near Chapel. We haven't dived that one, though."

"I heard that the cave diving course is long, and quite demanding…"

"You thinking of trying it out?" Emily asked.

"Me? Oh good lord, no. Embarrassed to say I'm not altogether comfortable *diving*, let alone doing it in a silty, enclosed space. I'm far too claustrophobic. But it still fascinates me. So, would you say you two are experienced cave divers? Comfortable with it?"

"Experienced? No, not really," Boone said without hesitation. "Comfortable… well, anyone who's done it will tell you there's nothing comfortable about it. But we've dived Giant Cave quite a few times, and I'm sure we'll do it some more. It's fascinating in there."

"Excuse me? Boone? Emily?" a voice came from the pier; Hannah, the diver Boone had helped with her motion sickness. "Augusto said to tell you… and he said I had to say these words…

61

he said to 'get your butts over to the grill and help or you won't get any lobster.'"

Emily shot up at comical speed. "Oliver, thank you *so* much for the delightful tour and the bottled water...and the lobsters. One of which I intend to eat."

Oliver laughed. "Go, go... get back to your group. Thank you for indulging me."

Boone rose to follow Emily onto the dock. "You're welcome to join us. They *are* your lobsters, after all."

"No, no... I have a date with the sunset." He picked his rum up and settled into the portside chair. He raised the glass in farewell. "Cheerio!"

Boone caught up with Emily as she reached the beach.

"Speaking of sunsets," she said as she untied her shirt from her waist, "with this breeze, it'll get chilly."

"Good point. I'll catch up."

Boone trotted back down the pier and boarded the dive boat, fetching his T-shirt. The sky to the west was glowing orange and Boone glanced across the pier to see if Oliver was enjoying the impending sunset. He wasn't. He wasn't enjoying his rum, either. The glass of pricy liquor sat unfinished on the aft table. Movement through the windows of the Sundancer's salon caught his eye. Oliver was on a cellphone, speaking animatedly, one arm sweeping the air with broad gestures. The salon door must have been closed, as Oliver's voice was muffled and unintelligible. Boone couldn't tell if he was angry or excited, but he suddenly realized he was eavesdropping, albeit visually. Pulling on his shirt, he made his way along the pier to join the divers for a sunset dinner.

**7**

"**S**orry you didn't get a lobster, Boone."

"S'ok."

"Yeah, cuz it was soooooo good," Emily said right into his ear. The two of them were wrapped together in a hammock, swinging gently in the evening breeze. "I mean, I've had lobster before, but this may very well have been... the *best* lobster I ever tasted. And you didn't have any."

Boone turned to face her, their noses nearly touching. Her eyes sparkled with mirth in the moonlight. *She loves busting my chops,* he thought. And if he was honest with himself, he enjoyed it. "Well, Emily... it's a basic math problem. There were only twelve lobsters. And we have twelve paying divers, so..."

"Good thing Hannah's allergic, yeah? Oh, bugger... that didn't come out right."

The pair burst into laughter and Boone hugged her tight, feeling her body shaking as she managed to ramp it down to a fit of giggles, shushing herself.

It was still early evening, but divers tended to crash early in the tropics, especially after a full day like today. Some of the tents were illuminated and voices spoke in low tones, so a few were still up. Boone and Em had picked a hammock a little distance from camp, planning to sleep under the moon and stars. The breeze was still strong, and mosquitos and no-see-ums were absent. A good thing, as no-see-ums—also known as sand flies—had a particularly nasty bite.

Emily extinguished the last of her laughter with a long sigh. "Oh my God, that was good." She bridged the inch of distance and gave Boone a lingering kiss. She withdrew, her eyes starting to sparkle again. "Remember our first night in Saba? The hammock…? When we…?"

"That was terrible."

"I know, right? The *worst*."

"That was *your* idea," Boone chided.

"Hey, I thought it'd be sexy!"

"I still have rope burn."

"You're one to talk! I thought you were gonna squeeze me through the mesh like Play-Doh."

"Thank God the hook broke."

"Spot of luck, that. Any longer and I'd have embraced celibacy."

"Hammock sex is bad."

"*So* bad," Emily said before lapsing into silence for several seconds. "Of course, if we were in Oliver Price's master stateroom… blimey, that bed? Eight hundred thread count."

"You only sat on the edge for a moment."

"A lady's legs know."

They swung gently in silence for a few minutes, the breeze rustling the palm fronds overhead.

After a moment Boone spoke. "So, we're not gonna…"

Emily laughed. "Oh, sod off. I'm too knackered and so are you." She started shifting in the hammock. "I think, before we go to sleep... and *nothing else*... before we go to sleep, I oughta visit the loo. Maybe grab a blankie, in case it gets nippy."

She had just swung one leg out of the hammock when a shape came alongside.

"Señorita, señor?" A metal object caught the moonlight as it swung and a sharp thunk sounded. Esteban was by their hammock. With practiced ease, the caretaker whacked off the top of the coconut in a series of angled cuts. The old man's gnarled hands bore several scars, suggesting he may not have always been so skilled. In seconds he held a freshly decapitated coconut in one hand, his machete in the other. "Coconut?"

"No, no, thank you Esteban," Boone said quickly. "Could you... sorry, could you give us some privacy?"

The caretaker shrugged and headed back to camp. Boone didn't like to be rude, but it had been necessary. At the sudden appearance of the machete and the sound of the first cut, Emily's entire body had tensed as if she'd had 3,000 volts put through her. Now her body was trembling uncontrollably, her chest heaving with rapid breaths. The moment Esteban was out of sight she burst into tears, turning in the hammock and pressing herself against Boone. He felt her heart hammering against his breastbone.

Boone gripped her firmly, willing her muscles to relax, her breathing to slow. "Easy... slow breaths," he whispered into her hair. Very quickly, she began to calm. Boone relaxed his grip as her breathing returned to normal.

"Yeah... so..." Emily had a slight tremor in her voice. "You're 'Mister Intuition.' I'm guessing you know what triggered that."

"It was the..." Boone didn't finish the sentence, not wanting to say it.

"The choppy thing, yeah. Well, he startled me, too. Bloody hell, I haven't had one like that in a while. Thought it might be over." She blew a little chuff of breath through her turned-up nose. "Honestly, *you're* the one who should be..." She slid her hand up his shirt, her fingers again finding the scar. "I mean, he nearly killed you."

Boone remembered all too well. Aidan, a lunatic they'd run afoul of in the Dutch island of Saba, had slashed Boone with a machete—the very implement he'd murdered a number of people with on several islands. If Boone hadn't jumped back at the moment of the strike, he'd have been disemboweled. As it was, the cut had left him with a broken rib and a cat's cradle of stitches. But what Emily had endured was on a completely different level.

"My scar's on the outside," Boone said. "What you went through, up on that mountain..."

"You needn't remind me, I was there," Emily said. "The weird thing is... well, it's kind of like what you said today. Something about the sharks triggered a panic attack and yet, that day, when you were rescuing Chad during an actual attack..."

"I felt calm."

"Yes! And there I was, being hauled up a mountain by a psychotic killer... and much of the time, I felt... well, not *calm* exactly... but nothing like what just happened."

"I don't think I've ever seen you like that before."

"That's cuz I usually feel it coming on, so I go for a walk, or hit the loo, or go for groceries. This time... well, it was the surprise, I guess."

"Has that happened a lot?"

"No... but enough times that I started seeing someone."

"Really? The person you were hinting I might talk to?"

"Yes. She's been great. Honestly, I haven't had an episode in months."

Boone frowned. He'd assumed Emily had been working through the ordeal and they had talked about it several times, but his intuition had missed the extent of the lingering trauma. "Em, I'm sorry I didn't... I feel like I failed you, not picking up on—"

"Stop. Don't do that. I didn't *want* you to pick up on it. This was something I needed to get sorted on my own." She ran a hand through his brown hair. "You're a fixer, Boone. And you can fix me dinner, or fix me a drink, or fix my sore back with a nice massage anytime you like. But I don't need you fixing this. That's on me. And the less you make of it, the better for me, 'kay?"

Boone looked into her eyes. "Okay." After a moment, he opted for a little humor. "Was this all an elaborate way of asking for a massage?"

A grin bloomed on her face. "A hammock massage? After what we learnt of hammock sex? Are you trying to murder me?"

❖ ◆ ◆

In the morning, the divers enjoyed a simple breakfast, gathered up their things, and loaded up the boat. The *Liquid Asset* was nowhere to be seen.

Before they left, Boone found Esteban and gave him a hundred-dollar tip. The dive shop budgeted sixty, but Boone slipped in a couple twenties of his own. "Esteban, I'm sorry I was rude last night. Emily and I..."

"*Si, si*, is ok. *La asusté.*"

Boone smiled. "Yes, you did startle her." He held his finger-tips, showing a tiny amount. "*Un poquito.*" He gripped the old caretaker's shoulder. "See you next week, *sí?*"

Esteban nodded, going back to the tents to ready them for the next group.

"Oh, Esteban," Boone said, turning back. "When did Mr. Price leave?" He pointed toward the pier.

"Late. After midnight."

"*Gracias.*" Boone returned to the dive boat and untied her dock lines, stepping aboard as she backed away from the little para-dise of Half Moon Caye. Emily was retrieving the fenders and he assisted her.

"Was Esteban miffed?"

"Hell, no. He was sorry he startled you. So, where are we off to first?"

"Hat Caye Drop-off."

"Another day, another dollar."

"Wonder where Mr. Wealthy McHandsome went?"

"Esteban said he left after midnight."

"That's a bit weird, yeah?"

Boone shrugged. "Guess he had somewhere to be. So, you thought he was handsome."

"Are you kidding? Fit bod, posh duds. And that *smile*... feck, you could eat pudding out of those dimples." Emily studiously avoided looking at him as she listed Price's finer qualities, but Boone could see the impish look on her face growing broader by the moment.

Boone shook his head and headed up the flybridge ladder to join Salvador at the wheel.

The skipper patted his stomach. "*¡Ay, dios!* That was a treat, getting some lobster before the late-June Lobsterfest. And did you see that boat? What I would do if I had that kind of money!"

———◆◆———

The day flew by, with two morning dives on the western fringe of Lighthouse Reef, a lunch break on neighboring Turneffe Atoll, and a final dive at Cockroach Caye Wall. Once everyone was aboard, the *Leeward to Seaward* swung north, heading back to Caye Caulker.

"All right, anyone here have a night dive tonight?" Augusto called out. Everyone shook their heads in the negative. "No? Good!" Augusto dug into the cooler. The ice had long since melted, and he came up with a dripping bottle of Kuknat Coconut Rum and a box of pineapple juice. "No dives means you can drink!"

"Everybody grab your cups!" Emily said, pointing to the bin of paper cups that each diver had written their name on. The dive shop discouraged any single-use plastic aboard and urged divers to use the same cup throughout the trip.

As the dive boat motored around the northern tip of Turneffe and angled west for the twenty-mile crossing to Caulker, Boone climbed to the flybridge with his binoculars, glassing the waters for dolphins or whales. A school of flying fish paced the boat for a short time, but nothing larger appeared. Nearing Caulker, Boone swept his binoculars to the south, scanning the shallows around Caye Chapel. No sign of Price's boat, but that didn't mean much—the little caye's marina was a square enclosure cut into the western side, and currently out of sight. A small private jet came in for a landing on the little island's airstrip, which took up the bottom third of the island. Boone glassed several of the multi-million-dollar homes on the northern shore. *It's the island equivalent of a gated community,* he thought.

After a quick stop in Caulker to unload the divers from there, the *Leeward to Seaward* headed away to the north for her berth on Ambergris Caye. Boone and Emily waved goodbye and then loaded up tanks and rental gear onto the tricycle cart Ignacio had brought over. The Go Slow owner said he'd close up shop and asked them to return the borrowed dive weights, having found replacements. Cycling away, Ignacio turned the corner onto Pasero Street, heading west to the dive shop on the lagoon side. Boone hefted the bag of dive weights and walked up the beach with Emily, planning to take Chapoose Street to go to Belize Diving Services.

"Bambooze is hopping," Boone remarked. The brightly painted beach bar was about half-full, which was impressive for late afternoon in the off-season. He switched the gear bag onto his other shoulder.

"Nice of BDS to provide the loaners," Emily remarked. She waved to a pair of women who owned one of her favorite craft shacks along the sandy beachside trail. Next door to them, a woman specializing in doing cornrows for the tourists beckoned to Emily. She smiled, waving a "no thank you."

"One of these days, Em…" Boone teased.

"Oh, you'd like that, wouldn't you?" She waggled one of her braided pigtails at him. Her long locks of blonde hair became tangled in dive mask straps if she wasn't careful, and she usually went for pigtails, braids, or a ponytail. Boone had let slip that he loved those looks, and so she had started getting creative with her hair-restraining methods.

"Yes, I suspect I *would* like that."

"If you promise me you'll never go 'man-bun' or mullet, then maybe I'll consider cornrows. 'Course, I'd require some sort of reciprocation... mayhaps... a temporary henna tattoo of my choice?"

"A tattoo of what?"

"*That's* your question? I woulda led with 'where will you put it?'" Emily flashed him an evil grin. "Oh, my, my, my... so many possibilities. I'll have to give this some thought. Maybe give the dive staff a poll, let them vote, yeah?"

"On second thought, cornrows are such a tourist thing..."

"Oh, no-no-no. I think this is a brilliant quid pro quo we've hit upon. And I'll hold you to it."

Ten minutes later they arrived at the BDS dive shop, where Emily flagged down Loretta.

"Oy, Loretta! Santa Boone has a sackful of lead for you. Oh bugger, that came out wrong."

Loretta laughed. "Hey, guys! You didn't need to bring those back so soon."

"Ignacio managed to scrounge up enough," Boone said. "Thanks for the loan."

"No problemo," Loretta said. "Actually, I was hoping I'd see you. Someone was asking about you."

"Me?" Boone asked.

"Actually, both of you. He asked for you by name."

"Who?"

"Some big guy. Sounded American." She pointed back toward the lagoon. "You shoulda *seen* the boat he had out there."

"What kind?" Boone asked, curious.

"Sorry, not really good at boat models. It was pretty, though. Anyway, he wanted to charter a dive trip with the pair of you. I told him you were with Go Slow down the street."

"Well, we've got a day off coming up," Emily noted. "I'm game."

"Did we just miss him?" Boone asked.

"No. He was here yesterday, right after you picked up the weights. I told him you were doing an overnighter at the Blue Hole. He said he'd swing by your shop and leave his card."

———————◆·◆———————

"No joy on some extra cash," Emily said as she exited Go Slow's office and joined Boone beside the equipment room, where he had just finished fixing a leaky valve on a regulator. "Ignacio said no one came by."

"Huh. It's just a two-minute walk," Boone said, pointing up the short, sandy street that linked the two dive shops.

Emily sighed. "Ah, well. We shall have to continue our frugal ways. Hey, maybe we could scoot over to Caye Chapel and ask Oliver Price for a loan."

Boone laughed. They were far from poor, but they weren't exactly rolling in dough, either. "I'll pass, thanks. Long as I've got sun, sand, and sea, I'm good."

Emily raised her eyebrows at him. "That all?" She tipped her sunglasses down. "Anything else on your must-have, can't-live-without-it list, hmm?" She gave one of her pigtails a gentle wave.

"Umm…" Boone feigned deep thought. "Beer?"

Emily turned on her sandaled heel and started away. "Right. I'm leaving you for Mr. Dimples."

Boone laughed and followed, heading back to their apartment along the packed-sand streets. He paused to pet a "potlicker" dog, a type of stray mutt found throughout Belize. This one always seemed to be at this particular corner. "Next time we see Ras, let's ask him if he knows anything about Oliver."

"Why?"

Boone rose from the dog and resumed walking. "Just curious."

"I think you're jealous."

Boone smiled, refusing to rise to the bait.

As they reached their apartment next to the bakery, Emily stopped him, sniffing the air. "They're still open... I could murder another Danish."

Boone smiled, opening the door of the bakery for her. "We can eat healthy tomorrow."

"Wake 'im up."

Cold water struck the side of Juan's head and he gasped.

"Good mornin', Sunshine."

The old Belizean fisherman's eyelids fluttered as he roused, wanting to see the owner of the voice—it sounded like the person had a pint of gravel in his throat, the accent from somewhere in the southern United States. Juan's blurred vision struggled to focus on the shape in front of him, the sickly light of a single, naked bulb illuminating the dark room.

"Howdy."

"*Qué?*"

"I said 'howdy.' As in 'hello,' '*hola*,' or 'pleased ta make yer fuckin' acquaintance.'"

Before him stood a man who towered over him, the garish print on his Hawaiian shirt blotting out the rest of the room. Juan blinked and tried to rise, but found himself attached to the chair he sat in. He struggled to remember what had happened. One minute he was strolling out of a local pawn shop with a wad of cash, headed for his favorite watering hole, and the next…

The man's face lowered and the brim of a straw hat brushed against Juan's forehead. "Where did you get… this?"

Juan squinted at the tiny green gem the man held between two fingers. The fingers moved and the object sparkled in the light from the overhead bulb.

"It… it was on the dock," Juan stuttered. "I found it after a man picked up some diving gear and got on a boat."

"What man?"

"I… I don't know. He was an American. He had on a wetsuit."

"You just described half the white people on the island. Real helpful. So, that's all you found?" The thick fingers left Juan's face and returned with a new object. "You sure you didn't find one of these?"

Juan stared at the small, green figurine, its eyes containing two stones identical to the one he had sold to the pawn shop. "No… I've never seen one of those before."

But he had. Much more worn and without the eye stones, strung on a necklace. And it belonged to a dear friend. Apparently, the recognition showed on his face.

"Never… seen one… before…" the man repeated back in a low voice.

"No," Juan whispered.

"Now, see… I'd like to believe that. But I don't. So, tonight's gonna suck for you."

The dimly lit room became very bright as the blowtorch ignited.

The next morning's dives went off without a hitch. Go Slow was combining divers from both cayes for the afternoon and night dives, so Salvador headed across to Ambergris Caye and docked the smaller dive boat, the *Laguna Azul*, in San Pedro. Boone and Emily made their way into town for lunch, turning south on the main drag. As they neared the paved plaza, Emily pointed at a yellow building on the right. Its distinctive entrance, a yawning jaguar's head, practically roared at tourists to stand within its toothy jaws for an Instagrammable photo.

"Ooh! Boone! I want to go dancing sometime—we have got to go there!"

Boone stopped, turning to Emily with a half-smile. "What's that place called again?"

Emily opened her mouth but snapped it shut. "Oh, sod off, Yank... just because you can't speak properly."

"What? It's the Jaguar's Temple Night Club, right?" He grinned at her. Em, being a Brit, pronounced the word "jag-yoo-er" and he loved to tease her about it.

"I refuse to participate in your pronunciation denunciation."

Boone laughed and started walking south. "Fine with me. Hey, I'm starving. Let's get some chips and salsa with some 'gyoo-ak-a-mo-lee' on the side."

"You looking for an arse-thrashing? Just for that, you gotta buy me one of those." She stopped and pointed.

Belize was known for its wood carvings, and all along San Pedro's main drag you could find locals selling beautifully polished sculptures, bowls, and walking sticks. Carved from Belizean hardwoods like ziricote, these crafts were often displayed on blankets, laid out in front of storefronts. Boone looked where Emily was pointing, noting the rows of sharks, turtles, birds, and bowls. Though some of the vendors sold mass-produced carvings from China, these looked to be legit ones from the mainland.

Boone gestured at the shiny, wooden animals. "What, my little carvings from Bonaire drinks aren't enough for you?"

"They're lonely and they need a new friend." As she squatted down beside the rows of carvings, the craftsman looked up from a smartphone, quickly pocketing it to begin his sales pitch. Emily smiled and nodded, perusing the menagerie. Suddenly her face lit up—then, just as quickly, she extinguished the smile and resumed the search.

Boone chuckled. *She spotted what she wants, but realized eagerness would double the price.* He decided to help out. "How much are the sharks?"

"Dese are forty dollars," the man said, pointing to several carvings shaped like sleek reef sharks. "Da big hammerheads are sixty."

"Belizean dollars?"

"Ya, mon. In US, dey twenty and t'irty."

*Very reasonable*, Boone thought but didn't say. "How about the turtles?"

"Forty Belize, twenty US."

"Hmm... I dunno..." Boone sighed and scratched his chin. He knew Emily had not been salivating over the sharks or turtles. At the moment, she was examining the bowls, a half-smile on her face. Boone had seen the exact carving she wanted, and she knew it. "Maybe we'll come back by after lunch..." He started to turn, then asked. "How about the manatees?"

"Dose are easier to carve," the man said, smiling. "Thirty Belize."

"I'll take this one!" Emily said, setting aside a bowl and snatching up a particularly adorable manatee carving.

"I'll wrap it for you," the man said, grabbing sheets from a San Pedro Sun newspaper while Boone fished out his wallet to pay the man.

As they walked away from the craftsman, Emily shouldered him playfully. "Nicely done. Your empress is pleased with her manatee."

"What are you going to name it?"

"Duh. Mana-Tina, of course," she replied without hesitation.

<hr />

They decided to have lunch at Caliente, the house restaurant for the venerable Spindrift Hotel. When they had first come to Belize they had stayed in this hotel—nothing fancy, just clean, reliable, and cheap. And there was another reason for popping by. Boone approached the front desk, retrieving an envelope from his cargo shorts containing brochures and some information on classes for dive certification.

"Excuse me. I'm with Go Slow diving... you have a guest here who requested some information. Manuel Rojas? Could you see that he gets this?"

The round woman behind the desk smiled. "I could. Or you could give it to him yourself. Señor Rojas just went into the restaurant for lunch."

Boone thanked her and he and Emily made their way through the bar to the entrance to the restaurant. Entering Caliente, they quickly spotted Manuel in the outdoor seating area and approached his table.

"Dr. Rojas," Boone began, "sorry to disturb you..."

"Ah! Boone and... Emily, yes? Please, join me!"

They sat and Boone offered up the envelope. "You mentioned wanting to learn to dive. Here's everything you'd need to get started."

"Oh, *gracias!* What brings you to San Pedro? You are on Caye Caulker, no?" He suddenly snapped his fingers. "Ah, you told me your company has a shop here, too."

"Yeah, we're diving from here this afternoon and evening," Emily said. "You enjoying the hotel?"

"I am now. The Museum is paying for my stay here and had put me in a room by the street. Far too noisy for me, so I paid out-of-pocket to upgrade to an ocean view room. It's delightful! Wonderful breezes. And the food is quite good here. I like to take lunch breaks back in town—take a shower and cool off. The Marco Gonzalez archaeological site I am working at is surrounded by mangroves. Quite hot and humid, not much breeze."

"Why would the Mayans have built there?" Boone asked.

"Well, it wasn't always in a mangrove swamp. We believe the site was first inhabited over two thousand years ago; at that time, sea levels were quite a bit lower and the site would have been on an island with beaches, ready access to the sea, and plenty of cooling breezes. As sea levels rose, the mangroves would have encroached, and the site lost its shoreline. It was abruptly abandoned about five hundred years ago."

"On the plane, you said it was a trading settlement?"

"Yes, we believe so. Its location would have been ideal for sending canoes between Mayan settlements on the mainland, and there are large amounts of materials there that don't occur on Ambergris Caye."

A waiter arrived to take their orders. Manuel told them that the homemade *mole* was quite good and Boone and Emily both opted for enchiladas smothered in the dark, sweet, earthy sauce.

"We've only been to one Mayan site so far," Emily said, after the waiter had brought them bottles of water. "Altun Ha? Am I saying that right?"

"Yes," Manuel said. "Do you know, Altun Ha is where they found the largest jade artifact ever discovered in Mesoamerica? A ten-pound bust of Kinich Ahau, the Mayan Sun God. They keep it locked away in a vault in the Central Bank in Belize City. Actually..." Manuel retrieved his wallet and took out a Belizean two-dollar note. As with all Belizean paper currency, Queen Elizabeth II was prominent on the front. Although Belize had declared independence, it was still a Commonwealth country and the Queen was the titular head of state. Manuel set the bill on the table and tapped the upper left corner.

"Oh yeah, I've seen that!" Emily said, peering closely at the stylized Mayan head in the corner of the bill.

"That was found in a cache with forty other objects. Altun Ha had so many jade artifacts, that it is thought it might have been a manufacturing center for the production and distribution of carved jade. Its proximity to the coast would have made it easy to ship the jade throughout the Mayan world."

"Have you found any jade at the site here?" Boone asked.

"Yes, a little, although not as much as I would have expected for a trading center. But Marco Gonzalez has been looted frequently. We've discovered numerous looting pits in the area."

"What, like a pit full of loot?" Em asked.

Manuel laughed. "No, no... it's what archaeologists call the haphazard holes that looters dig when looking for artifacts. Archaeologists excavate carefully and methodically. Looters tend to just dig a big hole."

"How long has this looting been going on?" Boone asked.

"Probably back when the site was abandoned. And perhaps some more occurred after it was rediscovered in 1984. There hasn't been much of value found during the time I've been working here, so the looting has pretty much stopped. The mangroves and insects are a deterrent too, of course. Would you be interested in a tour?"

"Sure!" Emily said. "We've been so busy diving, we haven't had a chance to do too much else."

"Our day off is coming up," Boone said. "Day after tomorrow."

"Good! Can you make it here on the morning ferry? The site will be much cooler the earlier we go."

"Sure."

Manuel tore off a piece of the envelope with the dive information and produced a pen. "Here is my cell phone number. Call me when the ferry docks. And speaking of tours, I'm glad you saw Altun Ha. It's a very nice site, but you really should go to Lamanai, further inland. I do some work there as well. The site is

far more extensive, its temple complex is wonderfully preserved…
and the jungle river cruise you take to reach it is very enjoyable.
There are monkeys, exotic birds, crocodiles…"

Emily coughed, choking mid-sip on her water. "I can skip the
crocs, but the rest sounds ace!"

"And you'll love the temples. There are three impressive ones
that have been fully excavated: The High Temple, The Mask
Temple, and The Jaguar Temple."

"I'm sorry, what was that last one?" Boone asked, glancing over
at Emily, a barely stifled smirk creeping into existence.

"Jaguar," Manuel repeated, pronouncing it the way most Amer-
icans said it.

Emily glared at Boone for a moment before breaking into a
smile of her own. "Manuel, would you like to see this awesome
manatee carving Boone got for me?" She started to unwrap it.
"Actually, he's going to be getting me *another* carving, too—what
would you suggest?"

—◆·◆—

An hour later, the *Leeward to Seaward* was moored in Shark Ray
Alley. Not a true dive site, this shallow area inside the reef was
for snorkeling. Originally a spot where local fishermen cleaned
their catch before going ashore, the area had quickly become
popular with huge numbers of nurse sharks and Southern sting-
rays looking for scraps. Now, the tradition continued with dive ops
and boatloads of snorkelers. Shark feeding was very controversial
in many areas, but given the docile nature of the nurse sharks,
most ops would bend the rules and participate at this location.

Augusto and Emily were in the shallows, dive mastering—or "snorkel mastering"—the group. Augusto had a small bucket of scraps and quickly had a number of rays and sharks clustered around him. In the distance, several other boats had similar groups of hungry sharks and rays, ringed by tourists. Boone remained up top with the skipper, watching a beautiful Formosa ketch with gleaming white sails and hull glide by on the ocean side of the reef, heading south.

"She's a beauty," Salvador remarked. "Can you make out the name?"

"Yeah." Boone adjusted the focus on his binoculars. "*Salty Dog*. Home port... Marathon, Florida." He lowered the binos. "They're a long way from home."

"You ever sail?" Salvador asked.

"Not really. Helped out on a few catamaran cruises in Curaçao, but I was green. Just did what they told me and tried not to get knocked overboard."

Salvador laughed, then looked at his watch. "Almost time for the chickens to come home to the roost."

"Almost. Let's pop down and get things in order." He started down the ladder and Salvador followed.

"We doing the Cut tonight?"

"Yeah," Boone replied. The skipper was referring to Hol Chan Cut, a break in the reef that led from the shallows out to the ocean beyond. A variety of marine life transited through that break from time to time, including dolphins, and the inner reef on either side of the cut was well suited to night dives. "Hopefully we'll get that school of eagle rays again—"

Boone was interrupted by a pair of fins sailing through the air and flopping onto the deck. A high-school-age boy scrambled up the swim ladder after them. His mask sat on his forehead, a sure sign of a novice.

"Whoooooo! That was awesome! I've never seen so many sharks! Man, there are even more today than yesterd—" He stopped talking, looking around the boat, then at Boone. "This isn't my boat…"

"Free beer," whispered Salvador, scrambling back up the fly-bridge ladder. He paused up top, looking down at Boone expectantly.

Boone had correctly guessed the fins were rentals and held one up, reading the markings. "Barrier Divers."

Salvador gave a laugh midway between gleeful and evil and vanished, heading forward to the radio. His voice was just audible over the sea breeze: "Barrier Divers, Barrier Divers… this is *Leeward to Seaward* with Go Slow…"

"What's going on?" the kid asked.

"Oh, just a little tradition among the dive ops in San Pedro. What's your name?"

"Blake."

"Hey Blake, I'm Boone. So, rule is, if a diver gets on the wrong boat, then the boat they belong to has to buy us all drinks."

"Or a case of Belikin," Salvador said, reappearing above. "We have the night dive, so they're just going to give us a case."

Boone smiled. Considering how cheap a case of the local beer was, Barrier Divers would probably come out better with that arrangement.

Far from being embarrassed, Blake thought the whole thing was hilarious. "Oh, man, I love that!" He reached up to pull off the mask. Boone now noticed that the kid was chomping on a wad of chewing gum, smacking the gum like a toddler who had just learned how to eat solid food.

*Where did he even keep that when the snorkel was in his mouth?* Boone was about to give a quick "Mask 101" lesson, but was distracted by the hand that grasped it. "What's with the duct tape?"

"Oh, this?" Blake held up his hand, the middle and index fingers swaddled in copious amounts of duct tape. "We were here yesterday. I got bit feeding a nurse shark. Cool, huh?" *Smack, chomp, smack.*

Boone shook his head. "You get it looked at?"

"Yeah. Some lady at the clinic put some stuff on it. They wanted to give me some stitches, but my dad said we'd wait to do it back in America. We leave tomorrow, so…"

"Duct tape," Boone said, deadpan.

"Yeah, my dad's like MacGyver, man."

Boone started to say something but stopped himself. *None of my beeswax.* Instead he pointed at a dive boat fifty yards off the starboard bow. "Your boat's over there."

"Thanks, man!" He reaffixed his mask and grabbed his fins. "Enjoy the beer!" he shouted. "You're welcome!" Blake hurled himself into the shallows with an inartful splash, nearly clobbering Emily, who was approaching the transom, leading their group back to the boat.

"Who the hell was that wanker?" she asked Boone from below, grabbing the ladder and pulling her green mask down around her neck.

"That was a case of beer by the name of Blake."

"Sweet as!" She removed her fins, watching the kid splashing toward the other dive op's boat. "Barrier Divers, eh?"

"Yep." Boone watched as she ascended the ladder. For a shallow snorkel like this, she had ditched her shorty wetsuit and was sporting one of her lime green bikinis, this one almost chartreuse yellow. As long as he'd known her, Emily had been enamored with the color green. *Frankly, she could deck herself out in mauve with polka dots and I'd be happy,* Boone thought, watching the beads of saltwater on her skin glisten in the sunlight. Reaching the swim platform, Emily pretended to trip, executing a ridiculous pratfall, complete with pinwheeling arms. Boone was "forced" to catch her and did so with a firm grip on her bare flesh.

"Oh, Mr. Fischer. You saved me!" She pushed free and shoved her fins into his hands. "Divers are coming in, so quit messing about and help, yeah? Still got a night dive to do."

# 9

The night dive had been largely uneventful, but the next morning's dives back in Caulker had borne fruit. Back aboard the smaller Caulker dive boat, the *Laguna Azul,* they had visited a sunken barge with a huge green moray in residence. An enormous Nassau grouper was known to visit from time to time, the pair seeming to have developed an odd friendship. Both were in rare form and the divers excitedly went over their photos and footage on the way back to the island.

"Boone, Em… come up top!" Salvador called out from the flybridge.

The two divemasters climbed the ladder to find Salvador on his cell phone.

"What's up?"

"Police. They want to talk to you." The skipper held his phone out to Boone.

"Hello?"

"Mr. Fischer?"

"Yes…"

"This is Superintendent Flores. I need to ask you a few more questions. Could you and Emily come by the Caye Caulker Police Station as soon as possible?"

"Umm… sure…" Normally, the *Laguna Azul* would continue around the island and dock on the lagoon side, but the police station was right by the ferry piers. "We're actually on our way in right now. I can have Salvador drop us off on the ocean side…" He looked to Salvador, who nodded. "Do you need us to call Ras Brook?"

"I have already spoken with him. I will see you shortly." The call ended.

"What was that about?" Emily asked, as Boone handed the phone back to the skipper.

"Apparently, the police superintendent from San Pedro has come down to Caulker. Wants to talk to us. Already talked to Ras."

"You want I should call him?" Salvador asked.

"Ras? No, that's okay. We'll be ashore in a couple minutes. But call Ignacio over at the shop, let him know we won't be there to unload. Augusto!"

The Belizean divemaster poked his head up the ladder well. "What you need?"

"I'm afraid Em and I are gonna bail on you. Can you and Ignacio handle things without us?"

Augusto rolled his eyes. "I've been doing this longer than you, *cabrón,*" he said with a grin before dropping from sight.

Five minutes later, the *Laguna Azul* came alongside an empty pier and Boone and Emily hopped across. The dive boat pulsed its engines a few times and swung away, heading north for The Split to cut around to the lagoon side. The police station was just up the beach, the bright yellow building easily visible through the fringing palm trees.

"Ah, good. Follow me," Superintendent Flores said without preamble the moment Boone and Emily entered the station. He left the front desk where he'd been hovering and ushered them into a small side office, closing the door behind them. "Please, sit," he said as he crossed behind a rickety desk.

"I'm assuming this is about the body," Boone said, as he and Emily sat in two plastic chairs across from the little desk.

"Yes. Do you know this man?" He opened a folder and slid a printed sheet of paper across, rotating it as he sent it toward them.

"Kevin Aldrich," Emily read. A copy of a passport photo looked up at them; a man with a youngish face and red hair. "I don't recognize him."

"Me neither," Boone said, scanning some of the information contained in the printout. "Address is St. Petersburg, Florida..."

"The deceased hasn't lived there in some time, according to the local police," Flores said. "I've already checked with Ignacio and he doesn't know the man either. He didn't come by your shop at any point?"

Boone looked at Emily, who shook her head. He turned back to the inspector. "Not that we know of... why?"

"Apparently, he is an amateur cave diver... or at least, that's what he told Loretta at Belize Diving Services. He wanted to rent some cave diving gear from them, but when they examined his certification card from—" He checked his notes. "—from PADI, she saw that it wasn't an Advanced card, so she refused."

"Makes sense," Emily said. "They're super serious about safety over there. You'd have to have loads of experience before they'd even let you participate in a cave dive with them, let alone rent you any specialized equipment."

"Mr. Aldrich claimed to be very experienced, saying he'd lost his Advanced card, and that he dived caves in Florida all the time, but couldn't provide any proof of that either. He then left the shop."

Boone frowned, thinking. "When was this?"

"Nine in the morning, the day before you found him."

"Well, he wasn't cave diving," Boone said. "If he really was experienced, he'd have had a two-tank side rig on him, helmet... probably a cave line reel... extra lights..." Boone stopped. *But he did have extra lights, didn't he? Both a wrist-mount and a big one in the BC pocket, that slipped out when the little statuette fell into the boat.*

"Besides, there aren't any caves up there in the mangroves," Emily pointed out.

"That we know of..." Boone murmured.

"What's that?" Emily asked.

Boone shook his head. *There was something else...* "He didn't have a weight belt on him."

"Ah, yes... our divers found a weight belt a couple hundred yards out in the channel. The belt must have come loose, and the body floated with the current into the mangroves."

"How much weight was on the belt?"

Flores glanced down at his notes. "Thirty-eight pounds."

"That's ridiculous!" Emily spluttered. "No one in a warm water wetsuit would wear that much weight!" As she said it, realization struck. "Unless someone had just shot you in the face and then stuck that belt on you, so you'd sink to the bottom."

Boone nodded. "The weights... threes, fours, and a couple fives?"

The superintendent checked his notes, then looked back at Boone with a suspicious expression on his face. "How did you know that?"

"Our shop had a bunch of weights go missing the other day."

The superintendent made a note, then continued. "The cause of death was a single .22 caliber slug to the brain, entry point in the center of the skull above the eyebrows. There was no damage to the mask, so it is believed that the individual was shot and then the mask was put on postmortem. There was minimal water in the lungs, which would be consistent with being shot before being weighted down and submerged. The coroner believes he was killed the night before, but it's hard to be sure with the amount of predation that occurred prior to discovery, both from the crocodile and smaller marine animals."

"Hey, that little figurine he had?" Emily said. "We met someone who thought it was just a souvenir…"

"Ah, that turned out to be quite interesting." The superintendent found another sheet in the folder. "It is a chacmool, and the staff at the Museum in Belize City also thought it was probably a souvenir… at first. But when they asked Dr. Felisberto, a specialist from the Belize Institute of Archaeology, to examine it…" He rotated the paper to Boone and tapped a paragraph.

"Object is composed of pure jade, consistent with the type found in artifacts at Altun Ha…" Boone read.

"Hey, Manuel said Altun Ha may have been churning out jade objects for other Mayan cities!" Emily said excitedly.

Boone kept reading. "The stone in the left eye socket is an emerald, approximately 0.5 carat. Examination of the empty socket revealed traces of tree sap, possibly a form of Mayan adhesive." He looked up. "How valuable would something like this be?"

The superintendent leaned back in his chair. "That's precisely what I wondered. Quite valuable. Perhaps he had more than that single statuette on him… and someone murdered him for it."

Heading across the island to the Go Slow shop, Boone and Emily popped by Errolyn's House of Fry Jacks for a quick bite to-go. Back on Bonaire, Boone had developed a taste for the *pastella*, an ABC Islands version of the empanada. Here in Belize, he'd discovered fry jacks; crunchy, flash-fried pastry stuffed with all sorts of fillings. Today he ordered two with bacon, eggs, and cheese.

"I don't know how you manage to stay so skinny," Emily remarked as she took a bite of her own "healthy" fry jack, stuffed with stewed chicken and beans.

Boone shrugged as he finished off fry jack #1. He'd always been thin, and with his height, "Beanpole" had been a common nickname growing up. He exercised regularly and his wiry frame was sculpted with lean muscle, but he had to admit that he wasn't the healthiest eater.

Emily reached over and patted his stomach. "How you eat that crap and never gain an ounce, I'll never know."

"Just my metabolism, I guess."

"Does your metabolism involve some form of unholy pact with Lucifer and his hellish minions?"

Boone was about to reply when a sound brought him up short. "You hear that?"

Emily looked around. "Yeah. Sounds like a dog."

A plaintive whine drew them to the side of the road. In the shadows under a light blue stilt house, bright eyes gleamed.

"Hey there, you." Boone crouched and spoke softly. "You want a bite of bacon?"

Another whine, but this one was punctuated with a single, short *Woof!* The dog had the long snout, cocked ears, and short coat of a typical Belizean potlicker, its color a café au lait tan. Caulker strays tended to have their own territories and Boone hadn't seen this one before along the route to the shop. It was quite small, half the size of most of the dogs in the neighborhood.

Emily crouched beside Boone. "Hey cutie! Who's a good dog? Come say hi!"

Tail wagging, the dog came forward tentatively. Boone fished a piece of bacon from his remaining fry jack, blew on it, and offered it to the potlicker. The dog carefully took the morsel in its teeth before stepping back and devouring it.

"Ooooh, you like that?" Emily said, lapsing into baby talk. "You want a wittle chicken?" She pinched some stewed chicken from her own fry jack and held it out. "I've never seen this dog around, have you?"

"No, first time I've seen him… or her…" He ducked his head down to ground level as the dog came forward for the chicken. "Him. No collar."

"He's so tiny. But he doesn't look like a puppy."

"Maybe the runt of the litter," Boone mused, finding a suitable chunk of egg in his fry jack and blowing on it to cool it. Above, a woman came onto the steps of the stilt house, fanning herself with a magazine as she looked down at them. Boone straightened and gave a little wave. "Excuse me, is this your dog?"

"No, today foist time I see it. Been under da house crying since dis morning. I put a bowl of water down dere for 'im. So many strays on da island, he's just anudda." With that, she turned and went back inside.

Boone fed the dog the piece of egg and followed it up with another piece of bacon. Finishing those, the potlicker commenced licking Boone's fingers. "Hungry little bugger, isn't he?"

Emily sat down and the dog left off licking Boone's fingers to plop down next to her, staring intently at the remnants of her chicken and bean pastry. "Oh, all right. Tell ya what, one more for me…" Em took a big bite of the fry jack. "And the rest for you," she finished, her voice garbled by the mouthful of food. She held the rest out on her palm and the dog devoured it, licking her hand clean once he'd finished.

Boone gave the potlicker a scratch behind the ears, eliciting more tail wagging. "Love those ears, buddy… like two floppy little bat wings." He stood. "We gotta go back to work, but we'll probably see you around, okay?" He started off down Pasero Drive and Emily joined him.

"I wish…"

"I know. But our apartment isn't really the best place for a dog. Besides, there are hundreds of strays all over the island. Hopefully someone will adopt him." There were a number of organizations that tried to place potlickers with visiting tourists.

"Maybe we should run him by the P.A.W. animal sanctuary," Emily said, pointing at the little compound as they passed it just before the dive shop. "I know they specialize in cats, but maybe they could give him a medical or something."

"Tell ya what… we'll swing by after the afternoon dive and ask." Boone glanced over his shoulder and smiled. "Someone's following us." He took a final bite of his fry jack and set the remainder on a cinderblock beside the sand road. As Boone and Emily reached Go Slow Diving, they watched their new friend trotting back to the stilt house with his pastry prize.

A t the crack of dawn, Boone woke to find Emily going through his shirts in the closet. It being their day off, he was hoping to sleep in a little, but that clearly wasn't going to happen.

"What are you…?"

"After we go see those Mayan ruins, you and I are going out. So no faded dive T-shirt for you. Ooh! This!" She selected a white guayabera shirt, holding it up to his bare chest as he rose from the bed. "Ace. And you do own a pair of trousers, right? Your jeans don't count."

"Yeah, got some khakis in here somewhere."

"Good, get dressed. The first ferry leaves at seven. We can grab coffee and breakfast in San Pedro."

"I think this is only the third time I've seen you in a dress," Boone said as they reached the sandy street outside their apartment building and headed north.

"Yeah, I'm more of a tanks, tees, and shorts kinda gal, but I can spiff up when I need to. You like what you see?" Emily spun around, modeling the pale green, spaghetti-strap sundress, its light material floating in the cool morning air. Her hair was down today and it floated free of her shoulders as she moved.

"Gorgeous. Dress ain't half bad, either."

"Good line," Emily said, ceasing her spins and continuing to stroll. "I've heard it before, mind you... but I liked it then, too."

"That gonna be okay for the Mayan site?"

"I looked it up online. It's not like we'll be slogging through a swamp. There's a walkway, so I should be fine."

"You don't have a purse or anything?"

"Why would I, man-with-pockets? I already stuck my ID and a credit card in your wallet and this—" She held up her cell phone. "—goes in here." She slid it into his right pocket and walked briskly away.

Reaching the end of their street, Emily started toward the ocean side of the island where the ferries were, but Boone stopped her. "Hey, let's go see if the dog is still there," Boone said. "We've got plenty of time."

"Okay by me." They had spoken to a worker at the animal sanctuary yesterday and discovered that Caye Caulker didn't have a permanent veterinarian on island, but that volunteers sometimes visited the sanctuary and examined animals. The sanctuary worker took their cell numbers, promising to let them know if they had one come in.

"Wait, one sec..." Boone crossed the intersection to Errolyn's and got a single breakfast fry jack and a bottle of water. "Gotta bring a gift," he said with a grin.

Reaching the blue stilt house, they called out softly, not wanting to wake the residents. No dog appeared. Boone crept closer, peering into the shadows under the house. "I don't see him."

"Probably out exploring."

"The water bowl is there... it's empty though." He filled the bowl with the water bottle and was about to leave the whole fry jack, then thought better of it, leaving half. He came back to the street, eating the remainder.

"What, you didn't leave all of it?"

"That dog is pretty small, and eating too much all at once might make him sick."

"Yeah, right," Emily scoffed. "Any excuse to eat one of those belly bombs." She started ponytailing her hair in preparation for the windy ferry ride. "Hey, don't get any of that fry jack on your shirt. We're having some proper food tonight and I want you presentable."

———◆◆———

After the half-hour ferry ride and a quick stop at The Junction for coffee and breakfast, Boone and Emily were sufficiently caffeinated to call up Dr. Rojas. He answered on the third ring.

"Ah, you made it! I hope you don't mind; I need to run an errand."

"Sure, no worries," Boone said. "We just got to your hotel, you want us to wait here?"

Manuel laughed, and the laugh came through both Boone's cell and the air as Manuel stepped out of the Spindrift, putting his phone into his pocket. An empty gallon jug dangled from his other hand by a hinged handle. "I'm so sorry, I had a late start. The hotel owner's daughter had her *quinceañera* at the hotel and I'm afraid I was up a bit late, enjoying some tequila with the parents."

"They had a party in the hotel? Bet the guests loved that," Boone said with a smile.

"Actually, it was quite clever. The owner is her mother, and she went around the hotel over the last two days, inviting everyone to her daughter's fifteenth birthday party. Free drinks and food."

Emily laughed. "Kinda hard to complain about noise when you've been invited to the bash."

Manuel nodded, wincing in the sunlight and retrieving a pair of sunglasses from his pocket. "Particularly when they were quite sincere about the free drinks. *¡Ay, caramba!*"

"Where are we off to, Doc?" Emily asked.

"Manuel is fine. Well, after I peeled my face off of my pillow, I went to the refrigerator in my room for some orange juice and discovered I was out. Do you mind?" He hefted the plastic jug. "There is a fellow on the north side of town who squeezes oranges for a very reasonable price. I'm afraid I have become addicted."

"Fine by me," Boone said. "Wanna make sure you're hydrated for our tour."

"It's only a couple minutes away by golf cart and I've got a rental." He gestured to a dingy, off-white golf cart.

"Shotgun!" Emily called out, scrambling aboard, leaving Boone to sit in the back-facing rear seat.

The trio trundled north along Barrier Reef Drive, golf carts, bicycles, and an occasional car passing them. As they drove by the yawning mouth of the Jaguar's Temple Club, Emily looked over her shoulder and shot Boone a warning look. He grinned and leaned over the seat to address Manuel. "How do you like San Pedro?"

"I love it! I realize it is more touristy than Caye Caulker, but it is still so quiet compared to resort towns in Mexico. And thank goodness they don't allow cruise ships to dock."

"Yeah, spot of luck there; the reef is too valuable to the tourism industry for them to allow that," Emily remarked. "Sometimes they anchor offshore, but usually they skip here and go to Belize City."

"They are a plague in Cozumel," Manuel muttered.

"It's not as bad as Coz," Emily said. "But one time we took a day off to go on a jolly to the mainland for some ziplining in the jungle. Alas, the cruise shippers had overrun that, so we went to a cave-tubing place instead—you know, where you get in an inner tube and float through caves on a jungle river?"

"Yes, I've done it. Did you enjoy it?"

"Didn't do it," Emily said. "The cruisies were there too."

Boone laughed. "When we arrived, there were so many brightly colored inner tubes, helmets, and life vests lined up in the river it looked like a ball pit at a Chuck E. Cheese."

"Yeah, so we gave up and went to the Belize Zoo instead. Bit of a drive, but we loved it! Those tapirs with their squishy noses were my favorites."

"Do the cruise ship shore excursions make it out to that mainland site you work at?" Boone asked. "Lamanai?"

"Fortunately for me, rarely. The river trip there takes too long for that." Manuel pulled over to the side of the road by a small, blue hut and shut off the golf cart. "No, the cruise ship tours usually stay closer to Belize City and go to Altun Ha."

"The one with all the jade," Emily said as they exited the cart. "Actually, on that subject…"

"One moment." Manuel approached the hut and waved to the wiry man inside. The interior of the little building contained several counters and a large, old-style juice press. Baskets of oranges sat nearby. *Hola*, Enrique!" He handed the man the jug. *"Un galón de jugo de naranja, por favor."* The man nodded and began rapidly slicing oranges.

Emily had taken the interval to look through her photos for the chacmool they had found on the dead man. She showed it to Boone and he nodded.

Manuel turned back to them. "Enrique is a fisherman by trade, but he started this juicing business on the side. Does very well! I'm sorry, you were saying? On the subject of jade?"

"You remember this, yeah?" Emily held out the phone.

"Ah yes, the chacmool souvenir you found while snorkeling."

Boone scuffed a foot through the sand at the side of the hut. "Yeah, about that... We weren't entirely, um... accurate... in our description of how we found it." He explained the full events of that morning, ending with the item falling from the diver's BC vest pocket.

Manuel looked stunned. "Well, I... I understand why you wouldn't have gone into detail on that short hop on the plane. Murder?" He shook his head. "Nevertheless, it still looks like a mere souvenir to me."

"That's what the staff at the Museum of Belize thought, too," Boone said. "But then they had it analyzed."

"We just learnt this from the police yesterday, but this little guy is made of pure jade," Emily said. "And it's consistent with the type of jade found in Altun Ha! And get this: that stone in one of the eye sockets was an emerald!"

Boone noticed the fisherman/juicer hesitate mid-squeeze and he motioned for Emily to bring her voice down. Meanwhile, Manuel was eagerly "reverse-pinching" the image on Emily's phone, zooming as close as it would allow. "Astonishing. Are they sure? I know many of the people at the Belize Institute of

Archaeology, I will call them this afternoon! But... *where* exactly was this found?"

"The northernmost tip of Caye Caulker. In the mangroves."

Manuel shook his head, handing the phone back. "There's nothing out there, to my knowledge. All the other Mayan sites on the cayes are here on Ambergris Caye to the north. Send me that photo, would you? I'll pass it on to some of my colleagues."

"Señor?" Enrique held out a full jug of fresh orange juice.

"*Gracias,* Enrique," Manuel said as he paid the man. "*Asta la próxima.*"

"*Si, claro.*"

Manuel climbed into the driver's seat and set the jug beside him. "I'll run this up to my hotel room refrigerator and then we shall go straight to the Marco Gonzalez site."

As the golf cart sped away to the south at a breakneck pace of ten miles per hour, Enrique—who spoke excellent English—dug a card from his wallet and made a phone call.

A gravelly voice answered on the first ring. "Yeah?"

Enrique squinted at the card. "Is this... Chuck?"

"Might be. Who's asking?"

"I am a fisherman. The other morning at the docks, an American man was offering fifty dollars for information about little jade statues we might find in our nets. Are you that man?"

"Depends on if you found one."

"No. But I know someone who did."

"Tell me more."

**11**

"You survived Hurricane Irma!" Manuel exclaimed as they drove south past the airport. "My goodness, that storm was huge, yes? I admit, I watch The Weather Channel somewhat religiously."

Boone laughed. *Everyone* in the Caribbean watches a lotta Weather Channel. At least from June to November. And yes, Irma was a big one; we were in Cat 5 winds for hours." He and Emily had given Manuel a brief rundown of their time on other islands during the half hour drive to the site, skipping over some of the more spectacular events of the last year. This was their day off; reliving their clashes with terrorists and psychotic killers was the last thing they wanted to do. But hurricanes were a popular subject in the islands, and Irma had indeed been a doozy.

"One of my workers is a local and was here for Hurricane Keith in 2000. Very bad. Much of this was flooded." Manuel gestured around them as they drove south, the buildings beginning to thin out as the foliage increased. "Here on Ambergris Caye, a third of the buildings were destroyed. I understand it was even worse on Caye Caulker."

"Yeah, the owner of our shop, Ignacio... he said there was a four-foot storm surge that came in from the lagoon side and completely swamped the island."

Manuel pulled over into a sandy parking lot on the right-hand side of the road. "From here we walk." He pointed at a pair of larger golf carts. "Looks like a tour group is in there already." Grabbing his pack, he got out and waved to a small, rustic building that was probably the visitor center. Alongside it were a number of bicycles. Manuel approached it and spoke to the woman inside, who handed him something. He waved them over, raising a small spray bottle. "The bugs haven't been too bad, but just in case... this eucalyptus spray works very well. He spritzed himself in a few strategic areas and handed it to Emily.

"Are we a bit... overdressed?" she asked, indicating her sundress. "Or *under*dressed, depending on your viewpoint," she added as she sprayed her bare legs, arms, and shoulders.

"You'll be fine. The path to the site is on a raised plank boardwalk and they are very good about cutting the mangroves back from it. Although I'm pleased to see you chose sensible footwear."

Emily waggled a green tennis shoe. "Yeah, even if we weren't doing this and just stayed in town, San Pedro roads don't play nice with a pair of heels."

Boone was glad he'd chosen sneakers of his own, and not his usual sports sandals. He sprayed himself and returned the bottle to the visitor center.

The trio set out through the brush and quickly came to a long stretch of uneven boards that stretched into the mangroves. Beautifully carved signs urged repeatedly to "Watch your step!" and provided information on the surrounding flora and fauna.

Near the road, the plants were short, but soon the mangroves rose over their heads.

"There are both red and black mangroves here. Much of this was above water during the time of Mayan settlement."

"Are there crocs in here?" Emily asked with a hint of nervousness.

"No, it's much too enclosed for them. The roots form a barrier. Most of the crocodiles in Ambergris Caye are on the lagoon side. The only thing to avoid here is the chechem."

"That sounds like an ominous beastie... what is that, a snake?"

Manuel laughed and pointed. "No, it's that." On an outcrop of dry land, an innocuous-looking tree had a sign nailed to it: "Chechem Tree. Do not touch!" Manuel paused to drink from a refillable water bottle. "It is a poisonwood tree. The bark has the same sort of oils as poison ivy. And as for snakes, the only one to watch out for is the *terciopelo*. You would know it as the fer-de-lance, but most locals don't call it that. Belizeans call it a Tommy Goff."

Boone chuckled. "I prefer that name. Kinda cute."

"Don't let that name fool you. They are an aggressive pit viper species with a nasty bite—but I don't know if there are any out on the cayes. I've certainly never heard of anyone seeing one here. But on the mainland at Lamanai, we keep an eye out for them."

A flash of red caught Boone's eye. He froze, peering into the mangrove trees. "Is that...? No way. A cardinal? We had those back in Tennessee!"

Manuel looked and spotted the bird, then pointed out its less flamboyant mate. "Yes, I was surprised when I saw them here. Although, one of my associates who works at San Gervasio, the Mayan site in Cozumel, told me she sees them frequently."

"Kinda weird seeing them in a tropical swamp. In my mind, when I think of a cardinal, I see it hanging out in the snow next to a Christmas tree."

"Whoa, it's gorgeous! And they've got pointy little crests!" Emily gushed.

"You don't have those in England?" Boone asked, incredulously.

"If we do, I've never seen one! But we've got hedgehogs, so that's something you two are missing out on."

After ten more minutes of "who's got the best animals," the walkway ended and they reached the Marco Gonzalez archaeological site, the terrain gently sloping up from the mangrove swamp.

Emily pointed at a sign with the name of the location. "Hey, I meant to ask… where'd the name come from? Was it one of the people who discovered it? Or… *re*discovered it?"

"Marco Gonzalez was a young local guide who led two archaeologists to the site. They named it after him."

"Hope they paid him, too." Boone said, looking around. "It's like a little island in the mangroves."

"Yes. The site is roughly an oval, about a kilometer across at its longest point. Centuries of settlement have left a lot of material here, so we're about twelve feet above sea level, higher than most of Ambergris Caye."

Over the next hour, Dr. Manuel Rojas gave them a detailed tour, pointing out foundations of the roughly fifty buildings that made up the settlement, mostly composed of limestone, there being no other form of stone to quarry on the caye. Even conch shells were used for building material in some structures. Pottery shards and bones were laid out in several locations, and he spoke about the types of items they continued to find.

Nearby, the voices of another tour competed with Manuel's, and Boone observed about a dozen tourists with their guide, a man with distinctive Mayan features, who was demonstrating some sort of spear-throwing stick. As Boone watched, he hooked a long, flexible javelin to the end of the stick, cocked his arm back, and sent the projectile into a nearby target with surprising speed and accuracy. Boone whistled with appreciation.

Manuel gestured for Boone and Emily to follow and started toward the group as the guide whipped another long dart through the air, its stone tip thunking into the target alongside the first. "Polo is one of our Mayan reenactors. He demonstrates indigenous techniques for hunting, craft-making, and survival skills." As they reached him, the man turned and smiled.

"Dr. Rojas! You want to demonstrate the *hul'che?*"

Manuel shook his head, grinning. "No, no… after those throws, I would look like a fool."

"I don't know, I've seen you hit the bullseye many times." He handed the stick and remaining darts to Manuel. "I need to finish up the tour. I will see you around, *amigo.*"

As the group continued through the clearing, Manuel held up the stick. It had a grip at one end, while the other curved into a notch with a peg. "Polo used the Mayan word for it, but this is an atlatl. It's a spear-thrower. It acts as an extension of your arm and the extra leverage it provides allows you to throw a javelin faster and farther. Here." He handed them each a slender spear, about two-and-a-half-feet long.

"They're so light," Boone observed.

"And wobbly!" Emily added, gently rocking the dart in her hand. The shaft bowed with each movement.

"That flexibility helps it travel through the air. You can reach about fifty yards with one. The Mayans tipped theirs with obsidian, but we use chipped stone here. Polo makes the practice points, demonstrating the Mayan tools at the same time he creates them." Manuel turned, nocking the back of his dart into the curved end of the stick and raising it level above his shoulder. "With this style of atlatl, you grip the stick with the bottom three fingers and pinch the dart with the thumb and index finger to hold it steady, and…" He reared back and threw. The dart hit the target fifty feet away with a satisfying thump.

"Nice shot!" Emily cheered.

Manuel blushed. "Not bad for a bookish archaeologist," he said, sounding pleased with himself. "Now you try."

Emily was up first, and her dart wobbled into the brush. "Oh, bollocks."

"Here, take mine." Boone offered her the remaining dart.

"No thanks, I'd rather see you do it. Try not to shish kebab a cardinal."

Boone laid the slender javelin up on the top of the stick, took aim, and swung his long, lanky arm forward. Perhaps due to the extra length of his limbs, the dart took off like a rocket. It didn't hit as close to the bullseye as Polo's, but the shaft itself penetrated the target to a depth of several inches.

Emily's jaw hung open as Boone handed the atlatl to Manuel, who looked at him askance.

"Either you've done this before—"

"I've done this before. Back in East Tennessee, my mom signed me up for a summer camp in Cherokee, North Carolina. The guy who ran the place… well, I guess you could say he was kinda like Polo, only he was Cherokee. He taught us a buncha skills during the week and they had some pre-gunpowder weapons. I thought the spear-throwing stick was pretty cool and the other kids were always hogging the blowguns and bows, so I had a lotta time to play with it."

"I want another go!" Emily declared.

Boone went to the target to retrieve the darts, searching first for Emily's errant throw. He found it next to a gumbo limbo tree. As he started back, he noticed one of Polo's tour straying far behind the group, looking back at Emily and Dr. Rojas, who were chatting animatedly. The man had his phone out and appeared to be filming. He looked Caucasian, a goatee and sunglasses visible under a straw Panama. His Hawaiian shirt and board shorts screamed "tourist," but something about that first impression seemed out of place. For one thing, his bulging arms clearly knew their way around a weight room. That alone didn't mean anything—fitness fanatics went on vacation like everyone else—but there was something about how he carried himself that didn't fit. Boone tried to remember if the individual had been in Polo's group before and couldn't recall seeing him. The man stopped filming and lifted the cellphone to his ear.

*Not going to get reception out here*, Boone thought, as the man gave up on his call, raising his polarized sunglasses to peer at the phone's screen. Boone pulled his own phone from his pocket, silenced it, then opened the camera app, zooming in on the man to snap a photo. He quickly pocketed the phone and turned toward Emily just as the man looked his way. "I found it!" he called out, stepping out of the brush and waving the dart.

As Boone walked to the target to pull the other javelins free, he spared a glance to the side. The man in the Panama hat was near the entrance to the site, joining the tour group as they returned to the wooden causeway. He did not look back at them and Boone relaxed a bit.

*Maybe he was just taking a last photo or video of the clearing,* he thought, as he reached Emily and gave her a dart. "Here ya go."

Emily took it and notched it onto the atlatl. She looked at Boone. "So… show me where to put my fingers."

Boone snorted a laugh. "Phrasing." He then arranged her fingers on the grip and took her through the throwing action in slow motion. Her second throw was worse than the first. Her third: a bullseye.

**12**

By the time Manuel returned them to town it was midafternoon. The archaeologist headed back to the dig to get some actual work done, leaving the divemasters to enjoy the remains of the day.

"Well, we have been sufficiently edified and educated—time for some fun!" Emily announced. She took Boone by the hand and started marching north.

Boone glanced over at her, watching her blonde ponytail swinging to and fro like a golden pendulum. "I thought you were going to let your hair down today."

"Oh crikey, I'm still in jungle adventurer mode." She shook her shining hair loose and teased it into a semblance of order. "Happy?"

Boone answered her brief question with a kiss. "Okay, Em, you're in charge. What's the plan?"

Emily's plan turned out to be quite simple. She took Boone straight to a little yellow spa out on a pier, where she had booked two hours of massage and mini-spa treatments. No cheesy spa music was needed here, as the sound of the ocean gently lapping beneath the boards provided the perfect accompaniment. Next, they went right back up the pier and straight into Belizean Arts, a gallery full of works by local painters, sculptors, and carvers. Then, next door to Fido's for a couple of watermelon mojitos, relaxing at a table overlooking the beach until Emily announced it was time for dinner.

"Where are we going?" Boone asked, dropping some Belizean bills on the table as they left.

"I'll give you a hint: a key lime pie fanatic like you would be happy with my choice."

Boone grinned and led the way around the block to Middle Street, officially known as Pescador Drive. They'd been to this restaurant a number of times and he never got tired of it.

Elvi's Kitchen was easily the most famous restaurant on Ambergris Caye, having risen from its humble beginnings as a burger takeout stand in 1974. The owner, Doña Elvia, had served food from a small takeout window underneath her house, situated beside a flamboyant tree. Her cooking was popular, and the business soon expanded; now, even in the low season, reservations were recommended. Unlike many "must visit" places in tourist towns, Elvi's had more than its reputation to recommend it: the food was some of the best Belizean fare on the island and the ambience was spectacular. Polished wood gleamed from walls, roof beams, and furniture. In the center of the sand-floored main dining room, the original flamboyant tree rose through the thatch-roofed ceiling, its trunk covered in white Christmas lights. And the key lime pie? In Boone's opinion, Elvi's made the best he'd ever had. They served it semi-frozen, and as the slice sat on your plate under a pillow of whipped cream, it seemed to get juicier with every bite.

After they were seated at a table for two behind the glowing tree, Emily ordered a glass of white wine and Boone chose a Belikin. The menu was pages long, and though they debated trying out various new dishes, they both opted for their favorite: Mayan chicken in adobo sauce, steamed inside a banana leaf.

The dinner was done, and they were waiting on their key lime pie when Boone remembered the man he'd observed at the end of their tour. He pulled out his phone and went to his pictures.

"Boone, no phones at the... oh, who am I kidding? I want a picture of the pie." She started to reach for her own smartphone, but Boone slid his across the table.

"Did you see this guy at the archaeological site? Weightlifter arms, loud tourist shirt."

She examined the picture and Boone watched her brow furrow slightly. "At the site, no, but..." She leaned to the side, looking toward the bar at the far end of the restaurant. "Is that him?"

Boone turned his head to follow her gaze and saw the man leaning against the bar, his back to them. His Panama hat sat beside him, revealing a severe buzzcut that made him look even less of a tourist, despite the Hawaiian shirt. Boone could just make out a diagonal scar across the back of his scalp.

"Well I'll be... that's him." Boone caught a glimpse of the individual's face amongst the bottles in the bar's mirror before the man looked down at his drink. Boone turned back to Emily. "Pretty weird coincidence..."

"What, that a tourist was doing two touristy things on the same day? This *is* the most popular restaurant on the island, Boone."

"Here's one of da reasons for dat," a waitress said as she brought the key lime pie, whipped cream piled high atop the hefty slices. "Enjoy!"

And they did. Three bites in, Boone stole a look back at the bar. The man was gone.

———◆·◆———

Strolling around the block to return to the main drag, Boone took Emily's hand. "So, this is *your* adventure. Ferries are all done. Did you get us a hotel, or are we gonna look for a fisherman to beg a night ride from?"

"Hotel. We'll take the six a.m. Belize Express tomorrow."

"Where are we staying?"

"Spindrift." She grinned up at Boone. "That story about the owner's *quinceañera* gave me joy. So, while you were off hunting for my spear, I asked Manuel to book us a room."

"Sneaky little minx, ain't you?"

"You don't know the half of it," Em said, mirth coloring her voice.

They hit Front Street, but when Boone turned right, he came up short, Emily's grip on his hand stopping him as she pulled him left. "Uh… Spindrift is right there," he said, pointing cater-corner across the intersection.

"Oh, we're not going there yet…" She tugged hard and Boone stumbled north toward the plaza.

"Then where are we…? Oh, no. No, no, no, no, no."

"Yes, yes, yes!"

Ahead, music pulsed, seeming to issue from the gaping maw of the jaguar's jaws as Emily dragged Boone toward the Jaguar's

Temple Night Club. The outdoor seating area was full up with revelers in varying states of inebriation.

"You've had this planned from the beginning."

"Since we walked by it the other day," Em said as they reached the door. "C'mon Boone, feed the jaguar!" she sang, pronouncing the big cat's name in all its British glory before dragging him inside through the roaring mouth.

Boone wasn't a fan of the noisier pursuits of resort towns, namely karaoke and clubbing. Unfortunately for him, Emily enjoyed both. *At least tonight isn't karaoke night*, he thought. The two-level club was hopping, the bass beat of the music pounding the air. *Feels like my organs are getting a sonic X-ray.* Flashing red strobes competed with green lasers, illuminating the gyrating crowd on the light-up dance floor. The whole scene had a haze hanging in the air, the product of fog machines and cigarettes. Emily threaded her way through the throng to reach the nearest bar, its shelves outlined in colorful LED strips.

"Beers!" she shouted, holding up two fingers. "Boone, pay the man." Belikins were quickly poured from a tap into plastic cups and Emily handed one to Boone, craning her head up to his ear. "People-watching beverage!" she yelled, and pointed to a corner.

They watched the smoky, pulsing room from the corner as they sipped their beers, occasionally sharing a shouted observation about someone's dance moves. The *punta* was on display, the gyrating hips of the Garifuna dance very much at home in this night club as men and women advanced and retreated with provocative pelvic pulsations. The club was mostly filled with locals, but a few tourists were here and there. Finally, Emily took Boone's cup and set their beers aside on a table. She beckoned for him to bend down so she could put her mouth near his ear.

"I know you're hating this," she shouted. "And it's a little much for me, too! A couple dances and we're outta here, okay?"

Boone flashed her the *OK* sign.

Emily grinned and the two of them headed for the dance floor.

———◆•◆———

The phone dinged and the man looked at the text.

*They are dancing.*

He quickly texted back: *Do it.*

Another text immediately appeared: *Wilco.*

The man in the Hawaiian shirt crossed the plaza and sat on a brightly colored bench with an unobstructed view of the entrance to the night club across Front Street. Setting his Panama hat on the seat beside him, he tapped his phone's screen and made a call.

———◆•◆———

"Hey!" Emily had been having a ball, dancing with wild abandon, when all of a sudden, a hand had gripped her ass through her sundress and squeezed. She swept an arm back to remove the offending hand, pleased that her swing connected with a pinkie finger. The grip released and she spun around to confront whoever it was—she knew it wasn't Boone. For one thing, ass grabbing wasn't in his DNA… certainly not in public. For another, they had danced apart during the last song. As she turned, she looked for Boone but didn't spot him. The groper-in-question was right there, boldly holding her gaze as he shook out the hand she had chopped. He wasn't a local. White guy, good shape, shaved head, a yellow T-shirt with a leaping marlin on a fishing line atop a pair of cargo shorts. The clothes looked new, the creases from a store-shelf fold still visible.

"You're a feisty one, ain't ya?" he shouted, a strong redneck accent twanging the vowels.

"Sod off!"

"Aw, c'mon baby, let's dance." He reached out and grabbed her arm.

On the island of Saba, Emily had had the good fortune to befriend Sophie Levenstone, a local firefighter and practitioner of Krav Maga, a brutally efficient Israeli self-defense technique. Emily had always been impressed with Boone's fighting skills, a mix of capoeira and Brazilian jiu-jitsu, and when Sophie offered to train her, she'd jumped at the opportunity. Here on Ambergris Caye, she'd found a place north of San Pedro to take a brush-up class from time to time.

The moment the man's fingers closed around her forearm, she struck, bringing her other arm across, gripping the man's pinky and lifting it in a sharp, twisting motion. She felt the finger give and the man screamed, clearly not expecting such a sudden and savage response. Emily swiftly shifted the grip to the hand and continued the motion, locking his wrist. The man was strong, and Emily knew if she hadn't caught him by surprise the wrist manipulation might not have worked.

"Bitch!" The man snarled through gritted teeth. Around them, dancers began scrambling away and she saw Boone tearing toward them across the strobing dance floor.

"Em!" he shouted, about to intervene, when a second man stepped into his path and took a swing at him.

*What the…? Who's this guy?* Emily thought, as she leaned her weight into the wrist, stepping in a circle around her attacker and keeping the pressure on the lock. She watched as Boone easily dodged the sucker punch from his broad-shouldered attacker and took up his capoeira stance, the bouncing *ginga* steps strangely at home on a club dance floor. She noted that this man was also Caucasian, hair close-cropped, and wearing a souvenir "I Heart Belize" T-shirt over khakis.

With a sudden roar, her own dance partner managed to turn his body enough that he broke the lock. She spun away from him, her eyes catching Boone's as she angled toward him, the bald redneck right on her heels.

The lanky divemaster feinted to his right, then tumbled in a swift cartwheel to his left when his attacker took the bait, snapping a quick *aú batido* L-kick into the onrushing face of Emily's opponent. Their combined momentum gave the kick enough juice that the man dropped like a stone and lay still. Boone used the impact to spring back the other way, coming to his feet to face the other man.

Emily spotted police near the entrance, trying to push through the crowd. "Coppers are here, you twat!"

The man flicked his eyes toward the entrance, then suddenly attacked Boone, snapping several punches at him as he advanced. The man kept his guard up as he did so, his stance grounded.

*He's not some drunken brawler,* Emily thought, as Boone blocked, ducked, and dodged. *He's got training.* But something about the man's attack seemed… *off.*

Finally, Boone left himself open and the man swung a haymaker. Boone ducked the swing by dropping to the floor, snapping a hammer kick to the man's leading kneecap as he landed, then planting and spinning his other leg in a *martelo de negativa* kick as his opponent buckled forward, slamming his foot into the man's temple and sending him sprawling across the floor. He came to a stop with his cheek pressed against one of the dance floor lights, his unconscious face glowing in a shifting array of colors.

A flash of movement caught Emily's eye. Her attacker was rising behind Boone, a flash of silver in his hand. "Boone! Knife!" As she cried out, she came at the man's flank and snagged his wrist, twisting it in a smooth motion. Perhaps he was still unsteady from Boone's kick, because the knife came loose with surprising ease. It clattered to the floor and Emily scooped it up.

Boone spun around and toppled the man with a simple leg sweep. At that precise moment, the song ended with a loud boom, confetti cannons showering the now-empty dance floor with sparkling scraps of paper.

"Oh, thank God!" Emily said, as the police broke through the crowd. She set the knife on the ground as they approached. "These men—hey, what are you doing?" The police grabbed Emily and pressed her to the floor, cuffing her. "They started it! Grabby McGrab-ass there!" She nodded her head toward the prone man who had groped her.

Boone was also swarmed, but he complied without a struggle. "It's okay, Em. They'll sort this out. Plenty of witnesses."

"Bollocks," she muttered, but watched with some satisfaction as their two assailants were cuffed as well.

"You okay?" Boone asked as they were lifted to their feet and frog-marched toward the exit.

"Yeah, peachy. You?"

"Fine." Boone laughed. "See, this is what you get when you drag me to a night club."

Emily sighed. "It was turning out to be a perfect day off, too." She ducked her head as the police put them into the back of one of the few San Pedro Police vehicles.

"It ain't over yet. Once they talk to the witnesses, we'll be on our way to the Spindrift."

"I s'pose." Emily let her head thump against the window, looking toward the plaza. There was some party going on and people were milling around several pop-up food stands. Locals mostly, but there were some tourists… and one tourist stood out. "Boone!"

"What?" He leaned forward to look out her window.

"Your friend is back."

As the police threaded their way into the evening flow of golf cart traffic, Boone and Emily watched the man in the loud Hawaiian shirt and Panama hat recede from view, his eyes locked on the police car, a phone to his ear.

"What time is it?" Emily asked from the hard bench against the back wall of the cell.

Boone looked at a wall clock through the bars he was gripping. "After two in the morning."

"What the bloody hell is going on?" Emily got up from the bench and paced, the cramped cell not allowing for many strides before she had to turn around.

Boone wasn't sure what the holdup was. He had expected they'd be sat down at a desk to answer a few questions and then be on their way. When they were led straight to a cell, he'd name-dropped Superintendent Flores, explaining that they were the ones who'd recovered the body and had met with him just the other day. The policeman who was locking them up appeared unimpressed.

"He's not in," he had said.

"Well... can you call him?" Boone asked.

"No."

"Look, we were attacked," Emily had pleaded. "Ask the people in the club!"

"We did. The ones we spoke to said *you* were the ones who started it."

"But… but that's not true!" Emily had shouted.

He pointed at Emily. "And *you* had a knife."

"It wasn't *mine!*"

*Something's not right,* Boone had thought. He'd laid a calming hand on Emily's shoulder. "What about security camera footage?"

"The club owner say the CCTV system was down."

*Well, that's convenient.* "Sir, I believe we're entitled to a phone call…"

The policeman had actually sneered at him. "You watch too much television." Then he flipped off the lights and left.

Now, hours later, they hadn't spoken to anyone since they'd been locked in the cell. Boone could see into the neighboring room and had watched a few policemen come and go, but now only one remained, his feet up on the desk, chatting on his phone to someone. From snatches of conversation, Boone guessed it was a girlfriend.

Emily joined him at the bars. "There's no way all of the people at the club would say we started that."

Boone looked at her. "You're right. There's no way. I could see how a few people might have gotten it wrong, but… no, something's fishy."

"And the guys who attacked us, didn't they seem… I don't know…"

"Not very touristy? Kinda like that other guy?"

"Yeah. Who goes clubbing in a souvenir T-shirt?" Emily asked. "I mean… I even got *you* to dress up."

Boone smiled at her, hearing the attempt at levity, but his mind was scratching at something else. "Those T-shirts… they were new. Like… brand-new."

Emily nodded, thinking. "I noticed that too, on the guy who grabbed me."

Boone sighed. "We might as well get some sleep. I don't think we're getting out of here tonight."

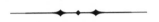

Raised voices roused Boone from slumber. Emily lifted her head from her makeshift pillow of Boone's lap and sat up on the bench.

"This is outrageous! Where is your superior officer?"

"He gone home."

"You arrested two employees of a local dive shop because of a bar fight in a night club? Where are the ones they were fighting with, hmm?"

"That posh accent…" Emily said, rising from the bench.

"It's Oliver Price." Boone went to the bars, Emily joining him. "What are the charges?"

"Drunk and disorderly, assault with a deadly weapon—"

"What?" Boone roared.

"It's complete bollocks," Emily shouted.

Oliver looked toward the cell from the other room and raised a calming hand. "What 'deadly weapon' are they charged with using?"

"The woman, she had a knife."

Oliver scoffed. "I seriously doubt that was hers—look at what she's wearing! Where did she stash it?"

The policeman shifted on his feet, looking uncomfortable. "There were witnesses…"

Price stepped closer to the man and spoke quietly. "I know these two and I vouch for them. I imagine you know who I am. I'm the one who donated all the new equipment to your department, including the new SUVs and police boat. You call your superior this very minute and tell him that I'm bailing them out. Do it now."

The officer looked cowed and after a moment he picked up his cell phone from a nearby desk and placed a call. Oliver strode toward the cells.

"Are you two all right?"

"Spiffy," Emily muttered.

Oliver's eyes took her in, lingering over the dress. "Night on the town didn't end well, I take it?"

"How did you know we were here?" Boone asked, moving closer to Emily.

"One of my associates was at the club and witnessed the whole row. I came over from Chapel as soon as I heard."

"Your associate… does he happen to enjoy Panama hats?" Boone asked. When Oliver looked confused, Boone continued. "White guy, hair in a military cut…"

Oliver broke into a smile. "No, no, it was Wilson who called me. African American gentleman. You met him on my boat."

"Your beefy bodyguard!" Emily blurted.

"Yes, that's him."

"And your boat's skipper," Boone remarked.

"Well, ordinarily, yes… but truth to tell, I drive my own boats, often as not. Wilson had the night off. And a good thing, too! Now, don't you worry, you'll be out of here in a jiff. I've got a bit of pull around here." He smiled broadly, perfect teeth shining in the dim glow of the fluorescent lights.

"Buying the police a boat can help with that, I reckon."

The smile faltered. "I fear that came across as somewhat boastful, but I figured reminding the man of it would produce the proper response. That new boat, by the way, was to aid in the policing of the marine reserves. There was quite a bit of illegal fishing and the poachers had little trouble outrunning the previous boat."

Boone felt Emily's hand on his arm. "We're grateful for your help, aren't we Boone?" She gave his arm a squeeze.

A jingle of keys interrupted Boone's response. "Okay, boss says he has Mr. Price's credit card on file for potential bail. You two are free to go," their jailer announced. He unlocked the cell and handed them a Ziploc of belongings. Without another word he went back to his desk and resumed texting.

Outside, the trio stood in the floodlights that illuminated the yellow and green police station on Middle Street. Boone took a look at his phone and saw it was three thirty in the morning.

Emily glanced at it. "Cor, it's half three. So much for a good night's sleep."

"The *Liquid Asset* is docked right there near the Phoenix," Oliver said, pointing toward a nearby resort. "I'll run you over to Caulker on my way back to Chapel." He turned to lead them toward the resort lobby.

"No, that's all right, we have a room," Boone said quickly.

"Don't be daft," Emily said. "We'd have to get up in a couple hours anyway to make the first ferry. Might as well take the free ride."

Boone started to object but couldn't explain why he didn't think that would be a good idea. "All right, fine."

Oliver smiled. "Excellent. This way."

Emily followed but Boone stayed put.

"What about our luggage?" he asked.

Oliver stopped and looked back. "Oh. Yes, of course. How silly of me. Where is your hotel? We can go fetch it."

"Boone, we didn't bring any luggage," Emily said.

Boone slapped his forehead with his palm. "Oh, right… sorry I'm an idiot. Guess I'm tired. Okay, let's go."

As they crossed through the grounds of the Phoenix, Oliver took out his phone and began texting. "Just letting Wilson know we're on the way. He decided to drive the boat, since he's due back today anyway." He resumed texting.

*Pretty lengthy text,* Boone thought. Ahead, he could see the shape of Oliver's Sundancer, moored at the far end of a pier on the edge of the dock's lights. In the gloom of the pier, Boone could see the glow of a cigarette. Its glow was joined by that of a smartphone as the man on the pier looked down at it. Then both extinguished, as the man pocketed the phone and flicked the cigarette into the ocean. *Where some turtle will probably eat the filter,* Boone thought, as he watched the man board the boat. Moments later the boat's engine started up and its running lights came on.

"All aboard for Caye Caulker!" Oliver announced, stepping across and turning back to offer his hand to Emily.

"Why thank you, good sir," she said and hopped across.

Boone waved to Wilson as the man exited the salon. "I can get the lines for you."

Wilson stopped and shrugged. "Fine by me." He headed for the bridge.

With practiced ease, Boone released the dock lines and tossed them across to Emily while Oliver watched with amusement.

"One would almost think you do this every day," he said with a chuckle.

"I'm also quite handy behind the wheel," Emily commented as Boone stepped across to join her. "Not this guy, though… boats will sink themselves sooner than let him drive them."

Boone shook his head with a smile. "The second part isn't true, but Em is a whiz at the wheel, no doubt about it."

"Really? Well, once Wilson gets us into the channel, would you like to drive her?"

"Do I want to drive a posh yacht? You better Belize it!" Emily crowed.

Boone groaned. "I can't believe you just said that."

Oliver laughed heartily. "You, my dear, are a delight. Very well, let's go to the bridge and Wilson can show you the controls."

"Ace!" Emily grinned and headed forward.

<hr />

Halfway back to Caulker, Emily was at the controls with Oliver at her side and Boone stepped aft for a breath of fresh air. Wilson joined him for some not-so-fresh air, shaking a cigarette from a pack. Given the hour, Emily was taking it slow and the man had little trouble firing up his smoke in the lee of the boat's main cabin and salon.

"Sorry to mess up your night off," Boone said.

"What?" Wilson looked at him, then shook his head. "Oh, yeah, nah, that's okay. That Leopard Club was too noisy anyhow."

Boone cocked his head. "Leopard?"

Wilson laughed, waving a hand. "Shoot, I meant Jaguar... I always get those confused. Anyway, good thing I saw what went down. And called Mr. Price."

"Yeah, that was a 'spot of luck,' as Emily would say." Boone nodded at the man's clothes. "You go clubbing in that?" Wilson was wearing the same black slacks and tight-fitting white polo shirt he'd had on at Half Moon Caye.

The man took a drag on his cigarette before responding. "Well, you know what they say. Chicks dig a man in uniform, and this is the only uniform I got."

Boone laughed. "Well, thanks, man. Glad you were there, or we might still be in jail. Wasn't right that we got locked up and the three guys who attacked us got off scot-free."

Wilson just looked at Boone. He took another drag and blew out a long stream of smoke before speaking. "Wasn't three guys. There was only two. 'Scuse me." He flicked his cigarette over-board and headed back inside.

Boone watched him go, then smiled at Emily as she came aft, Oliver close behind.

Em plopped down next to Boone. "That was brilliant! She handles like a dream!"

"Well, you're welcome to take her out on the ocean sometime," Oliver said, taking a seat across from them. "In the daylight, pref-erably. Take her through her proper paces."

"Throw in some lobster and top-shelf rum, and I'll consider it."

"Say, now that I've got you here... I was wondering. A friend of mine is looking for a pair of divers to help him with a little archaeological work. I don't suppose you'd be interested?"

"Your friend didn't happen to come asking for us at Belize Diving Services the other day, did he?" Emily asked.

Oliver thought a moment. "I don't know. I didn't think he was yet in country. Anyway, I'm sure you have a full schedule with that dive op of yours, but if you have any free time and would like to make a little extra money…"

"What's his name?" Boone asked.

"Archibald Welk."

Emily snorted a stifled laugh. "Oh, dear lord, I'm sorry."

Oliver grinned and waved a hand. "No, no, I quite understand. I thought the same thing when we first corresponded. With a name like that, you'd imagine he's more British than we are, with a monocle and an ascot."

"I bet he wears tweed," Emily mused.

"That, I can't attest to… but I *can* tell you that he's actually an American from the Bronx, without a British bone in his body."

"I wonder if Manuel knows him," Boone said.

"Ah, Manuel Rojas? The Mexican archaeologist who works on Ambergris?"

"You know him?" Emily asked.

"I know *of* him, but we've never met. Dr. Welk is with another organization, but perhaps they are acquainted, I wouldn't know. So, can I let him know you're interested? I understand he pays quite handsomely."

"Handsome is good," Emily said with a smile. "Well, I for one am all in favor of an infusion of cash. How soon—" Emily stopped as Boone slipped a hand onto her knee.

"Can we sleep on it?" he asked.

Oliver smiled. "Of course! But don't take too long. Plenty of other divers in Belize."

When Boone and Emily reached their apartment at five a.m., Em slipped out of her dress in one smooth motion and flung it onto the floor as she flopped onto the bed. "We can get a little sleep, yeah?"

Boone was already setting the alarm for half past six. Most days, that was "sleeping in," but it would give them enough time to get to the shop and set up for the morning's dives. He ditched his shirt and slacks and joined her.

"So? Wanna make some extra quid?"

Boone didn't answer, sifting through a jumble of thoughts.

Emily nudged him. "What are you thinking?"

"Jaguar."

"Oh, don't start that again."

"No... not the silly way you say it, the way Wilson said it. Or didn't say it. He called it the Leopard Club."

"So?"

"C'mon Em, it's one of the most well-known places in San Pedro. I don't think he's ever been there. And who goes clubbing in a polo shirt?"

"A guy who looks good in a polo shirt."

Boone chuckled. "Got me there." He thought a moment. "I tried to trip him up. I said we'd been attacked by three guys."

"And...?"

"He corrected me and said there were only two."

"Well, there you go."

"Yeah. Except he seemed pissed about it. Like he knew I was messing with him."

"He was probably pissed at having his evening ruined."

"I suppose."

"Look, we're both exhausted. I mean, you thought we had luggage over there, and—"

"No. I knew we didn't have luggage. But we'd just told Mr. Price we had a hotel room and yet he started to take us straight to the boat. Like *he* knew we didn't have luggage. I just wanted to see what he'd say."

"He said he'd go get our luggage! Look, I think you're being paranoid, Boone."

"Maybe." Boone sighed. "But before we sign up for... whatever it is, let's ask around. See if Ras knows something about this Archibald Welk guy."

"We could call Manuel, too," Emily suggested. "Now let's get some sleep."

All too soon, it was time to get up. After a quick cup of coffee and hastily wolfed breakfast, Boone and Emily hustled around the corner to the dive shop. Ahead, they could see two divemasters already there, loading up the boat.

"That's Cammy and Tim," Emily remarked. "What are they doing here?"

"Maybe we have a second boatload today," Boone suggested. Cammy and Tim were a pair of divemasters who subbed in at several of the dive shops on Caulker. "Let's check the board."

As they reached the shop, they were greeted by a somber-looking Ignacio. "Come inside, please."

"What's up, chief?" Em asked, a touch of concern in her voice.

Ignacio didn't reply, just turned and went inside.

Boone glanced toward the pier. Cammy and Tim were staring at them. Cammy managed a half-smile and raised a hand in greeting—Tim looked away. "Shit," Boone said. He and Emily entered the office.

Ignacio was sitting behind the little counter in the corner looking decidedly uncomfortable. "We have a problem…"

"Lemme guess. The arrest last night," Boone said. "Look, Ignacio, it was a misunderstanding."

Ignacio shifted in his seat. "That may be, and I understand you were bailed out, yes? But the situation is more complicated. Superintendent Flores is… well… he and my family go way back. And it has been suggested… suggested quite strongly… that I not employ you until this matter has been cleared up."

"But it *was* cleared up," Emily protested. "We had a witness contact Mr. Price, and he bailed us out."

"Oliver Price?" Ignacio knitted his brow, but then shook his head. "It doesn't matter. Making bail doesn't vacate the charges."

"But… innocent until proven guilty, yeah?" Emily said.

Ignacio cleared his throat. "There are other considerations. I am a member of the Village Council. I can't… look, this is difficult for me. I promise, once the police drop the charges, I'll hire you back and give you as much overtime as you need. But for now…" He looked down at his desk. "I'm sorry."

◆ ◆ ◆

"Sodding hell!" Emily's sandals tore into the sand-packed street as she trudged away from the dive shop, her gear bag swinging from a trembling fist.

Despite his stride being more than double the length of hers, Boone had to trot to keep up. "Look, it's not the end of the world. They'll drop the charges once all the witness statements come in and we'll be back to work."

Emily stopped at the corner and spun about. "Oh, yes, because the bureaucracy in this country moves with blinding efficiency, yeah? How long will it take before they get around to making these charges go away?" She kicked a chunk of sun-bleached coral, sending it skidding across the sand. "Un-Belize-able!"

Boone bit his lip, grinning at the word play.

Emily pointed at him. "Don't laugh! I know that was funny. And brilliant. But I'm not in the mood!" Her shoulders sagged. "Is it time to switch islands again?"

Boone shook his head. "It'll be all right. Look, I hate to admit it, but Mr. Price did say he had some pull with the police. These trumped-up charges, I'm sure he could..." He trailed off, a suspicion rising from the back of his mind.

"Could... what?" Emily prompted.

Boone was about to reply when a plaintive whine drew their attention to the light blue stilt house on the corner. The little pot-licker was back, bright eyes peering out from the sand under the house. The animal was trembling, and its whimpers sounded, to Boone's ears, like a dog's version of crying.

"Hey, little fella," Emily cooed, all talk of unjust incarceration and unforeseen unemployment gone to the winds.

Boone crouched and crab-walked closer. "Hey boy... remember us?" The dog scooted back a few inches, but halted and gave a half-hearted, hopeful tail wag. As Boone drew nearer, he spotted a wound in the dog's flank. "What happened to you, huh?"

"Is he hurt?"

"Yeah... looks like a dog bite..." Boone glanced up at the house. The windows were open, but he couldn't see anyone inside. Peering at the little water bowl near the dog, he could see it was dry. "Hey, Em, can you run over to Errolyn's and get a fry jack?"

"Back in a jiff!" Emily dumped her gear bag and dashed across the sandy intersection.

Boone dug into his own bag and came out with a beach towel and his water bottle. Extending a long arm, he poured the remaining water into the bowl. The dog watched him warily, but then crawled forward on its belly, like a World War One soldier sliding under barbed wire. Reaching the bowl, it lapped greedily.

Emily crouched alongside Boone. "They weren't open yet, but I talked them into giving me some eggs and bacon in a cup."

"Just as good." Boone sat on the sandy yard and Emily joined him. He spread the towel on his lap and took the cup, then waited until the potlicker was finished with the water before pinching some scrambled egg between thumb and forefinger. "Hey, boy… you hungry?"

The dog sniffed the air, then crept slowly out from under the house. Looking from one human to the other, he edged closer. When he stopped, a couple of feet away, Emily reached into the cup for a chunk of bacon.

"Baby steps, little pooch," she said, tossing the bacon close to the dog's snout. The potlicker tensed at the sudden movement but quickly gobbled the morsel up. "That's a good boy!" Emily said, her voice pitching up.

After a few more tempting offerings, the dog came to them and settled onto the towel on Boone's lap, where he fed the potlicker the remainder of the food, Emily giving encouraging words and ear scratches all the while. Occasionally, a flea or sand fly would jump ship from the canine's fur.

"Let's take him to P.A.W., yeah?" Emily urged, nodding at the nearby animal sanctuary.

"If he'll let us," Boone said, eyeing the wound on the dog's flank. It looked infected and he'd have to be careful and handle the animal gently. "There may not be a vet on-island, but maybe they've got some antibiotics." Gently, making sure to keep the swaddling towel clear of the injury, Boone stood and carried the animal the short block to the sanctuary.

A half hour later, Boone and Emily were walking south along Middle Street, having dropped off their gear at the apartment. The owner of the sanctuary had examined the dog and said she would call a friend who was a nurse to take a look—a nurse for humans, but beggars couldn't be choosers. She had promised to give them a call as soon as she learned anything. As they hit the street, Boone's cell phone dinged with a text from Ras Brook.

*Meet me at the I and I. Someone you need to talk to.*

The I and I Reggae Bar was a distinctive, three-story structure—a treehouse-like wooden tower, topped with a thatched roof and adorned with bright yellow, green, and red paint, three of the four colors of the Jamaican flag, the fourth being black. Caye Caulker had a sizeable Rastafarian community and Rastafari culture was on display at this popular club. The bar's name, "I and I," was a common phrase in Rastafari slang. A complex term, it meant "we" as in "you and I"—the oneness of two individuals, as equals. One Love. It was also not uncommon to hear it casually used to simply mean oneself, one "I" being the body and the other the mind.

Boone and Emily hadn't even turned the corner onto Luciano Reyes Street when the slow, pulsing tempo of a Bob Marley song filled the air, staccato guitar chords pulsing strongly on the off beats.

"Boonemily!" a voice called out from above. On the open-air, third floor of the structure, Ras Brook leaned over a railing and saluted them with a Red Stripe. "Come on up!"

Ascending the stairs, Boone and Emily passed numerous murals, a mash-up medley of Mayan images and tributes to Marley. Each floor was filled with rope swings, the wooden seats ranging from solo to bench-size. An occasional hammock dangled alongside the swings. It being mid-morning, the seating was largely empty, but for a few diners enjoying the inexpensive breakfast on offer.

Ras was leaning against the railing, looking out over the rooftops of the surrounding neighborhood. He turned as Boone and Emily topped the stairs and approached them, setting his beer down at a table as he passed it. When he reached them, he clapped a hand onto each of their shoulders and looked from one to the other. "I heard da news. I am sorry. But Jah always have a plan, and I and I will be all right. Seen?"

Boone knew that "seen" was a Rastafari way of saying, "know what I mean?"—kind of how Emily tended to tack "yeah" on the end of sentences. He smiled and clasped a firm grip onto the older man's strong hand. "Thanks, man. From your lip's to Jah's ears."

Ras smiled and nodded. "Ya, mon." He gestured to a table where a thin Mayan man sat on a swing. "Come. Sit." An ice bucket sat in the center of the table, bottles of Red Stripe perspiring in the warm air. Ras took two and popped the tops off on the edge of the table. Judging by the nicks in the wood, this wasn't the first time a bottle had been opened there. He offered the stubby bottles to them.

Emily raised an eyebrow above her green sunglasses. "Little early in the day, yeah?"

"It's not like you two got any diving to do," Ras said with a deadpan expression, before breaking into a grin.

Emily laughed and grabbed a Stripe. "Got me there. Cheers." She took a slug. Boone followed suit.

"I want you to meet someone. This is Luis Pacab. One of the oldest fishermen on Corker."

The man gave a small smile. "Not so old, *cabrón,*" the man said. And indeed, his sun-beaten face didn't reveal much in the way of wrinkles—Boone had guessed he was in his late fifties, at most.

"Luis, dis here is Boonemily." Ras swept a hand at the two divemasters.

Boone smiled. Ras had taken to referring to the pair of them as a collective unit, not out of line with the Rastafari concept of oneness among all things. "Pleased to meet you, Luis."

"Likewise," Emily said,

"Boonemily be like family. 'Me bruddah from anudah fahduh and me sistah from annudah mistah.'" Ras tapped a fist to his heart.

"Oh, Ras... you're making me blush." Emily tapped her own fist to her chest as she took a seat on a swing. Her toes barely reached the ground, so she made the most of it, starting a gentle rock.

Joining her, Boone's long legs turned his swing into a fairly stationary stool. "Ras here said we needed to meet you..." He took a swig of the Jamaican lager.

Ras nodded to Luis. "Show dem."

The man reached into the neckline of his weathered shirt and came up with a necklace, lifting the object on the leather cord in his fingers. It was largely featureless, but its overall shape was familiar. As was the color. It was green.

Emily ceased her swings. "Is that...?"

139

The man lifted the thong from around his neck and offered the object to her. She turned it over in her hands and then handed it to Boone, who rubbed a thumb across it. It had the smooth surface of sea glass, not unlike the Statian Blue Bead that he wore on a cord around his own neck.

"It's worn down, but this is definitely another little chacmool," he said.

"I t'ought so!" Ras crowed. "When you show dat little t'ing to Babylon in Belize City, I knew it look familiar. Took me a while but den me eyes open when I see Luis coming in from fishing dis morning."

"Where did you find this?" Boone asked, holding the object up to the light. It was definitely the same material.

"In the mangroves," Luis said, leaning back against the wall. "I was at the north end of the island, on the lagoon side. There is a spot where the water is deeper, and I like to fish there. In the shallows, I saw a dive mask on the bottom, down in the mangrove roots. Some snorkeler had lost it maybe." He set his beer down, reliving the scene with his hands. "I get in the water, keeping an eye out for crocodiles… I reach for the mask, and when I take it from the sand, I see this next to a root." He reached across and tapped the chacmool.

"When was this?" Emily asked.

"Almost twenty years ago," the man said. "A few days after Hurricane Keith."

"That would explain the lack of emeralds in the eyes, being batted around by a storm," Boone suggested. "Do you remember where this spot was?"

The man smiled and retrieved his necklace. "I don't like to reveal my fishing spots, but you are a friend of Ras, so…"

Ras Brook looked at the two of them. "Boonemily... you up for an adventure?"

"I'm game," Boone said.

Emily laughed. "As it happens, we have the whole day free."

———◆·◆———

Several hours later, Ras navigated his small boat into the mangroves on the lagoon side of the northern half of Caye Caulker. The sun was high in the sky and the sand and seagrass of the shallow bottom could be seen quite easily.

Boone joined Ras back by the outboard. "Hey Ras, I nearly forgot to ask... do you know an archaeologist named Archibald Welk?"

Ras shook his head. "No mon, and wit' a name like dat, if I knew him, I'd remember."

"How about Oliver Price?"

"Him I seen around. Live over on Chapel, I t'ink. Got a lotta frackles, dat one."

"I didn't notice any freckles on him..."

"Yeah, his skin is tan and perfect," Emily butted in. "Didn't you think so, Boone?" she asked, an innocent smile on her face. Boone didn't rise to the bait.

Ras laughed. "No, no... frackles mean money. Him very rich. Got a boat, a helicopter... but he give a lot to conservation and cultural groups in Belize me hear."

Luis Pacab pointed to the water off the starboard bow. "There is my spot. Good fishing, certain times of day."

Boone noted the bottom just off of the ledge wasn't that deep, perhaps thirty feet, but it was a noticeable drop from the mere feet of water that surrounded the mangrove shore. "And where was the dive mask and the chacmool?"

Luis pointed toward shore. "It has been many years, but it was over there, in the fringe of the roots. The water was up to my waist, I remember."

Boone and Emily grabbed masks and snorkels and hopped into the shallow water. Boone held his mask by the strap, simply looking down into the sand and seagrass.

"You're not expecting to just find another one of those things, twenty years later, are you?" Emily asked.

"I dunno." Boone flashed her a grin. "You got something better to do?"

"Schedule's fairly free at the moment."

Boone resumed his slow shuffle through the sand, scanning the bottom. "Luis said he found it shortly after Hurricane Keith. Hurricanes can bring things to the surface that have been buried for centuries. Besides…" Boone gestured around them at the completely undeveloped shoreline, gnarled mangrove roots making the actual contours of the land hard to determine. "This is not exactly a hot spot for tourist activity, so who knows? We may find something. That diver we found clearly did."

"But he was around the bend at the north point," Em clarified. "Over a mile away. So… whatever Luis found here might have come from up there."

"True…" Boone said, thinking. "But it works both ways… the diver's find could've come from here… and up there is just where he got dumped."

They spent a couple of hours searching, Ras and Luis joining them as well, but finally decided to call it off as the sun reached a lower angle in the sky. Loading back into the boat, Luis spotted a good-sized barracuda hanging in the water column near the drop-off.

"I should have brought my fishing gear," he remarked. "Although that spot is not a good place to drop a line. There is a cluster of dead roots from a mangrove tree that was uprooted during a hurricane. I have gotten snagged there many times."

Boone watched the bottom as the boat passed over the ledge, noting the cluster of sand-covered branches and roots, their surfaces covered in a fuzz of algae. His eyes transitioned back to the boat, landing on Ras's spotlight. As he thought back over the previous days, pieces began to fill in. "Wait... stop the boat."

Ras throttled down and Emily rose from her seat. "I know that look... what is it?"

"Luis, Ras... are there any caves around here?"

Ras shook his head. "Only one I know of is da big one near Belize Diving Services."

"But that one is huge, and probably connects to an entrance on Caye Chapel. If the cave system extends there..."

"Then why not here?" Emily finished.

"The diver we found... what was his name?"

"Kevin something," Emily said, thinking. "Aldrich."

"Yeah. He was an amateur cave diver, right?" Boone said, grabbing his mask and removing the snorkel from the strap. "And he had multiple dive lights on him when we found him."

"But we found him waaaaaaay up that-a-way," Emily said, pointing to the north.

Boone paused. "Correct. That's where we *found* him." He grabbed his fins. "Em, could you get my dive light for me?" He sat on the gunwale and slipped the fins on while Emily fished his light from his gear. He strapped on a weight belt he had brought, one that only sported a single pair of weights on it.

"Ah, you freedive?" Luis remarked.

Boone was an exceptional freediver and suspected the wiry old fisherman was as well. "Care to join me?"

The old man grinned and grabbed a mask and fins that looked to be from a bygone era. He suited up and sat on the gunwale opposite Boone.

"No weight belt for you?" Em asked.

Luis smiled. "Is cheating." He rolled backward into the water.

Boone laughed and followed. They both surfaced and held the side of the boat, taking a few moments to regulate their breathing before loading up their lungs and slipping under. The barracuda, which had taken up station under the boat, watched impassively.

Boone headed straight for the mangrove debris. He had a hunch and had long ago learned to follow his instincts. Kicking down to the bottom, he reached out and held onto a root, his eyes scanning to and fro. Luis joined him. Off to the right, Boone observed a small, yellow-and-black rock beauty, the angelfish's flank containing a bit of blue in the black splotch, indicating it was not long out of juvenile phase. The mangroves above would no doubt contain juveniles of numerous species, the labyrinth of roots providing safe haven from predators. Boone watched the fish travel into the roots of the fallen tree… and then vanish. He frowned. The debris wasn't so thick that he shouldn't be able to see it.

Luis nudged him and pointed off to the side. The fisherman kicked toward a cluster of roots and tapped three spots, root ends where the wood looked fresh. He descended lower and lifted a chunk of root that was mostly free of algae at both ends. He held it up to the ones he'd pointed out before.

Boone gave his fins a double flick and coasted to the spot. *Someone cut this. Recently, maybe in the last week.* Further in, he could see another series of cut roots and beyond that, shadow. He turned on the dive light and aimed it through the gap.

A tiny cave mouth greeted him, the rock beauty flashing away from the sudden light, vanishing into the darkness.

At sundown, Emily and Boone were sitting on the rickety porch of a nondescript house off Front Street, eating some freshly caught fish. Nearby, the owner of the house was in the sandy yard, busily tending the fire in a makeshift grill constructed from half an oil drum. Luis had recommended the place as good and cheap, the latter part of that description being of particular interest, given the current state of their employment situation. Inside the house, the owner's children were enjoying a game of checkers in their hybrid domicile/restaurant.

"Haven't you had enough of caves, after the Sulphur Mine in Saba?" Emily asked through a mouthful of coconut rice. "And that one was *above* ground!"

"Hey, I didn't penetrate this one... much. My fins never left the sunlight."

After the discovery of the cave mouth, Boone had returned to the surface for another lungful of air before examining the cave more closely. It was a tight fit, but he'd believed his lanky frame

147

would have little difficulty entering. After extending his arm with the dive light into the cave as far as he could, he had spotted a side passage angling upward toward the mangroves above.

"So, we'll swing by Belize Diving Services tomorrow?" Emily asked. "Find someone who knows what they're doing?"

"We could... but I wonder if there's another entrance above in the mangroves. The cave seemed to angle up, and the entrance I found was only thirty feet down." He took out his phone. "Although... I suppose we should call Superintendent Flores."

"Didn't Ignacio imply Flores was the one who strongly 'suggested' he not employ us?"

Boone hesitated. "Yeah, but... well, this might connect to a murder investigation. I'm sure he'll want to know what we found." He looked up the number for the San Pedro police department and after asking for the superintendent, Boone placed the call on speaker. After a moment, he was put through.

"Reyes."

"Oh. Um... sorry, we were trying to reach the superintendent."

"You have."

"But I thought Superintendent Flores was..."

"He's been reassigned," the voice said, all business. "I am Superintendent Reyes. What is this in regard to?"

"The murdered diver that was found on the north end of Caulker. We have new information."

"That case has been reassigned as well. Belize City is handling it now. But go ahead and give me your information and I'll see that it gets to the proper inspectors."

Boone laid everything out and the new superintendent didn't interrupt.

"Thank you, Mr. Fischer. This information may be very helpful, and I'll be sure to pass it along."

The call ended and Boone stared at the phone, his brow knitting. "I didn't…"

"Give your name? No, you didn't," Emily supplied. Then she shook her head. "They probably have Caller ID or something. Or maybe they know your number from the arrest?"

"Maybe," Boone said.

"Wonder what happened with Superintendent Flores?" Emily mused, assembling a bite of kingfish and coconut rice from the corner of the aluminum foil pouch. She waggled her plastic fork. "You think he got reassigned to Belize City to run the investigation?"

Boone shrugged, taking a final bite of his own. "I don't know how they run things here, but I suppose that makes sense. Let's get back home. It's been a long day, and I don't know about you, but I'm exhausted."

———◆·◆———

As it happened, Boone and Emily's day was not yet over. They arrived home just as the bakery next door was closing. The woman locking up jingled her keys at them. "A man was by, looking for you. There is a note." She pointed at a sheet of paper that was stuck into the jamb of the apartment door before waddling away down the street.

"Gracias," Boone called after her as Emily removed the folded slip of paper, which looked as if it had been torn out of a journal. It was addressed to Emily Durand and Boone Fischer, their names scrawled in pen. "What's it say?"

"Dear Sir and Madame… a benefactor of mine, Mr. Oliver Price, recommended I contact you about possible assistance with an ongoing project. If you're free this evening, please join me for a drink at the bar at The Split. I will remain there until 10 p.m. I promise it will be worth your while." Emily glanced up from the paper. "Respectfully yours, Dr. Archibald Welk." She looked back down at it. "He even writes like he wears tweed."

Boone took the paper and looked at it. "Guess he tore it out of something and wrote it when we weren't here." He pocketed the page.

"How did he know this was our flat?" Emily wondered aloud. "Let's go ask him."

———◆·◆———

Sandals and flip-flops in hand and feet in the sand, Emily and Boone headed along the shore toward the Lazy Lizard at the northern end of the developed southern half of Caye Caulker. Up ahead, a dimly illuminated sign greeted them, the words "The Split" spelled out in orange, three-dimensional letters. A line of painted geckos traipsed across the join between the two stacked words.

The Split was a popular hangout for locals and tourists alike. At one time, Caye Caulker had been a single island, but in 1961, Hurricane Hattie had come along. Depending on who you talked to, either the hurricane had carved the channel that split the island in two, or the storm had simply cut a shallow waterway that enterprising locals then turned into a deeper channel for small boats to transit between ocean and lagoon. Either way, The Split had widened with each passing year, as nature and erosion had dredged the waterway down to nearly a hundred feet.

Ahead, the strains of island music and a chorus of gleeful voices rose above the softer sounds of the ocean that lapped against Boone and Emily's feet. A sudden flurry of drums blotted out the sounds of revelry from the bar at the end of The Split as they passed by a pair of Garifuna drum bands, battling for supremacy. Originally from Saint Vincent, the Garifuna (or Garinagu) had been forcibly resettled onto the nearby Honduran island of Roatan, many later finding their way to Belize. Although the official Battle of the Drums was not until November, some Garifuna enjoyed getting an early start. Past the drums, the pulsing music from their ultimate destination once again took over the night air.

The Lazy Lizard had a motto: "A sunny place for shady people." And that may have been true at one time, but nowadays the iconic watering hole was full of middle-aged tourists and youthful backpackers, bringing to mind many of the bars over on San Pedro. The open-air bar itself was a hexagonal, two-story gazebo. The grounds around it sported many thatched-roof structures, including some tables in the water itself.

"Scanning…for… tweed," Emily announced in a robotic voice, looking at the patrons around them as they approached the bar.

"I hate to burst your bubble, you goof… but I bet that's our guy there." Boone pointed at a portly figure sitting at a solitary table near a sea wall, thick glasses on the tip of his nose as he perused a menu. His sweaty scalp shone under a bad comb-over. A journal sat on the table beside him, and a half-empty Belikin beer was alongside it. Far from being dressed in tweed, the man looked like a typical expat, with a light linen shirt and comfortable shorts. Sandals sat alongside his bare feet, the man's toes buried in the sand.

"Well, he has professory glasses, at least," Emily said.

"Dr. Welk?" Boone asked as he approached the man's table.

The man looked up. "Oh! You came! Sit, sit! Please!" He stood, gestured to chairs alongside his table, then thumped right back into his seat. "Anything you want is on me. You eat yet?"

"Yes, we..." Emily began.

"Well I haven't, and I'm starving. You think this coconut curry shrimp would be a good idea, or would it be... I dunno... risky?" Welk spoke with a pronounced New York accent that Boone hadn't often heard outside of mob movies—it didn't exactly bring archaeology to mind.

"Food's pretty good here," Boone said.

"Ah, screw it, who am I kidding? I'll get a burger like I always do." He shoved aside the laminated menu. "So... Mr. Price said he spoke to you about working with me on a project, and—"

"We told Mr. Price we'd sleep on it," Boone said.

"Before we got fired," Emily muttered off to the side, just loud enough so that Boone could hear her.

"What was that?" Welk asked cheerfully, his Belikin halfway to his lips.

"Sorry, frogfish in my throat," Emily replied, snagging the menu and studying it. A waitress came over and Welk ordered a burger and another beer. Emily tapped the menu. "Well, if you're buying, I can't very well *not* order something called The Dirty Naughty Banana, so... yeah. That."

"Just a Belikin," Boone said. "So, Dr. Welk... say we were interested. What exactly is it you have in mind?"

"I don't know if you are aware of the Mayan history in Belize," Welk began, "but at its height, the population of the various Mayan groups in Belize alone was nearly half a million. With a population that size, a lot of coastal trading centers were developed. Like Tulum, up in Mexico."

"Or Marco Gonzalez over on Ambergris Caye," Em said.

"We met an archaeologist who works there," Boone said. "Manuel Rojas."

"He's one of the reasons I'm here," Welk replied, accepting the beer that arrived. "I've read his research, and I believe Caye Caulker had a similar settlement at one time, opposite the one on Ambergris Caye—only this one is now completely consumed by the mangroves." He took a long drink before setting it down. "He doesn't agree, but that's not uncommon in our field."

"You know Dr. Rojas?" Boone asked.

Dr. Welk smiled. "He recommended you."

Boone frowned. Their tour of the site with the Mexican archae-ologist had only just occurred. "Really? We've barely met. When did you speak to him?"

"Well…" Welk took another drink. "I reached out to him this morning, after Mr. Price suggested I contact you."

"And he recommended that you hire *us*… to help you… with archaeology…" Emily said dubiously, sizing up the chocolaty-look-ing drink that was placed before her, a slice of banana on the rim.

"I don't need archaeologists, I need divers… preferably ones who know a little about cave diving."

"Then you should be talking to Belize Diving Services," Boone suggested.

"Well, I did… and you took classes there, as I understand it. But that's not the only reason I'm approaching you. I need someone who is not so high profile on the island. And Mr. Price suggested the two of you would fit the bill." He thought for a moment. "When dealing with a potentially unknown site and undiscov-ered artifacts, discretion is as important to me as diving expertise."

Boone sipped his beer, watching the man closely. "Where do you think the site is? The northernmost tip?"

"Close, but I believe it may have been more on the lagoon side."

"Have you found anything yet?"

"No, not yet. Well, not *nothing*… just nothing valuable." Archibald Welk waved a hand, as if to quickly correct himself. "That is to say, nothing valuable apart from its *historical* value. Some pottery shards, enough to know I'm looking in the right place."

Em took a long pull from her Dirty Naughty Banana, her cheeks caving in as she sucked the thick, boozy shake up the straw. "Cor, that's good. How much?"

Welk blinked at her. "Er… oh, the pay? Yes… I am prepared to offer you a thousand dollars a day—American dollars, not Belizean—divided however you wish."

Emily choked on her second sip. "A day?" she managed.

"Well, I'd only pay on a day I have you dive, of course."

"Oh, yeah, well that goes without saying," Emily said, her eyes wide as she drained half her drink. "Boone, what say you?"

"I don't know…"

"Well, I tell you what…" Archibald Welk said, as his burger arrived. "Think about it… call me tomorrow." He dug a card out of his wallet. "I'll give you until ten in the morning, but then I've got to put out other offers. And please, keep this conversation between us? There are some unscrupulous types in this line of work."

**16**

"Look, all I'm saying is… let's give it a go, yeah? If we don't like it, we bail." Emily poured a second cup of coffee.

Boone sat beside the open window in the little spot in the kitchen that they considered their dining room. The scents of freshly baked bread floated up from the bakery below as he turned the business card over in his fingers, then looked at it again. The card was ivory, with a Mayan temple graphic on the left side and writing on the right.

*Dr. Archibald Welk, PhD*
*Archaeologist*
*The Center for Mayan Lowlands Research*

At the bottom was a website and phone number. Emily snatched the card from him. "I looked at the website. It seems legit. Looks like they focus on Belize, Guatemala, and Honduras."

Boone sighed. "Okay, I tell you what. Let's call Dr. Rojas. Dr. Welk said he was the one to recommend us. Let's ask him what he knows about this…job."

"Fair enough. I have his number." Em grabbed her phone off the kitchen counter and placed the call to Manuel's cell. "Voicemail. I'll have him call us…" She waited, but then rolled her eyes and imitated automated speech. "The mailbox you have reached… is full."

"Call the Spindrift."

"Right-o." She looked it up and dialed, tapping the speaker phone option. A voice came on the line.

"Spindrift Hotel."

"Good morning, I'm trying to reach Dr. Manuel Rojas?"

"Ah, yes, we have him, but he is not in. He won't be back for a few days."

"Oh. But he's still checked in?"

"Yes, we are holding his room for him. He is on the mainland at Lamanai."

"That's the temple complex he was telling us about," Boone remarked.

The voice on the speaker phone clearly heard him. "Yes, they are beautiful ruins in the jungle off the New River. He should be back in a few days, if you would like to leave a message."

"No, that's okay. Thanks!" Em hung up. "Bugger. I could text him or email him, but first…" She started to look up another number. "Maybe there's a visitor center over there, or—"

Boone's phone suddenly rang, its vibration rattling his coffee cup, which sat on the uneven bistro table by the window. "It's the animal sanctuary," he said, recognizing the number and taking the call. "Hello." He listened, then said "Okay, thanks," and hung up.

"Well?"

"They'd like to talk to us."

"I'm sorry, but he's going to require a specialist. I think we can get the infection from the bite under control, but it turns out he has a separate issue. Almost certainly an intestinal blockage."

Boone looked at the little potlicker dog, who stared right back at him with soulful eyes, shining with moisture. The dog gave a half-hearted pair of tail wags, the tail thumping against the make-shift examination table. "Well, okay... so we get a vet," Boone said.

"You'd have to do that in Belize City," the sanctuary caretaker said. "And until the infection is under control, I wouldn't advise the water taxi. You probably should fly."

"Okay, fine," Emily said, gingerly stroking the dog's flank. "We'll do that."

The caretaker sighed. "This is a stray. The island is full of them. And you don't have insurance for him..."

"Well, no, of course not," Em said.

"The surgery won't be cheap..."

"How much?" Boone asked, holding the dog's gaze.

"Well, there is a shortage of vets. If I had to guess, it would be several thousand dollars."

The dog licked Emily's hand and she turned to Boone, moisture in her eyes.

"We'll call Welk," he said.

Dr. Welk was clearly pleased and asked to meet them for lunch to plan the next day's exploration. Boone and Emily decided they would split up, Emily taking the potlicker on the next available flight with Boone remaining behind to work with Welk. With their combined credit cards and the animal sanctuary's help, they contacted the Animal Medical Centre in Belize City and then arranged two airline seats down and one return seat to Caulker; the interisland puddle jumpers had virtually no under-seat room, so the dog would need to fly down beside Emily.

After he loaded them into a golf cart taxi, Boone gave Emily a lingering kiss and offered his fingers through the travel crate for the dog to give him a lick. "See you this evening."

"Back in a jiff," Em replied. The cart started up with a whine and headed south toward the airstrip. "Just so you know, since I'm saving the dog, I get to name him!" she called out as they receded into the distance.

———◆·◆———

"So… you don't actually know where this site is, but you think some cave diving might be needed?"

"Well, one likes to be prepared. And I do have *some* idea where to look."

Boone nodded. "Have you had any divers look for this site before?"

"No, I have not," Welk said. "I've actually been working on a site in Honduras until recently."

"So… why here, why now?"

Welk thought for a moment. "Well, there was a rumor that came to me that maybe some treasure hunters were sniffing around." Welk tore into a spiny lobster tail, the armored shell cracking with a crunch.

Boone sat back, staring at his half-eaten jerk chicken and thinking about the diver's body they'd found, along with its crocodile friend. They were sitting under an awning, eating lunch alongside the beach at Chef Kareem's. The food was considered some of the best on the island but suddenly he wasn't hungry. "These treasure hunters… are they still 'sniffing around?'"

Welk shook his head while he finished chewing, then leaned forward. "My source says something went sour… there was a fight among the looters, and one of them wound up dead. The police got involved, so they fled the area. I want to follow up on my previous exploration before anyone else shows up. And that's where *you* come in." He grabbed a bottle of Belikin and clinked Boone's water glass. "But you can see why I'd rather not involve too many people in this endeavor." He took a drink, then set the bottle down and steepled his fingers on his ample belly. "I am sorry Miss Durand couldn't join us."

"I am too, but it was unavoidable."

"The dog, yes… very good of you. I'm an animal person myself. And she's heading to Belize City, straight to the vet, and then straight back, right? She's not planning on talking about her upcoming work to anyone while she's there?"

Boone opened his mouth, then closed it. He shifted in his seat. "Look, Mr. Welk… she doesn't know anyone in Belize City. Other than airport staff, a couple taxi drivers, and the vet, I don't know who else she's likely to talk to, but if it sets your mind at ease, I'll give her a call and make sure she doesn't mention your project."

"Well, if it's not too much trouble…"

"No, no, you're paying us well." He took out his phone. "I'll text her to call me. She should be landing shortly."

———◆·◆———

"Easy, fella…" Emily cooed, her mouth against the bars of the travel crate, one arm completely inside. Her hand gently scratched the dog's back, but she kept her fingers well clear of the stitches on his flank. The plane was descending, and she could feel her ears pop. Since the puddle jumpers that traveled between Belize City and the cayes traveled at low altitudes, the cabin was unpressurized. "We're almost there…"

The dog whimpered as the plane shook from the vibration of the turbo props.

"Shh, it's okay… hey, how about we talk names?" She lowered her head to the dog's eye level. "You are definitely not a Spot or Rover, so let's nix those right off the bat, yeah?"

The dog gave a tiny woof and Emily giggled with delight.

"Right. Good to see we're on the same page. So, lemme think. Looking at your snuffling nose, I have a sudden desire to call you… 'Shmoogie the Wonder Dog'!"

The dog cocked its head nearly forty-five degrees at the sudden pitching-up of her voice.

Emily laughed. "But then I realize that your cuteness is clouding my mind and I simply *must* provide you with something more respectable."

The dog licked her hand.

"I see you agree." Her phone buzzed. *Must be very close to landing—got my signal back.* She pulled her hand out of the cage and dug her cell out of her pocket. A text from Boone.

*Call me when you land.*

The dog whined, his tone falling off from a high falsetto.

Emily quickly stuck her hand back in and gave the potlicker a reassuring ear scratch. "Oh, I'm sorry for the interruption. That was my boyfriend texting an incredibly unnecessary text. I think he's jealous of our love, wittle doggo."

Within ten minutes, the Tropic Air flight was taxiing to the tiny Municipal Airport terminal. Once the side door was opened and the stairs dropped, Emily carefully carried the crate into the terminal and retrieved her phone. Boone answered on the first ring.

"Hey, Em. Feet on the ground?"

"Yes indeed, and what lovely feet they are. Miss them?"

"And everything else attached…"

"Wow. I am both touched and sickened. We are definitely a couple."

Boone laughed. "The dog okay?"

"What… Shmoogie?"

"Oh… fuck no."

"Don't get your knickers in a twist, it's just a placeholder. He's fine. I'm about to grab a cab."

"Great. So, Dr. Welk is with me at the moment…" Boone said, his inflection telling her he wasn't entirely able to speak freely. "He's let me know that there may have been some treasure hunters…"

"Looters," Welk corrected, his voice also audible to Em.

"Looters," Boone amended, "who were looking for a Mayan site in the mangroves…"

"But they're gone now," Welk's voice added.

"They're gone now, but, just in case… we should avoid talking about our upcoming job."

Emily smirked. "Okay… I'll make sure I don't tell the vet I'm hunting for Mayan gold."

"Anyway," Boone continued, blowing right past her sarcasm, "Dr. Welk wants us to meet at six a.m. at the end of the road next to Wish Willy. We'll head out from there."

Emily thought for a moment. She didn't recall a dock at the end of that street. "All right, then. Anything else?"

"Love you."

"I meant, anything else I *don't* know?"

She could hear Boone smiling on the other end. "Name that dog 'Shmoogie' and we're done." He hung up.

◆ ◆

Emily reached the curb outside the little airport and was about to head over to the nearest taxis, when she spotted a slightly chubby man in a dress shirt and slacks holding a sign that read "E. Durand." He waved at her.

"Um... hi?" Emily said, approaching the man with the carry-crate held to her chest.

The man smiled. "Unless dere is anudda lovely lady wit' a dog, I'm guessing you da one I'm s'posed to take," the man said, his voice kissed with a breezy Belizean creole. "I'm Terry. Mr. Price hoid you were bringin' over a dog and wanted to be sure you got safely to de animal doctor and back."

"Well... that's very generous. Thank you." Emily knew that Belize City had one of the highest murder rates of any city in the world, but also knew that most of that was related to gang activity in the south of the city. Her route was entirely in the more developed northern portion, but a free escort wasn't something she was about to turn down.

The man stepped to the curb and opened the rear door of an old Cadillac. Despite the age of the make, it was well-treated, and looked like it might have just rolled off the assembly line. Emily got in and set the crate beside her, then opened up the notepad on her phone. "We're going to the Animal Medical Centre on Michael DeShield Lane."

"I know it well. Used to be a taxi driver 'til I started working for Mr. Price." He started the engine and moved smoothly away from the terminal. "Your foist time in Belize City?"

"I've been here a few times," Emily said, reaching back inside the cage to reassure the potlicker. "Been a couple months, though."

Terry laughed. "You ain't missed anyt'ing."

Emily petted the dog for a moment, then raised her head. "How did Mr. Price know I was coming here?"

"I don't know, Miss... he tell me who to pick up and I pick dem up."

Emily rubbed the dog's ears—the car seemed to be lulling the pooch to sleep. "Did Mr. Price have you pick up anyone else recently?"

"Ya, dere was a man from New York. Glasses. Fatter dan me."

"Dr. Archibald Welk?"

The driver thought a moment. "I don't remember dat being da name. I picked him up from de International Airport a couple days ago, took him to da Municipal Airport I just picked you up from."

A few minutes later, the car turned off the Northern Highway onto a sandy road and pulled up alongside a one-story concrete building. Emily looked out. "Is this it?"

"Yes, Miss. I wait here for you."

"Thanks! C'mon, Dog-who-shall-be-named." She extracted the carry crate and headed into the building.

———————◆◆

At sundown, Emily stepped off the last Tropic Air flight and found Boone waiting for her at the Caulker airstrip. He took the crate from her and led her to a waiting golf cart taxi.

"How'd it go?" he asked.

"Fine. They're going to get the infection under control before they do the surgery." She hugged Boone, her head against his chest, then looked up. "Hey, Mr. Price sent someone to take me to the vet."

Boone looked down. "Really?" He thought a moment. "Well, I'm pretty sure Price is bankrolling Dr. Welk, so… guess they talked." He laughed. "Saved us a few bucks, I guess."

Emily broke free. "Good. Cuz I'm starving and I need something more than the canned soup and ramen we've got in the flat. Let's go to Meldy's—I could murder a Chawita burger."

"Good morning!" Archibald Welk waved to them from the end of the sandy lane as they turned the corner.

Boone returned the wave, shifting his gear bag between hands.

"There's no pier here, is there?" Emily said through a smile, as she also raised a hand in greeting. They were still a hundred yards away from Welk.

"Not to my knowledge, but I can see a boat in the shallows, through the trees there." He pointed at the white hull that was visible between the branches.

And indeed, Welk started heading toward it. "There's a cut through the mangroves right here," he called out. "I didn't want to attract too much attention at a pier. Hope you don't mind getting your feet wet early."

Boone was surprised to see that the boat that was nosed into the sand was little more than a skiff. A skinny, Belizean-looking kid was waiting by the outboard. Boone didn't recognize him. The shirtless youth nodded a stone-faced greeting to them as he took their gear bags before helping Welk aboard.

"Gonna be a bit cramped, yeah?" Emily observed.

"Where are the tanks?" Boone asked.

"Don't worry, this is just to get us out to the main boat," Welk said. "Still, I wanted something that could get into the mangroves if we needed to."

Boone nodded. "I'll give her a push," he said to the young man once Emily was aboard.

"Kay. T'anks."

*Not much of a talker,* Boone thought, but he could make out Belizean creole in the voice. He noticed a tattoo on one side of the youth's chest. It looked like a stylized letter "G" with an "S" coming out of it, one head of the "S" ending in a snake's head, fangs bared.

In minutes they were heading into the lagoon. Welk had directed them to a spot fairly close to The Split, so there weren't many docks to pass as they headed north, but at the one off Hattie Street they spotted Ras Brook standing alongside his boat at the end of the pier, a touristy-looking couple beside him.

"Hey, Ras!" Emily yelled above the engine.

Their friend looked around, spotting them as they flashed by. He grinned and waved, but the wave faltered, and he shifted the hand to shield his eyes.

Boone kept his eye on him as they sped past and angled out to the northwest, the Rasta still watching them until the tourist lady tugged at his T-shirt sleeve and he turned to speak with her.

"Looks like Ras has some employment for the day," Emily remarked, as they flashed past the channel that led to The Split.

After traveling for a few minutes along the sparsely inhabited northern island, the skiff slowed as it approached an anchored dive boat, the name *Alhambra* along the side. Boone didn't recognize that boat as being one from any op he knew of. He was about to say so, when Welk answered his unspoken question.

"My organization picked her up at a police auction in Honduras for next to nothing," he said as they came alongside. "Apparently a dive company in the Bay Islands was running drugs for a mainland cartel."

"Kinda looks like the model Sea Saba was using, yeah?" Emily mused.

Boone examined the boat, noting the V-hull, enclosed cockpit, and canopied flybridge. "Think you might be right. Sure looks like a Delta Canaveral. What is she, thirty-eight? Forty feet?"

Welk shrugged. "No idea. Ask me what period a piece of Mayan pottery comes from and I'll talk your ear off, but I'm not a boat person."

Another young man was aboard the dive boat, a red T-shirt hanging loosely from his skinny frame and a backwards ball cap on his head. He fumbled the line their shirtless skipper tossed across and the two laughed, busting each other's chops as they prepared to try again.

*They clearly know each other*, Boone thought. He snaked a long arm up and grabbed hold of the dive boat's gunwale, helping to snug the skiff up to the stern. Red Shirt reached over to help Welk mount the swim platform as Boone stepped across with his and Emily's gear bags.

Emily hopped over right after him. "Nice boat you got here," she said to Red Shirt.

He nodded and smiled and stepped past her to help No Shirt climb aboard.

Boone moved his and Em's gear over to the shade of the small cabin enclosure, glancing at a number of tanks that were in place along the benches. "No Nitrox?"

"No, sorry," Welk replied. "I was pressed for time and this is what we had aboard. But any diving you do will be quite shallow, I expect."

*Not really the point,* Boone thought, but he shrugged and retrieved his regulator and BC and chose a tank. Em began setting up alongside him.

"I've got a general area I want to start in," Welk said, "if you'd like to… oh, you're already getting ready. Good!" He looked at their gear. "You're not using those side-mount rigs you asked me to get for you?"

Boone rapped his tank with a knuckle. "We'll start simple. If there even is a cave, we've got to find it first, right?"

"Of course." Welk turned away to join Red Shirt at the helm.

Boone turned the valve on the tank and looked at his gauge. Oftentimes, tanks would wind up with less than 3,000 p.s.i. in them and he wanted to be sure. His had that and a little more, as did Emily's.

Emily tipped hers forward, then rotated it side-to-side. "No dive shop markings."

Boone looked at his, too. "Huh. Guess they do things differently in Honduras."

"Well, if this boat came from a sham business…"

Boone nodded, trying to dredge a memory from the back of his mind. The cough of a motor caught his attention as No Shirt headed away from the boat, pointed south. "I thought we were going to use the skiff to get close in," Boone called out to Welk.

"Oh, he'll be back. Besides, we won't need it where we're going first."

<hr />

Where they went first turned out to be very familiar to Boone and Emily.

"It's Luis's honey hole," Emily whispered, looking down into the water.

The ledge and drop-off were easily visible, although Boone couldn't make out any underwater mangrove debris where the boat currently sat. Red Shirt was setting out an anchor and Welk rubbed his hands together vigorously. He took out a handheld GPS and examined the screen.

"This is the spot! A local fisherman told me he thought there was a cave down here somewhere."

"What was his name?" Boone asked.

Welk waved his hand dismissively. "I don't remember, something Spanish." He tucked the GPS back into his cargo shorts. Bursting with visible excitement, he was sweating profusely.

"Hey, Boss." Red Shirt held up a plastic bottle of water from the cooler and Welk took it, drinking greedily.

"Thank you!" he gasped, capping the half-empty bottle. "Got to keep hydrated!"

Boone leaned over the gunwale, looking along the ledge to the north and south. Glancing up at the shoreline, he thought a copse of mangrove looked familiar. Turning, he caught Emily's eye.

"Yeah. Think so too." Emily said from beside him, her voice low. He looked down at her and she nodded her head toward where he'd been focused. "Do we say anything?"

"Not yet. Let's get in the water first."

"Shall we get started?" Welk asked, approaching them.

Emily spun around, her smile shining. "You read our minds! Eager to hop in and have a look round!"

"You think Ras's friend Luis told them about the cave?" Em asked. They were at the water's surface, occasionally diving as they pretended to look around.

"No, I have a feeling *we* told them," Boone said. "When we called it in to the police. Kinda sounded like they owed Price some favors, so…"

Em looked back at the boat. "Anything about those two young blokes seem a bit dodgy to you?"

"I dunno. I don't think they're from Caye Caulker." Boone ducked his head under and then back up. He looked at the boat. Dr. Welk was on the phone.

"So, are we going to do this, or what?" Em asked. "I'm starting to feel a bit silly."

Dr. Welk lowered his phone and waved at them, then gestured for them to come back to the boat, which was anchored away from the ledge.

"Looks like the doc wants to talk to us." Boone swam back to the boat, Emily following.

"Find anything yet?"

"Not yet," Boone supplied.

"Well, look harder, because…" He waggled his phone. "I have some good news. That is, good news *if* you find what we're looking for. I've been talking to the higher-ups and they would like to speed things along. I think the rumors of those treasure hunters have them a little spooked. If you can find this site I'm looking for… *today*… then there's a bonus in it for you. Five thousand dollars. In addition to the daily rate."

Boone felt Emily pinch him beneath the surface. "Ow! I mean… wow. Um… okay! Guess we'll get back to it." He slipped his regulator into his mouth and signaled Emily to descend. Once they reached the sandy bottom, he pulled out his writing slate and scrawled a question mark. He held it out to Emily.

She took the attached pencil and scrawled on it for a while, then looked at him expectantly.

Boone turned the slate around and read it.

*I say yes. Our furry friend will be grateful.*

Boone looked up and nodded, raising his hand in an *OK* sign. He flattened his hand and signaled to head toward the cave. Once they reached it, Boone tapped his Aquinus dive watch and signaled "Five," and they settled in to wait.

◆ ◆ ◆

A shrill trio of whistle blasts sounded across the water. Boone let go of the safety whistle's lanyard and pointed down in an exaggerated fashion. Welk could be seen shouting at Red Shirt, who quickly took steps to bring up the anchor and reposition the boat closer to the spot Boone had indicated.

"What did you find?" Welk asked excitedly, leaning over the gunwale.

"Looks like a cave!" Emily shouted. Boone had instructed her to do the talking, since he trusted her acting skills far above his own. "There's an old mangrove tree partially blocking it. No wonder we had so much trouble finding it!"

◆ ◆ ◆

After some strategizing and preparation, Boone and Emily descended once more to the mouth of the cave. They had donned lightweight helmets with mounted lights and had changed into side-mount harnesses, with a single tank each. If it looked like they'd need it, they'd return to the surface to gear up with double tanks. As an added precaution, Boone had clipped a small Spare Air pony bottle at his side. The plan was for Emily to remain outside for the initial penetration, holding onto one end of the sturdy, nylon guide line that Boone had on a reel. A second spool of cave line was tucked into his vest, but he wasn't planning to use it. If the cave system turned out to be complex, he intended to return and reassess. Boone quickly went over his gear, checking the multiple dive lights and the backup pony bottle. He flashed an *OK* sign to Emily.

She swam closer and clipped the free end of the line onto her harness, then grabbed the back of his head and tilted her mask to his, their helmets clunking gently together. She backed off and waggled her fingers at him.

Boone turned and wormed his way through the roots to the mouth of the cave. He had brought his brightest dive light and now flicked it on, examining the entrance. *I think I can get through here without removing the tank,* he thought. He was successful, aided in part by his exceptionally lean body. Just inside, the cavern opened into an oval, the limestone walls slanting down to a sandy bottom. Boone was careful not to kick up the sand as he swiveled the light around the interior. The only passage he could see was the one he had spotted the other day. Off to the side, it slanted gradually upward at a slight angle.

*If it continues like that, it might reach the surface,* he thought. He moved closer to the passage and extended his arm into it, aiming the powerful dive light up the tunnel. After a moment, he decided to move forward to a spot where the passage narrowed. Sparkling bubbles from his exhalations clustered like little gems along the limestone ceiling overhead as he reached the curve. Arm outstretched, he extended the dive light again, angling it up this limestone artery. *Well, whattaya know.* At the edge of the beam, the light appeared to be striking the surface of the water.

Boone had only been inside for a few minutes, and at this shallow depth his air consumption would be minimal. A quick glance at his gauge confirmed he had used only a tiny fraction of the air in his tank. Looking at the narrow curve in the tunnel, he decided to uncouple the tank from the harness and push it ahead of him, sliding carefully into the tunnel like an eel. Once he was ready, he secured his handheld dive light and flicked on the helmet-mounted one. Taking his time, he inched his way up the passage. Almost immediately, he brushed against an object that moved when he contacted it. He froze, then looked closely.

*A turtle shell. Hawksbill, looks like.* A closer examination revealed a partial skeleton in the sand and a beaked skull. *Probably got stuck in here, trying to swim through.* He snagged the shell and backed out a few feet, tucking it off to the side before edging forward again.

In less than a minute, his tank broke the surface. Boone followed, rising out of the salt water. The regulator fell from his mouth.

The guide line had been gently tightening and slackening over the last fifteen minutes or so. Now, its movement stopped. Emily watched it. Watched it some more.

*Easy, Em. Boone can make that tank last two hours if he needs to.* Nevertheless, the stillness in the line made her nervous. *Sod it.* She grabbed hold and gave it two firm tugs, careful not to yank the line, in case it was snagged on something. They had agreed that two tugs was just to "check in." Three… was too close to two, so there was no three. Four would mean "I'm in trouble" if it came from Boone… and "get your ass back here" if it came from Emily.

Emily blew a relieved stream of bubbles when the line pulsed twice in reply to her questioning tugs. *Phwaw, thank God.* Above, a deep rumble drew her attention. A boat. Sound direction was difficult to determine underwater, but Emily had context. She looked up toward the dive boat to see if it was the skiff returning. It was. Em watched the tiny hull approach the dive boat, pause, then speed off to the north.

*Okay, that was weird.* But she quickly filed that away as the line began moving again. Boone might be returning. In minutes he emerged from the algae-covered roots. Even with a regulator in his mouth, she could tell that he was smiling. He took out his slate and frantically began drawing, sketching out what he wanted her to do.

———◆·◆———

Fifteen minutes later, Boone's head broke the surface of the water inside the cavern. He gently pushed his tank aside and turned to take hold of Emily's. Below, he could see her head lamp growing closer, until she too emerged.

"Welcome to the magic grotto," Boone said, lifting her bodily out of the water and giving her a hug, crushing her to his chest.

"Mm-whthfk?" She spat her regulator out. "Missed you, too." She sniffed the air. "Whew! Bit of a pong in here. Did you puff? If so, I'd get that checked out."

Boone laughed, pulling his mask down from his face to dangle at his neck. "No, no farts from me. That smell is just the vegetation and muck up above." He pointed at a few roots that pierced the ceiling overhead. "Bit rotten eggy in here, but the air seems pretty good." He shrugged out of his harness and set it aside.

The chamber they were in was a rough oval, about fifty feet across at its widest point. The water was only a small portion of it, the majority of the space being semisolid ground. Boone pulled himself out of the water and sat on the side of the little pool they'd come up from, pressing the butt end of his handheld dive light into the soft ground, to shine its broad beam on the ceiling. Stalactites and protruding mangrove roots mingled overhead. The megawatt light gave them plenty of illumination, so he flicked off his helmet-light and ditched his mask and helmet before sweeping his hand around. "I was about to explore, but I wanted you with me."

"What, didn't want to die alone?" Emily said with a smirk, slipping her harness off and joining him.

Boone grinned, reaching up to douse her helmet light and remove her mask. "And leave you to hook up with Oliver Price? Never." He crouched to retrieve something and then held out a clenched fist. "I kinda lied. Obviously, I explored... a little. Hold out your hand."

Emily's green eyes sparkled with anticipation. She held out her hand and Boone slapped his fist down into it and opened his fingers.

"Tada..." he said softly.

Emily's eyes grew even wider. "Bugger me sideways," she breathed.

**18**

Sitting in Emily's hand were two jade chacmool statues, their carved features unblemished, and a pair of glittering green stones in the eye sockets of each.

"Boone…" Emily breathed.

"As soon as I found those, I came for you. I think Dr. Welk will be verrrrrrry pleased." He pointed across the pool toward a shelf of limestone. "There's something over there, too… but I figured if I found too much more without you, you'd kick my ass."

"You got that right, Booney-boy," Em said, flicking on a small, wrist-mounted light she wore. Rising from the side of the pool, she began to walk around it. At under five feet in height, she didn't have to duck.

Boone followed, crouching a bit to keep from banging his head on intrusive mangrove roots and limestone stalactites.

Nearing the outcrop of limestone, Emily looked around. She swept her wrist light toward her feet… and staggered back. "Sodding hell!"

Boone reached her and looked down. *Bones. And a skull. And these don't belong to a sea turtle.* "Human," he said. "Except..." He crouched, examining them closely. "This skull... it's got an odd shape."

"Yeah, it's kinda squished."

"Y'know... this looks like old Mayan carvings, where the gods and kings have those long heads?"

"Oh! I asked Dr. Rojas about that. He said it was something only certain groups did, deforming the heads of their babies during the time their skulls were soft. And it was a class thing—usually just nobles and priests."

Out of the corner of his eye, something caught the light. Boone took Emily's arm and directed it to the back wall. "Gourds." He crouched beside the nearest grouping. Further along, the limestone curved back, and he could see more of them. He picked one up. "It's coated in something shiny. Like shellac. A hole at one end."

"These over here have some kind of cork in them," Em said, retrieving one closer to the wall. She gave it a shake, then popped it open. "Nothing but air." She tried another—it was also empty. "Maybe they were for food or water..."

Boone was staring down at the pool. "Actually," he said absently, "I think you were right the first time." He took it from her. "Air." He held the opening to his mouth, then lowered the gourd, turning it over in his hands. "This coating would keep it watertight."

"What, like a gourd scuba tank?" She shook her head. "I'll file that in the 'maybe' column, but I guess it's possible. If someone was coming in and out a lot." She aimed her light back at the limestone shelf. "You said there was something over there... hang on, yeah..."

Boone made his way over to it, careful not to step on any of the remains. On the outcrop were a few clay bowls and further along where the ledge angled up, he could see piles of green. He pointed. "It's a bit cramped up there. Monkey wanna climb?"

Emily was already climbing up. "Who you calling monkey. You're the one with the orangutan arms."

"Orangutans are apes."

"Oh, really? Very interesting, and you're a berk." She stopped. "Hello..." She dropped to all fours. "It's a whole pile of those chacmoolie thingies! Wait, two... three... Boone, there are a *bunch* of little piles of them. It's a treasure trove of those things! And there's a lot of this stuff..." She picked up something and held it down to him.

Boone reached up and took it. "Looks like... some kind of woven material." The scrap started to fall apart in his hands. "Those piles must have each been in a sack that biodegraded over time."

She came back down, holding a chacmool. "So, maybe a sack busted open and some of them wound up in the area outside the cave. Like the one Luis Pacab found. But why are there so many of them? And they're so small! Dr. Rojas said chacmools were usually huge stone statues, decorating temples. These? It's like they were... I dunno..."

"Mass produced," Boone said, taking the little figurine from her. "Something else Dr. Rojas mentioned... that temple complex, Altun Ha..."

"The one we visited a few months back, the one not far from the coast, yeah?"

"Yeah. He said it was a center of jade production. It's where they found that huge jade head, too." Boone peered into the tiny emerald eyes, then looked back along the rim of the pool. He took Emily's wrist and gently aimed her light back at the bones until the beam was centered on the weirdly shaped skull. "Priests..." He stopped talking, thoughts knitting together.

Em waited, watching Boone's dimly lit features. Finally, she spoke. "You've got it. I can see it in your face."

He looked at her. "Dr. Rojas said he thought that chacmool was a souvenir... and in a way, he might have been right. You know how, in the Middle Ages, Christians would go on pilgrimages and they'd end up buying stuff like... I don't know... shards of the True Cross or Saint Olaf's knuckle bone..."

"Relics."

"Yeah... and even today, people buy little silver crosses or Saint Christopher's medals..." He held up the chacmool. "I think these are kind of like relics... something the priests sold to the nobility who came to visit the temples."

"But... wouldn't this sort of thing be all over, then?"

"Not if the very first time it was done—say, at a temple complex known for making jade—not if that first batch went missing. Maybe they never made any more, if something they spent so much time and resources on just... vanished in the night." He knelt by the remains. "I think this person was a priest. *And* a thief."

———————— ◆ • ◆ ————————

"How many are there?" Dr. Archibald Welk asked excitedly, turning the sample chacmool over in his hands. Boone had also brought some pottery and one of the gourds, and Welk had spent a little time examining them, but it was clear he was very interested in the jade figurines.

"Hard to say. A lot."

They were back aboard the *Alhambra*. Boone had explained his theory and Dr. Welk had been impressed, even suggesting Boone consider pursuing a degree in archaeology.

"Well, let's begin bringing everything out," Welk announced.

"Really? It's an archaeological site, isn't it? Shouldn't you study it, as is?"

Welk shifted from foot to foot. "Well, here's the thing... I'm under a lot of pressure to secure everything before anyone else comes sniffing around. And, if your theory is correct... then this is not the trading settlement I thought might be here—it's really the cache of a looter. A looter who happens to be a Mayan. And furthermore, the site itself... well, it's a miracle it's still there, what with the encroachment you described in the limestone ceiling." He clapped his hands together. "So, let's get those artifacts safely out of there. Once everything is secure, we can return here on subsequent dives and map everything out in detail."

"Shouldn't we at least take in a GoPro?" Emily asked. "Document everything before we move it?"

"Excellent idea. Do that. And then load everything into these." He produced several large dry bags. "I've got some felt padding inside each one, in case you need to wrap anything. Just load as much as you can."

"The remains, too?" Boone asked. "I'm not comfortable with that..."

"Oh, no, no, of course not. Just focus on the chacmools and anything else that isn't too fragile. You can leave any pottery shards for now. Maybe tuck a few more of the gourds in there, if there's room." He laughed. "Scuba gourds. Clever."

"Where's the skiff?" Emily asked.

"Oh, I sent it to fetch us some lunch."

Emily cocked her head. "But, town is that way..." She pointed south. "And while I was underwater, I saw the skiff go *that* way." She pointed north.

Welk looked momentarily at a loss, but then Red Shirt spoke: "Him go fishing. I got a little grill."

Emily started to say something, then shook her head. "Well, the passage to get into the chamber is tight. We'll only be able to bring a single bag through at a time."

"Then we better get started!" Welk said.

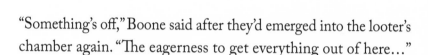

"Something's off," Boone said after they'd emerged into the looter's chamber again. "The eagerness to get everything out of here…"

"Maybe he's really afraid someone else will show up," Emily said, removing her gear. "And, look, if that dead guy we found… if that was a bunch of treasure hunters offing each other, and one of them had one of these chacmools, maybe they *will* return." She looked at Boone. "I don't know about you, but I kinda want to get this over with and not come back."

"Agreed." Boone lifted his fresh tank out of the water and set it alongside the pool, thinking for a moment. "Let's get our bonus and the day's pay." He got out his powerful dive light. "Your GoPro idea was excellent; we'll do that now. Document everything. Then we'll load up what we can and call it a day."

"Sounds like a plan."

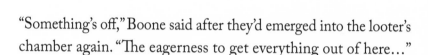

Between them, Boone and Emily managed to load up over half of the chacmool statues, but as they worked they came across more objects, including several golden totems, a gold mask with embedded stones, and several bowls that looked to be made of copper or bronze. It would definitely require a second trip. All the items looked to be ceremonial in nature, and solidified Boone's belief that a temple priest had robbed the temple and fled.

Making their way down the passage was tricky with the bag, but Boone managed to drag it along behind. Knowing that this would kick up a lot of sand and silt, he sent Emily down first while he brought up the rear.

As they exited the cave and pushed past the branches and roots at its mouth, Boone reached out and tapped Emily's shoulder. There was no need, as she was already looking where he was about to point. Up top, the skiff was back alongside the dive boat... but they had company. A third, larger boat was anchored nearby. Boone set the dry bag down on the sand and retrieved his slate.

Emily snatched the pencil and scrawled: *Looters?*

Boone didn't think so, and he held out his hand in a calming motion, then pointed a finger at himself, then two fingers at his eyes. He then pointed at Emily, held up a flat palm, then pointed at the sand. *I look, you stay.*

He kicked toward the boat along the bottom, holding his breath until he was underneath the dive boat, not wanting his bubbles to reveal his location. When he was on the sea floor beneath the boat, he resumed breathing slowly, the few bubbles he emitted clustering under the hull as he slowly ascended. Once there, he moved to the edge closest to the newcomer and raised his mask above the water, looking for the name on the side to confirm his suspicions. Satisfied, he returned to Emily, flashing an *OK* sign before writing on his slate.

She shrugged at him, palms up. *Well?*

He lifted the slate. *Oliver Price.*

"My goodness, you two have been busy!" the Englishman said cheerily as Dr. Welk extracted several of the figurines and examined them. "Didn't I tell you, Archibald? They were just who you needed."

"They've been great, Mr. Price. And thank you again for providing the funds to allow me to mount this expedition."

"The Maya are the cultural roots of Belize—if I make my home here, it's only right I contribute toward preserving their history."

Emily was waiting beside the cooler, eating an orange she'd found inside. "So, you just happened to be tooling around in your boat on the lagoon side of Caye Caulker..."

Oliver laughed, "Oh dear me, no... Archie here had told me he was planning to start this expedition today. He called me when you found the cave and I raced over from Chapel. Wanted to be here for the discovery. Can you blame me?"

Boone took a sip from his metal water bottle, glancing across at the *Liquid Asset*. The skipper, Wilson, was in the aft seating area enjoying a smoke, his shiny bald head soaking up the sun. His feet were propped up on a table, a wide-brimmed straw hat sitting alongside his dress shoes, his white polo shirt stretched across his chest.

"So... is there more?"

Boone looked back toward the group. "Sorry?"

Dr. Welk spoke again, gesturing at the bag. "Was this everything you found?"

"Oh... no, there's a lot more... I wouldn't want to risk moving some of it, but there are a couple more piles of the figurines, some copper bowls, and a few gold objects."

184

"Gold?" Price said with interest. "Really?"

"Yeah, but I'm concerned about bouncing the bag around during the exit."

"Then double up on the felt wrapping," Welk said. "We need to get the most valuable items out now, just in case."

Boone caught No Shirt's eye. "No grilled fish?"

The young man shrugged. "Not biting." He went into the wheelhouse to join Red Shirt.

"I have plenty to eat on board the *Asset*, if you'd like some lunch," Price offered.

"That's okay, we should get back to the cave, finish up. Gonna grab a power bar." He went to his dry bag, unrolling the top and digging one out. He noticed his phone had a couple missed calls and a text. He tapped it and saw it was from Ras Brook.

*The boy driving the boat when you wave to me this morning. Him a gang member from Belize City. George Street gang. Very dangerous.*

Boone stared at the message, then glanced up at the pair. No Shirt's tattoo, the "G" with the snake-like "S" coming out of it... *George Street*. Red Shirt's back was to him and beneath the flat bill of the backwards ballcap he could make out a tattoo on the back of his neck, also of a stylized "GS."

"Shit." He glanced over toward the *Liquid Asset*. Wilson was no longer at the table, but the Panama hat was. A chill rose up Boone's spine, as he suddenly remembered where he'd seen that hat. He turned to catch Emily's eye but found Oliver Price watching him closely.

"Oh dear..." Price sighed. "And it was all going *so* well." His hand came from behind his back, a small automatic pistol in his grip.

## 19

For a split second, Boone thought about lashing out and trying to disarm Price, but the mechanical sound of another weapon being readied extinguished that hasty instinct. Just as well, as it likely would have been suicidal. Boone glanced back and found that Red Shirt had retrieved a stubby machine pistol from a compartment near the wheel—a "MAC-10," he thought it was called.

"What's going on?" Archibald Welk looked equal parts confused and terrified. "Oliver?"

"Hands in the air, Dr. Welk," Price said.

Over on the *Liquid Asset*, Wilson had emerged from the cabin with some form of assault rifle. He called back over his shoulder. "Chuck! They finally got wise. Come join the party."

A buzzcut and goatee came into view as a burly man made his way up the steps from the stateroom. He snagged the Panama hat from the table where Wilson had been seated. The pistol he held dwarfed the one Price had trained on Boone.

"I almost tossed that stupid thing overboard," Wilson said with a grin. "What you doing, leaving that sitting there?"

"Figured you might want it for that chrome dome of yours," the man retorted in a gravelly voice, popping the hat atop his close-cropped hair.

"That's the guy who was following us in San Pedro," Emily said.

"And he's the one who called you from outside the night club after the police picked us up," Boone added, his eyes locked on Price. "After the bar fight that *you* staged. You had the police arrest us so you could bail us out… and I'm betting you had them lean on Ignacio to fire us."

"I needed you properly motivated. Money is a great incentive. Lack of money… even more so."

"And that diver we found… There were no other 'treasure hunters.' It was you." He nodded his chin toward Price. "Lemme guess. That gun's a .22?"

Price smiled. "Bit late now, to be putting the puzzle together. Pity you couldn't have remained in the dark a wee bit longer. It was the phone, wasn't it? Unlock it and toss it here."

Boone did so. Price looked at it and read Ras's text out loud. "Hear that, Willis? You are *dangerous!*"

No Shirt laughed. "Ya mon, you know it."

Price smirked. "Well, get your dangerous ass in the skiff and bring Chuck over here." He lifted the phone and squinted at it. "One little bar of signal. There shouldn't be any up here, but I suppose you got lucky with this spot. Or unlucky, depending on your point of view." He typed, speaking out loud as he did so.

"Sorry. Phone was off. Thought that guy looked shady, so we called the police. We are in San Pedro now. Everything is okay."

He hit send and tossed the phone overboard with a plop. "One less thing to worry about."

"You'll never get away with this!" Dr. Welk cried.

"Oh, give it a rest," Emily said. "Archibald Welk, my ass... I bet your name is Vinny."

Welk looked at her for a moment, glanced fearfully at Price, then dropped his hands, his face sliding into a grin. "Jimmy, actually." He went over to stand beside Price and broke into a laugh. "I'm sorry, Ollie, I couldn't hold it."

"That's all right, you had a good run. So, how's it looking?"

"Probably fifty mil for the emeralds alone. Y'know what? Mr. Fischer there actually had a pretty good idea about these statues being some sorta religious tchotchkes. As far as I can tell, they're probably late-Mayan." He suddenly snapped his fingers. "Hey, could be *very* late-Mayan. Maybe the priests got the idea of selling stuff like that from Spanish missionaries." He looked up and winked at Emily. "Don't let the goombah accent fool you, sweetness... I actually *am* an archaeologist." He picked up the gourd. "Only thing I can't figure out—why bring it all the way out here?"

"Because the trade routes passed through Ambergris Caye just north of here," Boone said. "And because pirates and thieves are always stashing their shit and hiding from the law on little, out-of-the-way islands. Caye Caulker..." He stared at Oliver Price. "Caye Chapel."

Price smiled. "You should see my place in the Caymans. Now here's what's going to happen." He gestured to Boone with the pistol. "You are going back to the cave to load up the rest of the valuables. Jade, gold—yes, definitely get those gold items you mentioned—precious stones, those metal bowls... anything carved, anything that looks largely intact. I expect the next bag to be bursting at the seams."

Boone's shoulders sagged. "Look… we'll get as much as we can, but—"

"*We?* Oh, no, no, no. Miss Durand will remain here as my guest until you bring every last scrap of loot out of that hole."

"I think this is the part where we ask: how do we know you won't just kill us anyway?" Emily's voice trembled.

"A fair point. But consider this. The police are already investigating the death of another diver. Perhaps this individual had been hired by a certain generous benefactor. Maybe this person dangled a pair of chacmools in front of said benefactor. Maybe he claimed he found the cave but then refused to tell us where it was unless we quintupled our initial offer and transferred the money beforehand. Mind you, I have *no* idea how that unfortunate individual happened to acquire that bullet in his head."

Boone ignored the obvious lie and remained silent.

"But, an additional pair of deaths would certainly draw far too much attention. Particularly if it happened to such an appealing pair." He smiled. "After this haul, it will be time for me to pull up stakes and move on, so I see no percentage in sullying my hands any further. We'll disable the motor on the skiff and leave you in it with an oar." He held up a finger. "Of course, if word ever reaches my ears that you were speaking about this little archaeological find or my involvement, or that of my associates—Well, the Belize City gangs are always eager to make a few extra bucks." He looked from one to the other. "Satisfied?"

"Not even remotely," Boone hissed.

Price shrugged. "Pity." He aimed his pistol at Emily's head.

"*NO!*" Boone took a step forward, but Chuck had boarded the boat and raised his own gun.

"Go ahead, *hero*. See what happens."

"Mr. Fischer," Price said loudly, his eyes and pistol locked on Emily. "If you bring me every last bit of that treasure trove, I promise... I swear... I will not kill either of you." His eyes left Emily's face and settled on Boone. "You have my word."

Boone looked at Emily, sudden tears blurring his view of her face.

"Plenty of other divers I can get if you decide to die," Price prodded. "But I'd very much prefer to get this done today."

"Fine," Boone spat. "I'll do it." He pointed toward his gear. "I'll need a fresh tank."

———◆·◆———

Boone was furious with himself. The signs had all been there and he hadn't connected them fast enough. He had ignored his instincts, blinded by their financial situation. Angrily, he tightened the straps on his harness. He looked back at Emily, who sat huddled under a towel on the opposite bench, her wetsuit not yet dry.

She looked at him with sad eyes and mouthed "I love you."

Boone answered her in kind, then turned to Price, who was holding out a large dry bag.

"Remember, I want every last scrap of—"

"If you hurt her, I swear..."

"You'll kill me. Yes, yes, very good. She'll be right here waiting for you."

Boone grabbed the bag from Price, then picked up his fins and headed for the swim platform. He had little hope that Price would let them go, but during the time the man had blathered on about guaranteeing them their lives to convince Boone to do his bidding, the young divemaster had come up with a plan. Donning his fins, he slipped from the stern and headed for the bottom, his eyes scanning the sand and sea grass.

Last Christmas, Emily had gotten him a slim, new phone case. Supposedly watertight, it would allow a recreational diver or snorkeler to take photos and video without the need for an expensive underwater camera. Boone's smartphone was too valuable to him to test it, but he had thanked Emily and put his phone into it, figuring it might come in handy if he ever dropped it overboard.

*Or if it was ever thrown overboard by some murderous bastard*, he thought, thankful that Price's arrogant need for physical histrionics had led him to toss it over the side—and additionally thankful that the Englishman had tossed it over the side nearest the ledge. *There!* Boone spotted the phone and angled steeply down. At this shallow depth, they might be able to follow his movements, so he simply snatched it out of the sand as he passed over it, tucking it into a pocket on his vest without slowing.

Ten minutes later, he rose from the water inside the cavern, swiftly stripping off his gear and pulling his mask down around his neck. He looked down at the phone. It was on! He tried tapping several apps, and the phone seemed functional. No bars, though… but Boone had expected this—the limestone would block any signal. Even outside of the cave, it might be difficult, this being the undeveloped part of Caye Caulker. Still, it was their only chance. And Boone had remembered the rank odor in the cavern.

He quickly made his way toward the ledge where they had found most of the artifacts. It was a tight fit for his tall frame, and he had to crawl at first, but then a section opened up above him, allowing him to rise to a half crouch. The smell of rotting vegetation was stronger here and Boone held out hope. He doused his light and looked up. *Yes!* Sunlight. Not much, little more than a pinhole, but it was something. He held his phone near the spot. Still no reception.

He set the phone aside and reached up toward the little gap, feeling a mangrove root beside it that had penetrated the ceiling. He turned on his head lamp again and examined it. Grabbing hold, he pulled hard. It gave ever so slightly. He repositioned his hands, taking a firmer grip. Assuming a wider stance, he closed his eyes, breathing slowly out, focusing his mind. When he was ready, he pulled with all of his might, lean muscles cording along his lanky arms. The root began to shift. Material began to spill out, bits of limestone and earth starting to trickle down, some of it bouncing off of his helmet with little taps. With a final, supreme effort, Boone yanked, leaning his entire weight away from the ceiling. Suddenly, the area above gave way, chunks of dirt and loose scree sliding down. He rolled away, falling off the edge of the ledge and into the water below.

Pulling himself back out, he returned to the ledge, examining the material that had fallen. He flicked the light off and looked at the ceiling. The sunlight was much more pronounced, and he scrambled back atop the outcrop, pausing to dig through the debris for his phone. *Didn't think that through,* he thought, cursing himself when the search took several minutes. Finally, he found it. *Still no bars.* He looked up at the skylight he had created. *Maybe...*

Holding the phone in his teeth, Boone snaked his arms up into the hole, grabbing for a root further up. Pulling at roots and clawing at the sides, he managed to rise several feet before becoming wedged tight, all forward motion becoming impossible as the shaft narrowed. He managed to get one arm free and took the phone in his fingers, extending his arm as far as he could.

He angled it just enough to see the screen. No signal. Or was there? He thought he saw some movement in the little indicator.

*Even if I didn't imagine that, it's not going to be enough.* He looked up. He was still a good twenty feet from the surface. Far overhead, the leaves of mangrove trees rustled in the breeze. Boone might possess an exceptionally lean figure, but with his great height he was still a large man, and simply too big to make it to the surface. But he knew a certain someone who could.

Once again, Boone left the mouth of the cave, a bulging bag of artifacts in tow. As he pushed through the cut roots and branches, he paused to let a piece of his gear drop to the sand. Ahead, he could see the trio of boats on the surface, a sturdy rope dangling from the dive boat. Boone hefted the dry bag and moved to the rope, attaching it to a carabiner that was affixed to the end. He ascended, reaching the stern of the dive boat and tossing his fins up.

"Did you get everything?" Price asked, watching as Red Shirt and No Shirt began hauling up the bag.

"Everything I could see," Boone said, climbing the stern ladder. "The only things I left were the remains of the priest and the gourds. Figured those would take up too much space." He glanced across to the *Liquid Asset*, anchored on the ocean side of the dive boat, and could see Welk—or Jimmy or whatever his name was—sitting on the aft deck enjoying a drink. Wilson was on the little flybridge, his assault rifle held across his chest, finger pointed straight out above the trigger. *Ex-military,* Boone thought. Chuck was on the dive boat, his large-caliber pistol trained on Boone. *Him too. Mercenaries.*

The bag broke the surface and Price rubbed his hands together with enthusiasm. "Excellent!"

Clear of the water, the bag was harder to manage, but the two gang members were able to bring it up over the gunwale, where it hit the deck with a thud.

"Careful!" Price shouted. He dropped to his knees and opened the bag. "Magnificent," he whispered.

The boat was oriented with its portside to shore. Boone went to that bench and secured his tank, under the watchful eye of Chuck. Emily was on the starboard side and Boone gestured for her to come to him. As she came across, he noticed she still had her little wrist-mounted dive light. *Good.* "Are you all right?" he asked.

"Still breathing," she muttered.

"Keep at it… slow, deep breaths," he said quietly, then flicked his eyes toward the water above the cave.

She followed his gaze, then looked back at him. "Maybe he will let us go…" she said hopefully.

"Maybe… but don't hold your breath." Adding "Yet," near her ear.

Chuck was stepping into the skiff with the heavy bag, Price following with his pistol at the ready.

"You're going to leave the skiff for us once you transfer over, right?" Boone called out.

Price smiled. "Yes, about that… there's been a change of plans." Chuck made his way to the outboard at the stern of the skiff.

"You bastard, you promised to let us go!" Emily shrieked.

Boone took a step away from her, his eyes flicking to the two gang members still aboard.

Emily continued her tirade. "You swore you wouldn't kill us! You gave your word!"

"My dear, I most certainly am keeping my word." He made a show of raising his pistol to the sky, the barrel leaving them. "I'm not going to kill you." He smiled. "*They* are."

Boone saw the MAC-10 coming up from Red Shirt's side, a long suppressor extending from the barrel. He had been expecting the double-cross and once it came, he acted with blinding speed.

When Boone had geared up, no one had noticed that he'd strapped on *two* weight belts, both his regular diving belt, as well as his lighter freediving belt. When Red Shirt started to move, Boone popped the quick release on the heavier belt, spinning his body as he did so and extending his arm as he completed the first revolution, the lead weights whipping through the air and striking the gangster's temple with a sickening thud. The man crumpled, a series of clacking sounds emanating from the silenced machine pistol as his fingers reflexively spasmed, sending bullets into the deck. Still spinning, Boone lashed out with a swift *armada* kick, the capoeira strike taking No Shirt in the chest as he was retrieving a pistol from his waistband, sending him tumbling to the deck. Boone completed the single revolution, grabbing Emily around the waist and pitching them both over the side just as he saw Price get off a single round with a sharp crack.

They hit the water and Boone arrowed down, letting their momentum carry them toward the sand. Muffled shouts of surprise could be heard from the surface as Boone strapped the heavy weight belt around Emily. She quickly assisted, pulling it tight around her waist as they plunged for the bottom. The *Liquid Asset* and the skiff were both blocked by the *Alhambra*, but that wouldn't last long once they made for the cave. He wanted to be as close to the thirty-foot depth the bottom afforded them once the bullets started to fly.

Boone had been a huge fan of the television show *MythBusters* while in college, and he remembered an episode where they had tested how water affected bullets fired at an underwater target— for instance, a super spy swimming away from a bunch of bad guys. Unlike most Hollywood myths, this one turned out to be true. The sudden increase in drag from the water rendered most bullets useless beyond about eight feet. Still, Boone wasn't about to test the limits of that theory, and they reached the bottom.

Above, muffled gunshots began, some booming and spaced far apart, others a staccato chugging. *Probably Wilson's rifle*, Boone thought. The temptation was strong to look back the way they had come, but he resisted the urge. Every second would count.

*Diving without a mask... not much fun.* Boone looked toward Emily. Her blurry face had a look of grim determination as she swam toward the cave. While Boone knew his own freediving abilities would probably allow him to reach the air of the grotto, particularly without having a bulky tank to push ahead of him, she would need a little help. He had briefly toyed with staging some of those corked gourds inside the passageway, but didn't want to try out such an unreliable air source, particularly when the whole thing was just a theory. No, he needed something dependable. *Hope I can see the damn thing.*

Squinting in the salt water, he spotted the piece of gear he had dropped when he left the cave mouth. Snagging the Spare Air pony bottle as he passed it, he grabbed Emily's arm and guided her hand onto the tiny tank. Above, the gunfire continued, though more sporadic now. Ducking through the fallen mangrove branches, Boone headed into the cave mouth. Emily followed, her wrist light coming on as she entered. She took a few breaths from the pony bottle and passed it to Boone. He still wasn't close to his freediving limits, but it seemed like a good idea to "gas up," so he used it before handing it back. He took Emily by the waist and pointed her toward the upward sloping passage, letting her lead the way. They were halfway up when the explosion hit.

Ironically, the same properties that protected Boone and Emily from gunfire could enhance the power of an explosion, as the water greatly amplified the shockwave from the grenade that detonated near the mouth of the cave. If they had been close to the opening, they would have been knocked unconscious or even killed. As it was, Boone felt a sharp pain as his eardrums compressed and he was pushed several feet up the passage. From the movement of Emily's light up ahead, he could tell she'd been affected as well. Quickly, he grabbed her heel and gave her bare foot a shake, worried she might have been stunned. Fortunately, she seemed okay. If anything, the speed of her ascent up the tunnel increased. In moments, they were back in the grotto, both of them gasping for air.

Emily looked to be having a dizzy spell as she reached the shallows and Boone reached out to steady her. "Whoa," she muttered. "Bit wobbly. You?"

"Definitely got my bell rung, but I'm okay, I think."

"What the sodding hell was that?"

"I dunno… dynamite? Actually, Price's personal goons looked military, so maybe a grenade."

Emily grunted, pulling herself out of the water. "I've heard of grenade fishing… isn't that something they do in your home state of Tennessee?"

"Nah, that's more of a 'Bama thing." He started toward her but felt a wave of dizziness of his own.

"Boone! You're bleeding!" Emily's wrist light was pointed at him and he looked down.

"Well, whattaya know," he said absently. The neoprene of his wetsuit was oozing blood out of a small hole in his left shoulder.

"Turn around!" Emily ordered. When he did, she hopped into the water, probing at the back of his shoulder. "There's no hole in back. C'mon, let's get you out of the water." She helped him climb out and sit beside the pool. Frantically, she unzipped his wetsuit, peeling it carefully back from his shoulders and pulling it down to his waist.

Boone winced. "Price got off a shot right when we jumped. Guess he got lucky. I was so pumped with adrenaline, I didn't even feel it." In the dim light, Boone could see the tears in Emily's eyes. "Hey... there are no vital organs in my shoulder. It'll be okay."

"The bullet's still in there, Boone."

"It's not bleeding too badly, though." He took hold of the empty sleeve of his wetsuit and pressed it to the wound. "Look, we just escaped certain death..."

"Yeah, about that. You got an endgame in mind? Cuz if they've got any more bombs, we ain't going back the way we came."

"You are correct," Boone said, grunting as he regained his feet. He went to the outcrop and retrieved something. "That Christmas present of yours? Best gift ever."

"Your phone!"

"When Price threw it overboard, it was the first ray of hope I had. Unfortunately, there's no signal in here. But..." He took her hand and led her to where he'd stashed the phone. Douse your light and look up there." He pointed.

"Sunlight!" Emily shouted. "But I don't remember that from before!"

"Had to do a little gardening. It leads to the surface. I tried my darndest and I can't squeeze through. But I know a certain girl whose parentage is half-pixie, half-leprechaun…"

Emily laughed and grabbed him by the back of the neck. "Normally I'd kick you in the bollocks for making fun of the altitude-challenged, but in this case…" She pressed a kiss to his lips. "Gimme the phone."

"Call Ras. We don't know how deeply Price has his hooks in the police department. It might only be one or two, but if one of them happens to take the call…"

"Right-o. It might take me a while to even get a signal, so… hang tight." She climbed onto the outcrop, flicking on her wrist light to peer up the chimney in the earth. She doused it and handed it down to him. "Here, take my torch. There's plenty of light up there and you'll need this to get back out once I bring the cavalry." She coiled and leaped, catching hold of something as her legs dangled for a moment before drawing up into the passage.

Boone watched her bare feet vanish up into the ceiling. "Be careful, Em," he called after her.

Her voice floated down from the roots. "Back in a jiff! Don't die while I'm gone."

**21**

Emily listened intently for several minutes, hunkered low in a thick stand of mangroves while she caught her breath. Even though the murky water here was only up to her shins, she could barely make out the bottom.

The climb up the tunnel had been strenuous and there were several cuts and scratches on her hands and feet from the jagged limestone that had poked through the mangrove-muck in places. *Good thing I wore the full suit,* she thought. Emily preferred to dive in a shorty wetsuit much of the time, but knowing they might be cave-crawling today, she'd opted for greater coverage. *Wish I'd kept my dive boots on,* she thought grimly, but she wasn't going to beat herself up about that—when she'd pulled those off aboard the boat, things hadn't yet gone south. Nevertheless, she had taken great care where she placed the sole of each foot during the climb.

Nearby, a deep thrumming could be heard. Cautiously, Emily crept forward, keeping low. Balancing on a mangrove root with her bare feet, she hugged a gnarled trunk and peeked around it. In the distance, the *Liquid Asset* was underway, angling to the south and the deeper waters of the lagoon. The dive boat remained at anchor, the man in the Panama hat leaning over the side, looking down into the water. A splash of color near the wheelhouse revealed that the red-shirted gang member Boone had decked with the weight belt was still down. Emily remembered the sound the blow had made and doubted he would be getting up anytime soon... if ever. *The Red Shirts are always the first to die,* her mind gibbered at her, and Emily felt guilty for thinking it—though, to be fair, the young gangster had tried to kill them.

The skiff was closer to the ledge, the shirtless gang member holding on to the side, his head and body underwater. His head came up and Emily saw a flash of bright green on his face. *The twat's got my mask!* She watched as the youth ducked his head under again, then pulled himself back into the skiff and motored back to the dive boat. Once there, he idled alongside, and the two men talked. It was too far to make anything out, but from their body language Emily didn't think they were about to pull up anchor.

Insects buzzed all around her and she resisted the urge to swat at them, wanting to avoid sudden movements until she was out of sight of the boats. *Not that they're likely to see me, with my involuntary camouflage,* she thought with wry amusement. Crawling out of that hole had left her coated from head to toe in smelly mud. She looked again at the phone. No bars. *Damn.* She looked out to the boat. *We had a teensy bit of signal out there, but I'm allergic to bullets and grenades.*

Emily glanced east over her shoulder toward the interior, where the mangroves grew into an impenetrable wall of gnarled branches and roots. *So... right or left... north or south?* Going to her right to the north would take her toward the passage between Caye Caulker and Ambergris Caye… south would take her toward The Split. *And toward the town's cell coverage. South it is.* Staying low, she moved to her left, occasionally glancing back toward the lagoon. Every now and then she would raise the phone high, hoping to catch a signal. Boone's phone had gotten the late messages from Ras at some point while they were at anchor, so she hoped she might not have to go too far.

In a few minutes, she was out of sight of the two boats and increased her pace. Up ahead, a tree drew her attention and she angled toward it. What had caught her eye was its height, and it appeared to be quite climbable. If she got higher up, she might be able to pick up signals from the developed part of Caulker.

It took her a while to reach the tree—she didn't think it was a mangrove, and it grew from a spot that was a little higher than the surrounding swamp of mangrove roots. She pulled the neck of her wetsuit open, sliding the phone down to her breastbone before starting to climb. Once she reached one of the higher limbs that was stout enough to hold her, she dug the phone out and stared at it. *Yes!* She pulled up Ras's missed call and dialed him back. She heard the ring immediately… but then she heard something else. An outboard motor.

*Bloody hell! C'mon, c'mon, c'mon!* The rings continued and the rumble grew louder, coming from the north. She looked toward the lagoon. The skiff came into view, skimming the shallows. The shirtless gang member was at the outboard, Chuck in the bow with a set of binoculars. *No!* Emily's branch was on the side facing the water and she willed herself to be invisible, just as Ras's voicemail picked up.

"Ras! It's Emily! We need your help! Boone's trapped in the cave, and I'm—"

A shout, carried on the wind: "There she is!" The motor's roar increased.

Emily clutched the trunk and tried to swing around to the interior side. Her heart skipped a beat as she bobbled the phone, managing to trap it against the trunk before it fell. She lifted it to finish the message but was greeted with the words "Call Ended."

*No no no no—shite!* A distant ripping sound was followed by several leaves flying off of nearby branches. Out of the corner of her eye, Emily could see the shirtless gangster taking his buddy's silenced machine pistol for a test drive. Fortunately, he didn't seem particularly adept at it. *Still... only takes one bullet,* Emily thought, biting onto the smartphone with her teeth and dropping to a lower branch and from there to the ground. Her bare feet sunk several inches into the wet earth. More shouts, Chuck yelling for the youth to "Get after her!" Emily shoved the phone back into her wetsuit and ran.

And promptly face-planted in the muck as her bare foot slipped on a wet root, sending her tumbling forward. She staggered to her feet, momentarily losing her sense of direction. There... sunlight on water, off to her right. She was still facing south. *If I go deeper into the mangroves, I may lose them, but I might just as easily trap myself in there,* she thought, looking at the foreboding wall of tropical foliage. *No... keep heading south.* Taking more time with her steps, she hopped from root to root through the mangroves, trying to put distance between herself and her pursuers while avoiding a broken neck.

"There you are, little girl," a rough voice called out from behind her.

Emily spared a glance backward. The merc named Chuck was visible through the trees, closing the distance. *How the hell did he catch up so fast?* Increasing her pace, she nearly slipped again, just catching herself from another fall as she grabbed frantically at a low-hanging branch. Laughter rose from behind, closer still.

"Oopsy daisy... guessing you didn't have any jungle warfare training, huh?"

Up ahead, an inlet from the lagoon cut a swath through the mangroves. Emily could see a narrow spot and she cut toward it, planning to use a fallen log to jump across. As she came closer, she came to a jarring halt. *That's no log...*

"Whatcha stopping for? I was just getting warmed up." Chuck was gasping for air, but he had closed the distance, the hand cannon of a pistol held in his grip.

Emily spun around and stood with her back to the inlet, shaking with fear. She grabbed a dead branch from a cluster of roots and held it up to ward him off.

Chuck stopped, looking at the stick. Sneering, he holstered his pistol. "Easy, young lady... that's a deadly looking twig you got yourself there. You know how to use it?"

Emily swung the stick in the air, her voice quavering. "Stay back!"

"Careful... ya gonna hurt yourself with that." Chuck reached to a sheath at his back and withdrew a wicked-looking survival knife. "How 'bout I whittle that down for ya?"

At the sight of the knife, Emily's demeanor changed, her terrified features going slack. She slowed her breathing, looking from the knife to Chuck's face.

"Deer in the headlights," he said, more to himself than to her. "I can work with that." He started forward.

Emily stood frozen in place, the stick falling from her fingers. Chuck moved in. "Hold still. This may sting a bit." He lunged.

And so did Emily. Instantly dropping the terrified-damsel act, she spun to the side, taking Chuck's wrist in both hands and yanking in the direction of his thrust, twisting the wrist and angling her pull just slightly so that his leading foot caught a red mangrove root and tripped him up further. His momentum carried him into the inlet, right onto the "log"—the armored back of the crocodile Emily had nearly played a game of *Frogger* on.

"You're right! It *might* sting a bit!" she shouted hysterically, her voice skirting the border of laughter and tears.

The croc was a big one. Emily had an idle thought that it might be the same one she and Boone had come across when they'd found the diver's body. The reptile thrashed to the side, startled by the impact.

Chuck cried out, splashing frantically as he tried to reach shore, managing to grab hold of the roots along the side just as the crocodile turned... and struck. The massive jaws clamped down on the mercenary's ribcage and yanked him back into the inlet. Chuck's screams were extinguished as the reptile's death roll pulled him under.

Even though her plan had panned out exactly as she had hoped it would, the carnage of the result was jarring, and for the second time Emily felt herself begin to freeze up. When Chuck had caught up with her, she had played the frozen-in-fear act to the hilt—but when the knife came out it had ceased to be an act. She had suddenly found herself back on the hurricane-lashed island of Saba with a machete-wielding psychopath named Aidan. Fortunately, she had snapped out of it in time before Chuck had skewered her.

The water of the inlet frothed with the struggles of predator and prey and Emily shook herself, turning away and running for the lagoon... only to come face to face with the skiff, its bow against the mangrove roots of the shoreline, its motor idling.

No Shirt lifted the machine pistol, but the rumble of the skiff's idling motor was joined by the sound of another boat, its roar rising in pitch as it approached. Emily couldn't see it through the thick foliage, but the gangster clearly could, his head turning to the north, his eyes growing huge. He swung the barrel of his weapon, triggering it too early. The unwieldy barrel coughed with a *thup-thup-click*. Only two rounds had remained.

Emily watched as sudden movement flashed through the gaps in the trees and a familiar shape rushed into view. Ras's little fishing boat smashed into the smaller skiff's stern, capsizing it and sending the gunman flying into the water of the lagoon. As the man struggled in the shallows, Ras maneuvered his boat around, stepping into the bow to heft an oar and smashing it down onto the gangster's head before he was able to recover his footing.

"Don't kill him!" Emily shouted. "He's just a stupid kid."

"Doan worry, Miss Emily... I and I not da killing type." Ras grabbed the unconscious youth by his belt and managed to haul him into the boat.

Emily spared a look back toward the inlet, making sure the croc didn't have any friends, then dashed through the shallow water toward Ras's boat. A flash of lime green in the water beside the upended skiff caught her eye: her mask the kid had been using. *Yoink!* She snatched her mask by the strap and jumped into the boat alongside Ras, who was busy trussing up the gang member with some mooring line. "Thank God you showed up!"

"I got dis text from Boone saying you was okay and in San Pedro, but it didn't sound like him, so I come lookin'. Den I got your voice message when I was approachin' a dive boat near da cave. Saw dat little skiff rushing to da sout' and recognized dis blood clot here. Figured dey were after you." Ras hesitated. "Where is Boone?"

"That dive boat... we escaped from there, but Price shot Boone when we jumped. He's still in the cave! We've got to save him!"

Boone opened his eyes. Very little light greeted him in the near-to-tal gloom of the cavern. A tiny glow came from the vicinity of the chimney Emily had ascended, but that was all. Boone had doused the wrist-mounted light she had left him, conserving the batteries. He had been meditating for the past half hour, breath-ing slowly and listening intently for any sounds from above, all the while trying to push his fear for Emily's safety to the furthest corners of his mind. He wasn't having a lot of luck with that.

Boone struggled to his feet, wincing as he rose. The wound he'd received didn't seem to be too serious; then again, his first-hand knowledge of gunshot wounds had been zero, up until about an hour ago. Machetes to the torso, now *that* was something he had a vivid frame of reference for... and this injury wasn't half as painful—or bloody—as that wound had been. Still, he'd found a jagged bit of limestone and ripped part of a sleeve from his wetsuit to create a rudimentary dressing, then pulled his wetsuit top back on and zipped it up—partly to hold the homemade bandage in place and partly for warmth.

The greatest discomfort he was experiencing had nothing to do with the threat of hypothermia or torn flesh. No... the great-est discomfort he felt was the uncertainty—the ignorance—of Emily's situation.

The minutes ticked by and Boone felt his heart rate rise. He paced. *Goddammit Em, come back to me!* All he wanted right now was to hear her voice and know that she was safe. His pacing brought him up against the limestone ledge and he looked up at the glow from above. *It should have been me. We could have dug into the sides of that passage, widened it… I should have gone!* Furious, he kicked the base of the outcrop… and it gave.

Cautiously, he flicked on the dive light Emily had left him and aimed it at his feet. He crouched, examining the hole his dive boot had made. It was a neat aperture, crumbled chunks of limestone lying around it. He reached out, extending his long arm into the hole. He felt something hard, smooth, and cool to the touch. His fingertips closed on the object and brought it into the light.

**22**

"Boone!"

"Emily!" Boone's shout came right on the heels of Emily's own.

"Oh thank God, are you okay?"

He laughed, relief flooding his voice. "I was about to ask *you* that. I'm fine." Suddenly, he tensed. "Wait!" he hissed. "We shouldn't be yelling—"

"What, you worried 'bout dem bad bwoys?" a familiar voice floated down. "Dey gone."

"Ras! Good to see you, man! Wait, what do you mean gone?"

"Dem George Street bwoys, we capture one, de udda is dead."

"And Price and his men buggered off on his little yacht," Emily said. "Well, except one... and he... he won't be a problem. Tell you all about it later. How you feeling? Need me to come in?"

"No, I've been ready to get my ass out of here since the minute you left," Boone called up. "The shoulder's stiff, but I stopped the bleeding. I can make it out, no problem."

"You've still got plenty of air in that backup tank, yeah?"

"Yeah, we hardly used it. The dive boat still where it was?"

"Yeah…"

"Good. Meet me there."

"Wait, what about that grenade?" Emily asked. "Could it have collapsed the entrance?"

"I'm betting not. I think we'd be dead if the explosion had been that strong. But if I'm not at the boat in about fifteen minutes, come on back to my little Hobbit hole and we'll talk Plan B."

"Okay, see you at the boat!"

"Oh, and that rope they used to haul up the chacmools? See if there's another one of those bags that Welk had and send it down to the sand below the boat. I found something else."

---

Boone was thankful to see that the cave mouth was intact, albeit cloudy from sand particulates stirred up by the earlier explosion. After a quick visit to the bag that lay on the bottom beneath the *Alhambra*, Boone surfaced at the stern of the dive boat and came up the ladder. Off to the side, he could see Ras's boat at anchor, No Shirt trussed up and lying in the bow.

Emily grabbed him the minute he hit the swim platform, hugging him fiercely.

"Whoa!" Boone pulled back.

"Ohmigod, your shoulder, I'm sorry, I—"

"No, the shoulder's okay, it's that *smell!*" He stared at her and laughed. "You look like Schwarzenegger in *Predator*."

She looked at herself. "Oh, yeah… I am a bit whiffy, aren't I? Trust me, I was a *lot* worse before I fell in the water a couple times. Climbing out of that mucky hole… I felt like an active participant in a colonoscopy."

"You're a little young to be talking colonoscopies."

"Well, a girl can dream. Come on, we need to jump in Ras's boat and get you to a hospital."

"Not yet. Ras, can you pull up the rope?"

"Ya mon."

While Ras began bringing up the bag, Boone's eyes fell on the fallen gang member. He went over and knelt beside the body. Reaching out, he touched his fingertips to the youth's neck. He didn't need to—it was crystal clear that the man was dead—but he felt he should.

Emily laid a hand on his shoulder. "He didn't give you any choice…"

"I know. Still…" He rose, looking down at the body. "What do we…?"

"First thing we're gonna do is get you to a hospital. We'll leave the one we captured on board and Ras will call this in to the police. Claim he heard gunfire coming from this boat as he passed it."

"And leave Boonemily out of it," Ras said, as he hauled on the rope. "Babylon got Price's men on de inside it seem."

"Careful with that," Boone said, when the dry bag broke the surface. He joined Ras at the gunwale and took hold of the bag, unclipping the carabiner.

"What is it?" Emily breathed.

"Close your eyes and hold out your hands."

"This again? All right, I'm game."

Ras gasped as Boone removed the object from the bag and placed it into Emily's hands. She opened her eyes… then opened them wider.

"Cor…" she breathed. Then mouthed "blimey," but no sound came out.

Sitting in Emily's hands was a massive jade head, exquisitely carved, almost exactly like the one Dr. Rojas had told them about.

"Dat's like da one on our money!" Ras shouted.

"That other head came from Altun Ha… and I have no doubt this one came from there, too. If I had to guess… when our skeleton priest friend in the cave loaded up on those chacmool trinkets, he grabbed a little something extra."

"Holy shit, Boone…" Emily stuttered. "What do we…?"

"We get this to Manuel Rojas," Boone said without hesitation. "After the last couple days, I've got some trust issues."

◆ ◆ ◆

Caye Caulker didn't have much in the way of medical facilities, and despite being the most popular tourist town in Belize, San Pedro on neighboring Ambergris Caye did not have a hospital. It had a clinic but, after their arrest a couple nights before, Boone didn't want to show up there with a gunshot wound. After a ten-minute stop in Caulker for Ras to gas up, and for "Boonemily" to quickly shower and grab some essentials from their apartment, the trio settled in for the hour-long boat ride to Belize City. During the trip, they made several attempts to reach Dr. Rojas, but he didn't answer, and his voicemail still wouldn't pick up. The text thread that Emily had started with his number remained barren of replies. Ras brought them ashore in the neighborhood of Buttonwood Bay, where he directed them to a private hospital not far from the shore. He announced he'd anchor in the bay and "do some fishing" until they called for him. The massive jade head would remain with him, hidden in a fish box.

Apparently, a bullet wound didn't raise many eyebrows in Belize City medical facilities. Boone and Emily had concocted an elaborate story of a mugging—and how they'd already talked to the police—but after only a few sentences they were ushered to an examination room where a doctor set to work. As it turned out, the wound was shallow. The .22 caliber bullet hadn't done a great deal of damage and the slug was easy to remove. An hour later, they were in a recovery room and Boone's credit card had taken a wound of its own.

"Too bad we didn't get money up front from that Welk guy," Boone said, as he signed the slip the nurse brought in. "Between this, and... oh! Hey, while we're here, we should check on our potlicker friend."

"Surgery is scheduled for tomorrow," Emily said. "Besides... we need to stay on task and see if we can reach Manuel. Fortunately, while you were in there blubbering as they took the bullet out—"

"I wasn't... I barely felt it!"

"While you were weeping like a toddler with a splinter, I found... this." She held her smartphone up, showing an entry on Google Maps.

"Women's Group Arts and Crafts..." He looked up from her phone's screen. "I'm not buying you any more carvings—we have no money!"

"It's a gift shop at the Lamanai site, you berk. Maybe they can get Manuel for us." Emily dialed the number and tapped the speaker button.

"*Hola...?*" a woman's voice spoke, sounding uncertain, perhaps confused as to why anyone would be calling them.

*"Hola! Por favor,* we are looking for Dr. Manuel Rojas? At Lamanai?"

"Ah… Manuel, si, si. Nice man. His phone… something wrong. I take your number, have him call."

Emily gave it and their names and hung up. "Well, that was easy." She sat on the side of the bed. "Now I guess we just wait—do something to pass the time…" She started to lean in for a kiss but stopped herself. "Whoa… déjà vu."

Boone laughed, remembering his recovery in a hospital in Saba. "Yeah. Different island, different weapon, but your eyes are the same beautiful shade of green as last time."

Emily smiled and leaned in again.

------------◆·◆------------

The following morning Emily's phone rang. Its custom ringtone—the chorus from Panic! at the Disco's "The Emperor's New Clothes"—jarred the couple awake.

"Jesus!" Boone sat bolt upright, nearly spilling Em onto the floor. "I hate that ring."

"But you love the song. That's why I chose it!"

"Not when it… *ambushes* me like that."

"It's the gift shop," she said, picking up and tapping the speaker option. "Hello, Dr. Rojas?"

"Yes, is this Emily?"

"Yes, and Boone… the divemasters you took on the tour?"

"Of course. So good to hear from you. Marisol said you have been trying to reach me? I'm very sorry about the state of my communications. Something happened to my cell phone a few days ago and I haven't been able to receive calls or texts. Even my email seems to be down. Maybe I've been hacked. What can I do for you? Would you like a tour of Lamanai?"

"No... I mean *yes*, probably, at some point. But that's not why we wanted to talk to you. Um, you know that head you talked about? The one on the Belizean money?"

"Yes, the bust of Kinich Ahau, the Sun God. The largest jade object ever found in the Mayan world."

"Yeah, that one. So... what if it wasn't?"

There was a pause. "Wasn't... what?"

"The largest."

"I don't follow."

"Well, thing is... we—hey!"

Boone snatched the phone and muted the speaker setting. "One second, Doctor," he said, holding Emily's gaze. He held a finger to his lips, then sent the finger around the room, tugged his ear, then shrugged. *We don't know who's listening.* With all of their diving together, the pair had become adept at using simple signals in everyday situations.

She nodded, pointing at the phone and spinning her finger. *Go on, then.*

Boone resumed the call. "Dr. Rojas... how long will you be at Lamanai?"

"Just today and tomorrow."

"Maybe we *would* like a tour... any chance you'll be available today?"

"It is short notice, but I can accommodate. How will you get here, though?"

"Uhhhh... I don't know. How *would* we get there?"

"Well, usually you book a tour. I like Eco Adventures, myself. But this is last minute, so best to go there and ask around. If you take the Northern Highway to Carmelita in the Orange Walk district, after you pass through town, two turns before the toll bridge, there is an area of docks on your left. Don't take the last one before the bridge—that's the old compound of that software billionaire… McAfee? The one who fled Belize after his neighbor was murdered?"

"Yeah, we've certainly heard about him," Boone said. "That murder was in San Pedro, though, wasn't it?"

"Yes, he had a house there. This compound was where he supposedly had a company working on medicines made from jungle plants. The Gang Suppression Unit raided it… and not long after, several of the buildings burned down. He's not there anymore, of course. He escaped to the United States… ran for Libertarian president and lost to Gary Johnson. I believe he is in Canada now."

"Okay, so… we go to the docks that are *before* the old McAfee compound…" Boone prompted, steering them back on topic.

"Yes, just go there and ask around… see if Ian Fuente is there. Tell him I sent you. He will take you to Lamanai for about a hundred-fifty US dollars. Cash, of course."

"Just as well. I suspect the ol' credit card is groaning under the weight of charges as it is."

"But if you are on Caye Caulker, you won't reach here until—"

"Actually, we're in Belize City," Boone said, sparing the details of exactly why they were there.

"Oh… well, once you have a car, it will take you about an hour-and-a-half to get to the docks on the New River, and the river cruise takes a couple hours."

Boone glanced down, seeing that it was just after seven in the morning. "Okay, thanks! We'll see you soon." He hung up and relayed what Manuel had said to Emily.

Boone had been officially discharged the night before, but the hospital had said they could remain in the room until morning at no extra charge. This was generous… although it may have just been to avoid any liability if two discharged gringos stumbled out in the wee hours and blundered into an actual mugging.

Emily gathered their things. "So, what's the plan?"

"Let's call Ras. Grab the jade head and find some transportation."

◆ ◆ ◆

An hour later, they were on the road north, the dry bag containing the artifact on the seat between them, their backpacks alongside. As it happened, Ras had a cousin who was a cabbie, and he'd met them at the shore after a quick call from Ras. King was about the same age as Ras, and while Ras Brook definitely enjoyed his ganja, King took it to another level. Boone and Emily had to roll down their windows for most of the drive to avoid spending the rest of the day high as kites from the musky cloud that lingered around the driver's seat. But the music was jammin', and they made good time, passing through Carmelita at half past nine. A couple minutes later, the toll bridge came into view and the cab slowed.

A thousand feet from the bridge, King pulled off of the main road into a sandy cut. "Here ya go, me bruddah an' sistah."

Boone had his wallet out. "How much do we—?"

"Nutting," King said, his words riding on a stream of herby smoke. "Brook say Boonemily ride free, so dey do. He do for me if I do for him—everyt'ing irie, seen?"

"Seen and heard and appreciated," Emily said, snatching up the dry bag. "But we owe you too, okay?"

"All right, me sistah. Jah bless." With a crunch of tires, the cab pulled away, turning to the right and heading back toward Belize City.

"There are the docks," Boone said, pointing through the tropical foliage that encroached on the sand-packed driveway. He started toward the river.

"Oy, this is heavy!" Emily said, scurrying up to his side and pressing the dry bag into Boone's chest. "Here, you take Jaden."

"Jaden?"

Emily didn't say anything, just grinned at him with anticipation.

"Oh. Because the head's made of..." He couldn't see Emily's eyes behind her sunglasses, but he knew they'd be sparkling with mirth. Boone just shook his head.

"Oh, c'mon, that's good, right?"

Boone started walking again.

"It's just a placeholder, yeah?" Emily trotted along beside him, playfully shouldering into him. "I mean, they'll eventually name it after some Mayan god or king or god-king or something, but for now... you carry-eth his royal highness, King Jaden... ruler of Dry Bag."

Boone's attempts to maintain a stoic look failed him and his face cracked into a smile as they reached the docks on the shore of the New River. The river itself was a murky green, a stark contrast to the turquoise and cobalt blues of the waters he and Emily were accustomed to. Actually, it reminded him a bit of some of the rivers in Tennessee. The humidity reminded Boone of his home state as well, the lack of sea breezes this far inland lending the air a heaviness that was largely absent on the cayes. A man of medium build and tan complexion was working on an outboard engine aboard a small center console. He looked up and smiled as they approached, and Boone raised a hand in greeting. *"Hola!* We're looking for Ian Fuente?"

"You found him," the man said. He spoke with a Belizean creole accent, and his ancestry appeared to be a mix of several groups. "Manuel gave me a call, said to keep an eye out for a very tall man and a woman who was..." He hesitated, then indicated their respective heights, looking a bit embarrassed. "Sorry..."

"S'okay," Emily said. "I'm small in height, but positively titanic in spirit."

The man laughed. "Yes, he said you were the funny one."

"Hear that Boone? What does that make you, hmm?"

Boone handed Emily the dry bag, aiming it into her stomach and eliciting a little "oof" from her. "I'm Boone Fischer, and Chuckles McGee here is Emily Durand." He reached out to shake the man's hand.

"You want to go to Lamanai, uh?"

"Yes, please."

"I just need to change out a spark plug and we can get going right after." He pointed back at a small shack. "The lady there sells some snacks and water for the ride."

"Thanks," Boone said. He debated offering to give the man a hand with the engine—he was quite handy with marine engines, having done repairs on nearly every dive boat he'd ever worked on. But it was clear Ian knew his business, so he resisted the urge and started for the shack.

"I'm guessing I should avoid any references to Jaden, yeah?" Emily said quietly.

"Yeah... I'm sure Ian's fine, but honestly the fewer people that know, the better."

"Slow down, Willis… say that last part again."

"Okay, but you gonna bail me out, right?"

"Of course," Oliver Price said. "As soon as we're off the phone, I'll make a call and have you out of there."

Price, Wilson, and the man known as Archibald Welk were sitting at a roadside café in Belize City, waiting on a local contact to arrange the sale of the antiquities they'd taken from the cavern. In fact, when Price's phone rang, he had expected it was the broker, but instead it had been Willis, one of the two George Street gangbangers that Price had hired for a little extra muscle. Price had wondered why they hadn't heard from them or his own man, Chuck. Now he knew. Chuck was croc-bait, the other gangster's body had been recovered rather than disposed of, and Willis himself was calling from prison in Belize City. And… the two divemasters had gotten away.

"Okay, so, we were waiting for dem…" Willis began.

"No, no, skip to the end… you said they brought something up?"

"Yeah… dey pull up a bag, like we were doing with dose little statues… only what dey had in dere wasn't no little statue. It was big."

Price sat forward, the plastic patio furniture giving a squeak as one of the legs flexed and scooted along the floor. "What was it?"

"Well, I was tied up in dat rasta's boat, so I couldn't see real good… but it was green. Same green as dose statues. And… y'know what it look like? Dat head on Belize money."

"What did they do with it?"

"I don' know. Dey had it wit' dem when dey left. Dey leave me on de dive boat and go south."

Price's excitement grew. "Listen, Willis… I will have you out of there in the next hour… but you must keep your mouth shut about this. All of this. Do you understand?"

"Yes, boss."

"Good. Hang tight." He hung up and looked at Wilson. "Our remaining gangster seems to have gotten himself locked up. Fortunately, he's at the police station here. I'll make a call and you go bail him out. Then kill him."

Wilson nodded, as if he'd been asked to pick up the dry cleaning.

"But first… it appears as if our intrepid treasure hunters have escaped and found themselves a large jade head."

"Like the Sun God head from Altun Ha?" Welk asked excitedly.

"Sounds like it. Now… where would they take such a priceless treasure…" Price trailed off, then suddenly brought up his phone, seeking and finding a number. He dialed. "Hello, is this the Spindrift Hotel? I'm with the British Museum, and I'm trying to reach a Dr. Manuel Rojas… Yes? Where? Okay, thank you very much and have a pleasant morning." He hung up and turned to Welk. "I've always wanted to tour Lamanai."

**23**

"Your first time touring Lamanai?" Ian asked as they motored south, shortly after leaving the docks. The river here was quite narrow and winding, the mangroves encroaching in places.

"Yeah," Boone said. "Actually, except for Belize City, we've only been to the mainland a few times."

"Oh, you're missing most of Belize, then!" He gestured around them. "So much wildlife here, beautiful jungles, rivers… mountains in the south. And many, many Mayan sites… though you are on your way to see the best, I think. Well, in Belize at least. My wife and I went to Tikal in Guatemala." Ian whistled. "The main temple there is the tallest Mayan structure in the world."

"Ooh!" Emily waved her hands. "They used that in *Star Wars*, I heard… the rebel base near the end? Sorry, I am a fount of useless trivia."

Ian laughed. "It's all right, I know this! My son pointed that out to me when we were watching it. But at Lamanai, the Temple of the Jaguar is quite impressive, I promise you."

"The Mayans loved their jaguars, didn't they?" Boone asked.

Ian nodded. "You speak truth. Seems like every site has a jaguar temple. Except for the bigger crocodiles, the jaguar is the top predator in Belize and the biggest cat in the Americas. In the world, only lions and tigers are bigger."

"Are there any j... any of those cats... around here?" Emily asked, clearly avoiding saying the animal's name in her accent.

Boone grinned at her, earning himself a punch in the arm. He was grateful she'd targeted the one that didn't connect to the wounded shoulder.

"I have seen one or two along the river," Ian said. "But most of them live further out in the interior. There is a lot of jungle surrounding the Lamanai site, so perhaps there."

The river continued to wind in unpredictable ways. Boone had to keep checking the sun to figure out their direction. Most of the time, they were heading south, but sometimes they almost seemed to be backtracking.

"The river was green when we started, but it's starting to look blue," Boone noted.

"Yes, there seems to be some sort of pollutant that is getting worse up near Orange Walk. No one is sure what it is. But the river is in better shape down here. And there is more wildlife." He pointed off the starboard side. "There, in the mangroves... you see there? Crocodile. Should we go in for a closer look?"

"I'm good, thanks," Emily said quickly.

"Yeah, let's just keep going," Boone added.

As Ian slowed to make the turn at an abrupt bend in the river, a low rumble rose to compete with the idling engine, seeming to come from all directions.

"What on earth is that?" Emily asked, looking around.

"Oh, good, I was hoping we'd find some," Ian said with a smile. He cut the engine. "If you look carefully, you'll find out for yourself."

The sound continued, an unearthly roaring. Boone peered into the trees and spotted black shapes in the branches. "Monkeys." He could make out the faces of several who were close to the river's edge. Their mouths rounded into a perfect "O," they were blasting out an unholy amount of sound.

"Howler monkeys," Ian said. "Very common in Belize."

"They are *so* loud," Emily said, laughing as the roars seemed to get even louder now that the boat was stopped.

"Yes, one of the loudest animals in the world. They have a big bone in the throat, and they can expand their necks. Even though they are only about fifteen pounds, they can roar louder than a lion. But only the males scream like that."

"Sounds about right," Emily said.

"And here's a fun little fact a zoologist friend at the Belize Zoo taught me: louder calls, smaller balls."

"What?" Boone turned from the trees. "You're kidding."

"She swore it was true. Someone researched this. The ones with the smallest testicles are the loudest."

Emily doubled over with laughter. "Oh my God, that's brilliant! That is absolutely too good!"

"Um, how did these researchers…?" Boone began. "Actually, y'know what? Never mind. I don't need to know."

"They're not gonna fling poop at us or anything, are they?" Emily asked, looking askance at one howler that had swung to a branch overhanging the river.

"It happens," Ian said.

"I wonder if there's a correlation there, too?" Emily mused, keeping a wary eye on the one above. "Do the ones with the tiny balls fling the most shite?"

Nearly an hour later the river began to widen, and Ian increased their speed.

"The New River…" Emily was in the bow, looking back at Ian. "That sounds very un-Mayan. What did the Mayans call it?"

"Ah, smart lady. Yes, the Spanish changed it to the El Rio Nuevo, and when the British took control it was changed to the New River. But before that, the Mayans had another name for it. Forgive me, I don't know the actual Mayan word, but they thought they saw faces in the water, so they called it The River of Strange Faces."

"That's… not creepy at all," Emily said with a visible shiver.

Boone had a flash of memory: the dead diver in the mangroves. He shivered as well. Ahead, the river opened up wider still and Ian angled for a dock near the shore.

"Here we are!" Ian called out as he slowed. "Lamanai."

"What is 'Lamanai' in English?" Boone asked.

"It means 'submerged crocodile.'"

"Of course it does," Emily muttered.

After handing over two hundred dollars to Ian—fifty of which was a well-earned tip—Boone and Emily left the docks and headed inland along a sandy lane. Emily pointed at a little shack, adorned with brightly colored T-shirts, blankets, and scarves.

"Women's Group Gift Shop," Emily read from a sandwich board sign by the door.

"*Hola,*" a woman inside said, rising from a stool. "You are the ones looking for Manuel, yes?"

Boone stepped inside the shop. "Yes, thank you for having him call us."

"He is out working on a new site and said to send you to the ball court by The High Temple. He will come there at *mediodía...* twelve noon?"

"*Gracias,*" Boone said. They still had a half hour.

The shopkeeper bent over behind a small counter and came up with a stack of papers. She took one and returned the rest. "Here is a map he gave me. It is better than the ones the museum gives out." She set it on the counter.

Boone had looked up Lamanai on the internet and found that most information about it spoke of three or four temples, but this map showed just how extensive the original city must have been. Obviously, there were many structures that had not yet been cleared, and perhaps many more not yet discovered.

The woman pointed to a rectangle at the leftmost edge of the paper. "Manuel is working here. But there is no trail, so you wait for him here." She tapped a spot on the map that showed a cleared area. "Nice grass, not as many mosquitos." She offered Boone the paper.

He took it and gestured around the shop. "Your business is lovely." Even with their dwindling funds he felt they should buy something, so he leaned over to Emily. "We can swing a T-shirt..."

"On it." Em selected a shirt with a Mayan wheel calendar on it and "Lamanai, Belize" underneath. She handed over some cash and thanked the woman, joining Boone outside.

Following the map, they made their way along several paths to a well-maintained area, shaded by the surrounding foliage.

"Says this area was a Mayan ball court," Boone read from a sign.

"Whoa…" Emily whispered, pointing toward the far end of the courtyard. Through the trees, a massive stone structure shone in the sunlight. "It's stonking huge!"

"That must be The High Temple," Boone said. He glanced at the time. "We've got a few minutes."

Emily was off like a shot. She came up short at the foot of the stepped pyramid. "The Mayans sacrificed people up there, didn't they?"

"Uh… I know they practiced human sacrifice, sure, but I don't know how often it actually happened."

"Back on Saba, I was carried up a pyramid of sorts…" Emily mused.

Boone remained silent. Emily was referring to her involuntary journey up the slopes of Mount Scenery. Her captor had intended to sacrifice her at the summit. Boone could see the connection here, but back on Half Moon Caye, Em had insisted this was something she needed to work through on her own. He watched her as she looked up the tiers toward the top.

"On the other hand, Aidan was mad as a bag of ferrets… and this… this is a beautiful pyramid. And I want some photos. C'mon!"

After a quick scramble up the staircases on the tiered sides of the pyramid and a flurry of selfies and panoramic shots across the jungle canopy, they returned to the ball court.

"I wonder what that is?" Boone approached a pair of rocks that lay in the center of the ball court, one of which looked quite flat and rounded.

"That is where offerings were made." A local wearing a green shirt that proclaimed him a "Tour Guide" stubbed out a cigarette and approached them. Boone was pleased to see the man tuck the extinguished butt into a fanny pack at his waist. "Archaeologists found a small vessel full of mercury underneath. Perhaps an offering before a game."

Boone introduced himself and Emily. "We're waiting for Dr. Rojas," he said.

"Oh, okay," the man said, extracting a fresh cigarette and lighting up again. "I thought maybe you were part of a tour group."

"We haven't seen that many tourists today," Emily remarked.

"No, it's very slow. No cruise ships today. I heard a helicopter landing in Indian Church to the south, so maybe a small tour group is coming, but I don't know. Rain is coming."

Boone silently cursed himself for not looking at the weather forecast. Even outside of hurricane season, it was a daily habit for divemasters, but with all the excitement he'd forgotten to do it. *Getting shot can certainly throw a wrench in your routine*, he thought.

"So… this ball court… is this the game where the loser gets sacrificed?" Emily asked the tour guide.

"Only the team captain."

"Oh, well, that's okay then." Emily looked around at the sloping masonry on either side. "Where's the goal?"

The tour guide gestured to the center of the walls on either side. "There could be several on either side. Some ball courts have permanent stone rings. This one might have had ones that were brought in for a game, perhaps made of wood." He took a puff, then continued. "The balls were solid rubber, almost ten pounds. And you couldn't use your hands or your feet… just elbows, hips, or knees."

"Ouch," Emily said. "Makes football seem like child's play."

Boone smiled. She meant the game he knew as soccer, rather than American football, but either way… the Mayan ball game seemed brutally difficult.

"Ah, you made it!" Dr. Manuel Rojas approached from the direction of The High Temple. "Are you ready for your tour?"

"We actually got a little tour from…" Boone gestured to the guide.

"Filipo," he said. "But I'm on break," he added with a smile, turning and walking off toward the gift shop.

"Actually," Boone said, "maybe you could show us what you're working on right now? This new site?"

"Oh, I don't know about that. It's out of the way, in some fairly rough jungle terrain. Nothing much to see, yet. We're still excavating—"

"Out of the way is actually good," Boone interrupted. "We've got something to show you… and *just* you. Best not to be in an area where some tourists might show up."

Dr. Rojas raised his eyebrows. "I am intrigued. Very well." He dug a small canister from a pocket and tossed it to Boone. "Here."

Boone caught it. A can of bug spray.

◆ ◆ ◆

"Lamanai is actually the longest inhabited Mayan settlement in the world," Dr. Rojas said. They had just crossed the courtyard toward the west and stepped onto a path that was barely discernible. "We think it was established about 900 BC, and when the Spanish arrived in 1544, the Mayans still lived here. Contrast that to many other Mayan sites that were abandoned long before. The Spanish tried to Christianize the Mayans here, but they rebelled in 1640 and burned the churches." He came to a halt on the path and gestured ahead. "We haven't really cleared the trail yet, so..." Reaching to his side, he drew a short machete from a canvas sheath.

Boone felt Emily stiffen beside him. He reached out a hand to reassure her, but she brushed him off and moved alongside Manuel.

"Excuse me, Doctor? Would you mind if I take that and do the choppy-choppy? It's been a long week and I could use a little therapeutic carnage, yeah?"

Dr. Rojas shrugged and handed her the blade, pointing west. "Just head through there, towards that rise."

"Right-o." Emily threw Boone a meaningful look as she hefted the machete and started forward, cutting through the brush.

Boone watched with pride as his empress hacked and slashed, carving a path through the jungle. *That's one way to face your fears,* he thought.

"So, do we go up that hill?" Emily asked, pausing her murderous botanical rampage.

"That is no hill... it is a temple," Dr. Manuel Rojas informed her.

They were at the foot of a mound, its slope covered in trees, roots, and vines. It bore no resemblance to the grand temple structures in the curated parts of Lamanai.

"Only a small portion of the Mayan world has been uncovered. The jungle has a way of reclaiming the land in a very short period of time." Manuel led them around the side of the mound. "This temple here is one we discovered with some of the newer satellite software." Through the trees, a small folding table was set up along with a couple of camp chairs and a tent. "I've been taking preliminary measurements and searching for entrances. I don't believe this temple will be as grand as the ones in the main temple complex, but who knows?"

Emily sunk the blade of the machete into a rotten log. "No wonder you carry bug spray," she said, swatting at an insect.

Boone sniffed the air. A pungent tang of ozone. *Rain is coming.* "Is it just you out here?" he asked.

"Yes, at the moment." Manuel reached the table and grabbed a towel, mopping his brow. "There is a little cooler over there if you would like some water." He sat in one of the camp chairs and gestured around them. "So… we are alone. What did you want to talk to me about?"

Boone looked at Emily, who nodded. He opened the dry bag and removed the head, though it was currently wrapped in every remaining scrap of felt they had managed to find back on the dive boat. Boone set the artifact on the table and carefully unwrapped it.

Manuel sucked in a gasp of humid air. *"Madre de dios,"* he breathed. He rose from the camp chair, wobbled a bit, then steadied himself and adjusted his glasses. "This is…" He leaned in, peering closely at it. "Surely this is a fake…" He swallowed and straightened up. "But it isn't, is it?"

"Do you think it came from Altun Ha?" Boone asked. "Another bust of the Sun God?"

"It appears to be sculpted from the same type of jade, and the carving looks to be by the same sculptor, but this isn't the Sun God, Kinich Ahau." Manuel rotated the head and pointed to a small figure carved at the base alongside the head.

"That looks like a bunny rabbit," Emily said.

"Correct. And here, on the top of the brow, a serpent's head. If I had to guess, this is Ix Chel, goddess of the moon and fertility. She is often depicted as old... but sometimes young. The waxing and waning of the moon as a representation of the stages of fertility. Her younger self is often accompanied by a rabbit... and her older self usually has a snake crest." He looked up at them. "Do you know, in Cozumel there is a shrine to her? One of the most important pilgrimages in Mayan culture was associated with an oracle there."

"Perhaps these heads were created together at Altun Ha," Boone surmised. "A sun god and a moon goddess."

"This is a phenomenal discovery!" Manuel blurted out, his professorial manner shattered by boyish excitement. "Where did you find this?"

Boone and Emily recounted the events of the last few days. Manuel was particularly interested in the cache of chacmool figurines and was impressed with Boone's hypothesis.

"Hmm... religious totems to take back from a pilgrimage. That's not a bad theory. And your guess that the remains you found could be from a priest sounds plausible."

"Oh! And I brought this!" Emily took her GoPro out of a pocket of her shorts. "They left our gear when they buggered off... guess the gang members were planning on selling it all. This contains footage of the cavern and quite a few closeups of the items that were there."

Manuel watched a few minutes of it. He sighed. "But all of these chacmool statuettes and the other artifacts... Mr. Price and his men have them?"

"They took everything," Boone said. "I found the head later."

"I am so sorry for what you had to go through with those people. I wish you had contacted me before you went to this cave!"

"We tried," Emily said. "But you had already left San Pedro, and every time we called your cell, we got a 'mailbox is full' message."

"Which I'm starting to think was no accident," Boone mused. "The 'archaeologist' that hired us claimed you had recommended us. They must have taken steps to make sure we couldn't verify that."

"This archaeologist, what was his name?"

"Archibald Welk," Boone said.

Manuel frowned. "I know no one by that name. Sounds British."

"Yeah, but really he's some guy from the Bronx," Emily said. "Talks like he walked out of a Scorsese movie."

Manuel's eyes went wide. "Fat man? Thick glasses? Balding, with hair combed over the top?"

"Yeah," Boone said. "Said his real name was Jimmy."

"James Cavelli." Manuel shook his head, looking disgusted. "He was kicked out of an archaeological dig the British Museum was conducting in Tunisia. They discovered he was trying to line up buyers for some of the items they had excavated. It made all of the archaeological newsletters. He was actually quite brilliant, but after this scandal he was stripped of his doctorate. I thought he would be in jail by now." He reached out and touched the head. "All of those other artifacts you found... we must contact the authorities!"

"Yeah, about that..." Emily said. "We're going to need to figure out who we can safely contact."

"We think Price has someone on the inside of the police," Boone explained. "Probably several people... and possibly high up in the ranks."

Manuel thought for a moment. "I know someone who can help. He can get this head safely to the vault where they keep Kinich Ahau." He began rewrapping the head. "I will call him from the museum phone near the entrance, then I will contact Ian and have him come back for us at first light."

"I don't think we have that much time," Boone said. As Dr. Rojas had been speaking, Boone had noticed activity in the tree branches to the east. Monkeys or birds, disturbed by something moving through the jungle. Through the foliage Boone spotted a flash of white. The movement passed by a gap in the leaves and Boone got a better look. A polo shirt. *Wilson.* Boone suddenly remembered the tour guide, Filipo, mentioning a helicopter. He whirled to the table and stuffed the wrapped head into the dry bag.

"What is it, Boone?" Emily asked.

"Price is here."

# 24

"How did he find us?" Emily hissed.

"I don't know," Boone said, pulling out half of the items in his backpack and stuffing the dry bag inside. "Dr. Rojas, you said you were looking for an entrance to this temple—did you find one?"

"Yes. A small gap leads to an antechamber a few feet across."

"Good enough. Take the GoPro and hide in there. If they find you, tell them we ran off with the head." He opened the cooler and grabbed a stainless-steel water bottle he found inside, handing it to Emily, who put it into her pack. He glanced toward where he'd seen Wilson, then turned the other way. "What's west of here?"

"A mile or two of jungle. Eventually there is a road. It leads to Shipyard. A Mennonite community to the northwest."

"Okay, we're taking the head there. We'll find a way back to Belize City. Go buy a burner phone and call Go Slow Diving to get our numbers and a number for a friend of ours, Ras Brook. We'll hook up later."

The sounds of movement through the trees grew closer. Multiple people were approaching.

Emily pushed Manuel toward the mound. "Go!" she whispered.

Manuel needed no urging and moved quickly toward the buried temple.

"There they are!" Wilson's booming bass voice cut through the chatter of jungle fauna.

Boone pulled the machete from the log and handed it to Emily, slinging his backpack onto his shoulders. Without a word they began to run into the jungle. All around them, a rushing sound arose as the heavens opened up, heavy rain lashing the canopy overhead.

———◆ ◆ ◆———

It was slow going at first, but Boone was lucky enough to spot an animal trail, the slight thinning in the foliage caused by various creatures using the track over time, and they were able to pick up their pace. The thick jungle canopy protected them from the downpour for a little while, but eventually they were soaked to the skin.

"Are we still going west?" Emily asked.

"Think so… hard to tell with the sun blocked by the rain clouds." He glanced back. No sign of their pursuers.

"Did we lose them?" Emily asked.

"I dunno. They may have paused at Manuel's camp to search."

"I hope he's all right."

Boone froze, grabbing Emily's shoulder to bring her to a halt. "Wait. Listen."

"All I hear is rain…"

"There's something else." He scanned the trees behind them to the east but something in his peripheral vision drew his eye. To the south... movement. A glimpse of a man in camouflage. He crouched, pulling Emily close. "They're flanking us," he said into her ear. "A man over there." He pointed.

Emily nodded. Keeping low, she moved off the trail and headed north, Boone close behind. Once they had added some distance, Boone picked up the pace and soon they were running as fast as the foliage would allow.

"Whoa!" Emily came up short, her feet slipping out from under her.

Boone snaked out a long arm and snagged Em's backpack to keep her from falling. And a good thing, too. The reason she had stopped was readily apparent: a muddy slope dropped off precipitously.

"Do we go around?" Emily wondered aloud. She turned to Boone in question but then cocked her head. "What in blooming hell are you grinning at?"

Boone didn't even realize he'd been smiling, but he took her arm and sat her down. "Back in East Tennessee, we had a lotta hills and there was this one place... when it got really muddy from a heavy rain... well... it was kinda like sledding."

"Are you having a laugh? That's steep!" She looked down incredulously, but her expression quickly changed. "A lot to grab onto though, roots and little trees... we can do it in chunks, yeah?"

"Yeah. Ladies first."

"It was your idea, *you* first!"

"See ya at the bottom." Boone shoved off and slid along the mud for about thirty feet before he snagged a branch.

Emily zipped by him, grabbing a root further down. "I think we've discovered a new cruise ship shore excursion."

Boone scouted ahead for another muddy lane between trees and launched himself on a second run. Below, a creek was visible, swollen from the tropical cloudburst. He grabbed hold of a tree about halfway down.

"I'm going for the finish line," Emily said from a nearby bush. She let go and slid toward the bottom, going airborne at the last second and landing in the mud at the edge of the creek. She came up grinning, breathing hard. She rose from the mud and lurched back toward the cliff. "That wasn't so ba—aaaah!!"

Boone saw a flash of movement from the leaf litter and Emily's face contorted with pain. "Em!" Boone hurled himself down the remainder of the slope, crashing into a tree at the bottom. Wincing, he staggered upright, preparing to rush to Emily's side.

A cry of animal rage rose from Emily as she brought the machete down in a whistling arc, severing the head of the snake before it could strike again. She followed up with additional blows. "Sodding…" *Whack.* "…hell!" *Whack.*

The snake was nearly five feet long, its diamond-checkered body now writhing and coiling in its death throes. The scales were mostly variations of brown with a yellowish underbelly. The flat, large-eyed head worked its jaws in the air, sizeable fangs flashing. Boone kicked it aside as he threw himself onto the ground beside Emily.

"Boone…" Emily said, eyes filled with tears. "I don't want to look…"

"Easy…" Boone glanced at her mud-slathered legs, then took off her backpack and retrieved the metal water bottle. "Where did it—?"

"Left leg. Calf, I think. It hurts…"

Boone poured water on her left calf and two puncture marks were revealed, oozing blood. "Okay… you're going to be okay…"

he said, fighting panic, trying to remember the snakebite treatment he'd learned at that summer camp in Cherokee. *Don't cut into it, don't try to suck the poison. Keep the victim calm so the venom won't spread. Bandage the wound.* He spied the souvenir T-shirt Emily had just bought and pulled it out of the backpack. Quickly scoring it with the tip of the machete, he tore a long strip from the shirt and tied it over the wound.

A sound from above. A snapped branch, a curse. And a man in camouflage slid down the slope, landing in a heap about ten yards away. Struggling to his feet, he readied a short, military carbine of some kind. Boone was already rising, stretching his hand down to grasp hold of the decapitated snake as he closed the distance. He hurled the mindlessly writhing body and the man instinctively reacted in horror as five feet of headless viper thudded into his face and chest. His hands flailed at it to toss it aside. Boone reached him as the gun started to come up. Lashing out, Boone struck the man in the throat, then twisted the gun from his grip and slammed the butt of the carbine into the man's temple. The mercenary crumpled, fumbling at a holster at his side. Boone struck him again and he was still.

"That's... that's the man who grabbed my arse in the night club." Emily had struggled to her feet.

"Em... the venom! You can't move around."

"Well, we bloody well can't stay here!"

"You're right." Boone handed her the rifle. "Here. You're our gunner."

"I've never shot one of these!"

"First time for everything." Boone lifted her off the ground and held her against his chest. "You can't run. I've got to keep your heart rate down."

"Fat chance," she muttered.

"Manuel said the jungle went for a mile or two... we've been zigzagging a bit, but I'm pretty sure we've come at least a mile."

"So it could be *another* mile to a road? You expect to carry me all that way?"

Boone didn't answer, adjusting his grip on Emily's petite frame as he looked at the stream. Even with the rain sluicing down into it from the slopes, it seemed manageable. He started across.

———◆·◆———

"Funny little world this is..." Emily said distantly.

Boone looked down at her. *Is she delirious? Going into shock?* "Em... you okay?"

"Sorry... it's just... last time I was carried through tropical foliage by a strapping gent, it was up a mountain by a lunatic during a hurricane. This... this is better. Well, except for the snakebite. That part sucks."

"Freeze!"

Boone stopped dead in his tracks. The voice had come from behind him.

"Don't move." Footsteps approached. "Put down the girl and turn around slowly."

Boone looked down. Emily had the carbine ready, concealed by Boone's body. At his feet, the jungle grasses would hide her somewhat. "She's been bitten by a snake," he said loudly.

"I don't care, put her down now and turn around."

"Do it," Emily mouthed, determination in her eyes.

Boone set her down and turned around, hands raised. The mercenary was the other man they had fought in the staged barfight in the night club. He had a weapon trained on Boone's face.

"Where is it? And if you say 'where is what?' I'm gonna put a bullet in each of you right now."

"Backpack." Boone said.

"Toss it here."

Boone shrugged out of the straps and gently set it at his feet.

"You deaf, dive boy? I said to toss it here."

"It's a priceless artifact. I don't want to break it. Your boss would be pissed."

The man hesitated. "Fine. Back off."

Boone did, moving slightly to the side as he backed away. When the man stepped forward Emily opened fire, riddling the man's chest with rounds from the carbine. He fell back, cursing. Boone saw that the mercenary was wearing body armor and grabbed the backpack by a strap, swinging it down onto the man's head. The felt that swaddled the heavy artifact kept the blow from being lethal, but the merc went limp. Boone put the backpack back on.

"Did I… did I kill him?" Emily's voice sounded shaky.

"No. He had on a bulletproof vest of some kind. I hit him with a moon goddess." He scooped her back up and the rifle clattered from her fingers.

"I can't… I can't hold that… feel a bit woozy…"

"It's okay, we're almost there." Boone had no idea if that was true, but he set off all the same. Overhead, the rain was letting up. *Small favors*, he thought.

Ten minutes later, as the vines and trees crowded closer, Boone was regretting leaving the machete behind. *Not that I have a free hand to swing it.* He paused, scanning the near distance. *There!* A strip of brown in a sea of green. *Another animal trail.* Boone glanced up at the treetops. The sun was quite low in the sky and he was pleased to see that this new trail ran toward it. He adjusted his direction to follow the new path.

Boone hadn't gone more than five minutes when something rushed from the brush and crashed into him. He lost his grip on Emily and heard her grunt as she fell limply onto the trail. Rolling to the side, he spotted a flash of white above him and realized Wilson had caught up to them. Remaining prone, Boone scissored Wilson's legs into a *tesoura* takedown, sending the burly man face-first onto the ground.

Wilson struggled to his knees. "Nice one… but I'm gonna—"

Boone interrupted the man's boast with a *martelo de negativa*, whipping his foot up from the jungle floor and snapping the man's head to the side.

Wilson spat a tooth and launched himself at Boone, slamming the lighter divemaster to the ground before he could rise. "I'm gonna fuck you up, pretty boy!"

Wincing at a flash of pain as he grappled with the larger man, Boone felt moisture blooming at his left shoulder. *Stitches on the bullet wound must've popped loose*, he thought. He struggled to position himself for a jiu-jitsu hold, but carrying Emily for the last mile had drained much of the strength from his arms. *That's what legs are for,* he thought grimly, trying to snag one of the man's arms with a scissor lock.

◆ ◆ ◆

*Hello, little ant. Where are you going with that leaf?* Emily watched as the little leafcutter ant marched past the tip of her nose. In the near distance, other specks of green wobbled past. *Oh, look, you've got some ant friends.* The view blurred and Emily tried to refocus her vision. The side of her cheek felt moist. *Why am I on the ground?* Slowly, memory returned. The snakebite, the bad guys. Then something hit them and she fell. "Boone!"

Emily raised herself onto her elbows and a wave of dizziness threatened to overwhelm her. She shook it off and focused on the struggle happening in the leaf litter nearby. Emily tried to rise to her feet, but her knees buckled, and she fell beside one of the huge buttress roots of a kaway tree that stood alongside the animal trail.

"Your boyfriend is doing very well," a voice said from overhead.

Emily sat up and leaned against the flat root. A figure in a khaki hunting shirt wavered in her vision. She squinted and the image resolved. Oliver Price stood in the middle of the trail, watching the fight.

"No, truly... I've seen Wilson take out three men all by his lonesome. I confess, this whole mano-a-mano fisticuffs thing is beyond me. I say put a bullet in the brain and be done with it, but he insisted." Price held a handgun loosely by his side. "His wife left him, I think. He just needs to blow off some steam." He glanced at his Rolex. "Wilson! Hurry it up, I'd like to get out of here before dark."

Emily tried to speak but only managed a mumble.

"You don't look so good. What on earth happened to you?"

Emily took a breath. "One of... one of your cousins bit me."

Price crouched beside her. "What are you prattling on about?"

"S... snake..."

"Oh. Yes, probably one of those fer-de-lance beasties they have here. Nasty way to go." He rose. "Wilson, finish it!"

When the bodyguard glanced back toward Price, Boone lashed out, smashing the heel of his palm against the bridge of the man's nose. Wilson roared, drawing a hunting knife from a sheath at his waistband. Boone kicked both legs out, driving the man off him and gaining separation, readying himself for round two.

"Enough!" Standing over Emily, Price raised his pistol, aiming at Boone as the two fighters got to their feet.

Emily had watched Boone practicing his capoeira on many, many occasions. Truth to tell, she thought his "dance-fighting" sessions were sexy as hell, but it wasn't just voyeurism on her part. Remembering a particular takedown move, she gathered her remaining strength and clamped her legs on Price's own as she torqued her body. Price yelped in surprise, pitching forward as he pulled the trigger. The exertion sent a starburst across her vision and Emily blacked out.

◆ ◆ ◆

Boone had just managed to break loose from Wilson when a shot rang out. Overhead, monkeys burst into a cacophony of noise. The bodyguard looked confused as a large spot of red bloomed in the center of his white polo shirt. Wilson looked down, then turned toward where Boone had dropped Emily.

"Motherfucker, you shot m—"The big man stopped in mid-sentence and collapsed like a puppet with its strings cut.

Boone dashed forward to discover Oliver Price rising to his feet. Emily lay slumped against a tree. Boone screamed and rushed the man, but Price swung his gun and pointed it at Emily's head.

"Stop!"

Boone froze, raising his hands.

Price looked toward Wilson and shook his head with a tsk. "Good help is so hard to find. What's more… I actually liked him." Price's cool composure slipped, and rage danced in his eyes.

He stepped back from Emily, continuing to level his gun at her still form. "Where is the head?"

Boone figured if he gave up the artifact, they would be dead in the next minute. "We left it with Dr. Rojas."

Price smiled. "I doubt it. Where is the good doctor, anyway?"

"Back at the main site, calling the cavalry."

Price paused, then waggled his pistol at Boone but swiftly returned it to Emily's face. "Come over here with Ms. Durand and have a seat." He took a few steps back.

Boone moved cautiously toward the tree, gauging the distance. *No way I can reach him before he gets off a shot. Or two.* Boone examined Price's weapon—it looked quite large. *Looks like he's abandoned his little peashooter from before… if he hits me with that, I'm going down.* Reaching Emily, Boone was relieved to see her eyes open and blinking, although she looked dazed. He crouched beside her and sat her up against him.

"Em…?"

"I'm sorry…" she whispered.

Boone put a hand to her forehead. *She's burning up.*

Price took a few steps to the side, gun still trained on them. He walked backward to Wilson and nudged him with his foot, then took a couple of steps toward the tree, cocking his head to the side. "It's in the backpack isn't it?"

Boone said nothing.

"Open it." When Boone simply glared at him, Price adopted a two-handed shooter's stance. "Your friend might survive that snakebite, but she definitely won't survive a bullet to the brain."

Out of options, Boone began to unshoulder the backpack. In the treetops, the monkeys abruptly ceased their shrieks. They had been active since Price had shot Wilson. Boone glanced up at a thick branch extending out from the tree he leaned against and felt an odd mix of hope mingled with terror. A deep rumble replaced the silence.

Price raised his eyes. The rumble became a savage roar and a spotted shape shifted on the branch above him. Oliver Price screamed as two hundred pounds of jaguar slammed him into the jungle floor.

Boone scrambled to his feet, hauling Emily onto his shoulder as he sprinted for the animal trail. Glancing down, he spotted several cat-like paw prints. *Hopefully that was the only one using this trail,* he thought as he ran to the west. Behind, mingled screams and roars receded into the distance.

**25**

"Stop…" Emily's weak voice came from over Boone's shoulder. "Stop… I'm going to be sick. Put me down… for a second." Boone gently lowered her to the ground. "Okay, here you go…" Emily knelt and retched into the leaves at the side of the trail.

Boone crouched beside her. "We're almost there. The jungle is thinning out and I think there's a dirt road just through those trees." He reached into his pack and dug out a water bottle. "Here… drink."

"Probably just… park the tiger again if I do…" But she took the water and drank. "What happened… back there?"

Boone brushed a sweaty lock of blonde hair from Emily's face. "A jaguar," he said, meticulously pronouncing it in her British fashion.

Emily managed a smile. "Nice to see… you've learnt 'ow to speak proper." She raised her brows and gave her head a shake to clear the cobwebs. "The dashing Oliver is cat food, then?"

"Yep."

Emily's dimples popped into existence and she snorted a laugh. "Heh… Fancy Feast." She laughed again, but her face suddenly lost its smile. "Boone? I don't feel so good…" Eyelids fluttering, her pupils rolled back in her head and she flopped backward into the jungle muck.

"Em!" Boone looked down at her left leg. The area around the T-shirt bandage was an angry red and he saw swelling topping her sneaker. *Damn! Should've taken the shoe off.* He unlaced it and gently removed it. The foot was definitely swollen. "Come on… we're gonna get you to a hospital." He sat her up and she moaned softly. Gently, he took her in his arms and rose to his feet. Shadows were lengthening—sundown was less than an hour away. He lurched forward toward what he hoped was a road.

◆ ◆ ◆

Fortunately for Boone and Emily, there was indeed a road, albeit a small one. The surface was chalky white, a form of crushed limestone common in Belizean roads. On the far side, farmland stretched to the horizon, occasional trees dotting the landscape. Boone remembered Manuel saying that the town of Shipyard was to the northwest, so he turned to the right and started that way. He looked down at Emily—she was deeply unconscious, her arms and legs dangling limply. He choked back a sob and picked up the pace.

On the horizon to the north, a cloud of chalky dust appeared. Something was coming down the road. Boone stood in the center of the track, holding Emily in his arms. The first shape that appeared was a horse… a buggy rolling along behind it. As it drew nearer, the driver brought the horse down to a gentle trot, then came alongside. The sole occupant of the buggy was a boy, probably no more than twelve years old. He wore denim overalls and a light-blue, button-down shirt. A white straw hat sat atop a mop of shockingly blonde hair. *"Kann ick di hülpen?"*

"Please... help."

The boy blinked. "Yes." He patted the passenger side of the bench he sat on. "Bring her here."

Boone climbed into the buggy, arranging Emily on his lap. The boy snapped the reins and they trundled south.

"Wait," Boone looked back over their shoulder. "Isn't the town that way?"

"Yes, but this road is a dead end. Just fields. Faster this way." The boy glanced over at Emily and Boone was struck by his bright blue eyes. "What happened?"

"Snake bit her."

"Ah. Lancehead. Or... umm... fer-de-lance. Our farmers sometimes get bitten in the fields. Very bad snake. How long ago did it bite?"

Boone thought. The events of the last hours were a blur and his sense of time was completely distorted. "I'm not sure. Two hours?"

The boy snapped the reins, coaxing a little more speed out of the horse. "I know where to take you. We have a doctor who can help." He looked at Boone. "Please do not worry." His eyes slipped down from Boone's face. "You are bleeding."

Boone glanced at his shoulder, noting the blood that stained his shirt. "It's nothing." He kissed Emily's forehead and his lips were greeted with alarming heat. "How long will it take us...?"

"The horse is well-rested. About forty minutes. But on the main road, we may come across a truck that can take you faster."

*Forty minutes may be too long!* Boone brushed aside a clump of sweat-soaked hair from Emily's face. She took a sudden, shuddering breath and Boone felt a stab of panic, his heart rate suddenly racing. *Another panic attack? No, not now!*

"Mister… are you all right?"

*You're taking her to get help. Focus on something else!* Boone breathed out a long, slow breath. "I'm fine. My name is Boone… this is Emily."

"I am pleased to meet you. My name is Levi."

"You speak excellent English, Levi."

"Thank you. I also speak Spanish."

"When you drove up, you spoke to me in German?"

"*Plautdietsch.* It is a dialect of Low German… a little like German but also a bit Dutch."

"So, you are Mennonite?"

"Yes."

Boone knew there were over 10,000 Mennonites in Belize. He thought back to Bonaire, where he had met a pair of non-practicing Mennonite brothers from America. "Do you happen to know any Claassens?"

The boy chewed his lip. "I think there are some in Upper Barton Creek, but I don't know any in Shipyard. We are Old Colony… in Barton they are Old Order."

Boone felt his pulse slowing and the sense of panic began to ebb. Conversation was helping. "What's the difference between them?"

Levi smiled and shook his head. "We only have forty minutes," he said with a laugh. "Mennonites are not some big group that all act the same—there are many different colonies, each with its own rules and beliefs. For instance, our group cannot drive any personal vehicles with a drive train… except we *can* drive tractors to farm the land… but those have to have steel wheels instead of rubber. But over in Barton, they can't use tractors at all."

"You said we might come across a truck on the main road?"

"Ah, yes, but it won't be driven by one of our order. A local will be at the wheel... but a Mennonite *can* be in the passenger seat."

Boone nodded, digging into his backpack for his phone. The battery was dead. "What about cell phones?"

Levi flicked his eyes over at Boone, then back to the road. "Well... we are not supposed to have them... but some do."

"Do you have one?" Boone asked excitedly.

"Oh, no," the boy said quickly. "I am too young. But where we are going, there will be one."

They reached a larger stretch of road and Levi turned right. On the horizon of flat farmland ahead, the sun was about to set. In a few minutes, a rumble sounded from behind and the boy brought the buggy to the side of the road and stepped out, waving his hat. The truck pulled up alongside and a burly, bearded man leaned out from the passenger side. He also wore denim overalls with a white hat, and he spoke a stream of what Boone assumed was the Plautdietsch that the boy had mentioned. He caught the name "Levi" in the man's questions, so he assumed they knew each other. The man nodded and exited the truck.

"This is Isaac, one of our elders," Levi said. "He will take you to the doctor."

Boone stepped down from the buggy and carried Emily to the truck. Isaac helped him climb inside, then leaned across to the mestizo driver. "I will sit in the back," Isaac said. "Luis, we are going to Dr. Penner. *Rapido.*" He placed a strong hand on Boone's shoulder. "We will be there very quickly."

"Thank you," Boone said, exhaustion creeping into his voice.

Isaac climbed into the bed of the truck and thumped the roof of the cab. Luis stepped on the gas. As the truck's tires crunched, gaining purchase in the limestone of the road, Boone leaned out of the window and waved to Levi. The boy watched them drive away, his hat over his heart.

Boone sat back, clutching Emily tightly. "Hang in there, Em."

"The worst of the danger is over," Dr. Penner said. He was in his late fifties, a shorter beard than Isaac's framing his face. "One of the greatest worries is infection, but I've administered antibiotics."

Boone looked down at Emily. She was breathing slowly, sleeping deeply… but her delicate features contorted on occasion.

"Is she in pain?"

"A bite from a *terciopelo*… or lancehead, or Tommy Goff, or fer-de-lance… all the same snake, you understand… a bite can be quite painful long after the envenomation. I've given her painkillers, fluids, and a mild sedative." The doctor handed Boone a bottle of water. "Drink. You look severely dehydrated yourself."

"Will she…?"

"I have treated numerous patients for bites from this snake. Believe me, she is in better condition than many. I believe the envenomation was moderate. Your estimate of the size of the snake leads me to believe it was a mature adult, and older snakes are able to control the amount of venom they inject. This wasn't a dry bite, but it wasn't as bad as it could have been. The swelling has already gone down a little, which is a good sign. But the antivenom can have its own adverse side effects. And also, with this snake, there is a danger of necrosis in the tissue."

"Necrosis? You mean… she could lose the leg?"

Dr. Penner raised a hand and spoke calmly. "I don't see anything to indicate that. But we should get her to a hospital immediately." He pointed at Boone's shoulder. "And you, too. Let me take a look at that?"

"Just some stitches that came loose. It can wait 'til the hospital." Boone was having trouble concentrating, his thoughts fuzzy. "What time is it?"

"A little after midnight. I have spoken to Isaac and he will have Luis drive us to the hospital in Orange Walk."

"Wait... do you have a phone?"

"Yes, I do..." He fished a basic flip-phone from his pocket and handed it over.

Boone thanked him and reached out to Emily's face, brushing his fingertips along her cheek. "Be right back, Em." He stepped outside the tiny clinic, racking his brain for Ras Brook's phone number. Dredging it up, he dialed.

"Hello? Who dis?"

"Ras, it's Boone."

"Boone! Been trying to reach you for hours, mon! T'ank Jah, we were fearin' da worst! Are you in Shipyard?"

"Yes, we're... wait, how did you know that?"

"Dr. Rojas call me. Said you were gwonna try to get dere. You get away from Mistuh Price, den?"

"Yes, but Emily... a snakebite..." Boone felt his voice hitch. "She's in a bad way, Ras... we're going to leave for Orange Walk... there's a hospital there."

"No, no, no, stay right where you are... wait one second..."

Boone could hear Ras speaking to someone and he realized that during this entire call, Ras's voice had been pitched like he'd been shouting. A noise in the distance caught Boone's attention, a thumping sound in the air, approaching from the east. Dr. Penner stuck his head out of the clinic door.

"We have to leave. Isaac and Luis are driving over right now."

"Hang on, doc... I have a feeling we're about to get a ride." He waggled the phone at the doctor. "Hey, where would a helicopter land around here?"

Dr. Penner looked up into the night sky, clearly hearing the approaching chopper. "The Three Star Feed Mill, just up the road. Most of the helicopter pilots know it. I'll get Emily ready." He vanished back inside just as Ras came back on the line.

"Okay, Boone..."

"You're in a helicopter, aren't you?"

"Yeah, mon. Your Dr. Rojas has some juice! We need a place to land, den we can take Boonemily to the hospital in Belize City."

Boone gave him the location of the landing spot and he heard Ras relaying the information before coming back on the line.

"Got it. Be dere in three, pilot say. And Dr. Rojas is here, one moment."

There was a rustling, then: "Boone, we are going to take you to Belize City. They have the best snakebite unit there. I know, I've been bitten myself."

"Okay. Thank you. Oh, and... the other thing... I've still got it with me."

"Well, I wasn't going to ask... but thank you for letting me know. I've made arrangements for that, too."

Isaac's truck pulled up beside the clinic and Boone headed inside to help with Emily. "Got to go, Manuel... see you shortly." Overhead, Boone could hear the approaching helicopter change direction, the rotor beats receding to the north.

A different helicopter sat in an empty field… twelve miles south of Shipyard. Under the starry sky, James Cavelli, a.k.a. "Archibald Welk," smoked the last cigarette from his pack. *Something's gone wrong. They should have been here hours ago.* Around noon, they had landed just south of Lamanai… now it was after midnight. Price had headed for Lamanai with three of his mercenaries, leaving Cavelli at the helicopter with the pilot. The last communication he'd had from his employer was just after one in the afternoon. Price had talked to a tour guide for the site and knew where the divemasters had gone. Now… twelve texts, ten calls, and four voicemails later… nothing.

He looked back at the pilot, who had been dozing in the chopper. "When I finish this smoke, we're outta here, capisce?" The pilot didn't respond, so Cavelli leaned into the cockpit. "Hey, you *comprende* me? We're—" He stopped talking. The pilot was staring, wide-eyed, out of the front of the helicopter. Cavelli dropped down from the door and looked toward the tree line. A figure was approaching, staggering like a zombie from a horror movie.

"*El diablo…*" the pilot breathed.

Cavelli dug at the holster at his hip, drawing a pistol. He turned it sideways, staring at it, trying to find the safety as the figure lurched into the dim light that emanated from the cockpit.

"Wha' the fuck are you plannig on doig wi' tha…?" the thing slurred wetly.

Cavelli lowered the handgun. Although its speech was horribly distorted, the voice was familiar to the disgraced archaeologist. "Oliver…?" The figure came closer and Cavelli recognized the clothing the creature wore, although the hunting vest was now more rust-colored than khaki, caked in dried blood. The man held a large hunting knife that looked a lot like the one Wilson carried.

"Star' the helcoptuh..." the figure said as it reached them. The light from the cockpit's instruments now illuminated it enough that Cavelli involuntarily gasped.

Oliver Price's face was a horror show. Half of his lips hung from his face, one cheek was open to the bone, and the ear on that side was entirely gone. The jaguar had clamped down on Price's head near the end... but the end had come for the cat, not the man. Oliver raised the hunting knife. "Good ol' Wilson... thoughtfu' of him to die wi' this nex' to him..." He tossed the blood-soaked blade into the helicopter and raised his other fist. "Here... hol' this... don' lose it."

Cavelli held out a shaking hand and Price slapped something cold and wet into his palm.

"Ge' me the fuck outta here," Price slurred, pushing past Cavelli and climbing into the helicopter. "My compoun' in Honduras... I'm done wi' Belize..."

Cavelli opened his hand. A massive fang of a tooth lay on his palm, blood clinging to its root.

# 26

oone paced the waiting room, glancing up at a clock on the wall. Nearly two in the morning. Emily had been taken into the I.C.U. and was being examined by a snakebite expert who had just arrived at the hospital.

"She will be all right," Manuel said from a chair against the wall. "Dr. Hernández worked on me when I was bitten. He is excellent." On his lap, he held the dry bag containing the head, the bag's sides coated in mud.

Ras rose from his seat beside the archaeologist. "Boone-mon, sit here wit' us and try to get some sleep... you look like you 'bout to fall down."

"I'm fine..." Boone said, although his exhaustion was near total. Every muscle felt heavy and his vision seemed to have receded to a tunnel.

"How's da shoulder, brudda?"

"What? Oh. Fine." Boone moved his arm and the loose hospital gown slipped from his shoulder, revealing a fresh bandage.

His bloody T-shirt had met its demise shortly after he entered the hospital, a nurse consigning it to a trash can. His wound had been re-stitched and Boone had been given antibiotics and pain-killers. The drugs and mind-numbing fatigue coated his brain in a fog. Footsteps from down the hall drew his attention. A lot of feet were making that noise, coming at a fast clip. Alert, Boone turned to face the oncoming sounds but felt a hand at his shoulder.

"It's all right, Boone." Manuel said. "The cavalry has arrived."

Walking with purpose, a group of men and one woman turned the corner from the elevators. In the vanguard were a pair of Caucasian soldiers dressed in camouflage and boonie hats, assault rifles slung at their chests, barrels to the floor. Two more took up the rear. In the center came a pair of Belizean men; one was wearing a military uniform but the other looked as if he'd just rolled out of bed. Alongside them, the Caucasian woman was smartly dressed in slacks and a blazer, her hair in a ponytail. One soldier peeled off to speak with the nurse's station while the rest of the group entered the waiting room.

The man who looked the least well-dressed spoke first. "Dr. Rojas! We got here as soon as we could." He addressed Boone and Ras. "I'm Dr. Goldson with the Belize Institute of Archaeology. Given the nature of what you've found and what I was told about the... uh... police situation, well... I pulled a few strings and called BATSUB." He gestured to the soldiers. One of them, who seemed a bit older than the others, stepped forward.

"Lieutenant Barkley, British Army Training and Support Unit Belize." His accent wasn't quite as strong as Emily's, but Boone guessed he was a Londoner. "We've been asked to escort a certain item to a secure location." He nodded to the uniformed Belizean. "Major Collins of the BDF is in charge of this operation."

"Do you have it?" the Major asked.

Before Manuel could reply, Dr. Goldson cleared his throat. "Why don't we move this conversation to the consulting room I've asked to borrow?" He led the group out of the waiting room. Manuel followed but Boone remained rooted.

"I... I should stay here..."

"But... this was *your* find," Manuel said. "And I'm sure they have some questions for you."

"I certainly do," the woman said, with what Boone easily recognized as a Dutch accent.

"Ras placed a hand against Boone's back. "S'okay mon, I will stay here. Come right away and get you if dere is any news. Promise."

Boone nodded, his eyes distant. The group swept back down the hall and crowded into a small room, three of the British soldiers remaining outside.

Manuel set the bag on the table and carefully extracted the jade head. "Here it is."

"My God," Dr. Goldson blurted, "it's just as you described!" He peered at it closely. "Ix Chel, perhaps?"

"That was my assumption," Manuel replied.

"And the rest? The video you sent me from that GoPro... there were other artifacts, yes?"

Manuel hedged, then looked to Boone.

"Oliver Price has them... *had* them..."

"Where is Mr. Price?" the woman asked.

Boone hesitated. "Well..."

She held up a bi-fold wallet and flashed a badge. "I am Greta Pyke with INTERPOL. Although he has been going by various aliases, we have been looking for your "Oliver Price" for some time. That alias was a new one to us, and he may have been operating here for some time. He must have, to have built up the network he appears to have had in place. I understand he was pursuing you in the jungle. Do you have any idea where he is now?"

"Partway through the digestive system of a jaguar, would be my guess."

"What? This is no joking matter, Mr. Fischer."

"No joke, ma'am. That jaguar is the only reason Emily and I..." He stopped talking, thinking of Emily on the stretcher as they brought her into the hospital, an oxygen mask on her face.

"Then the artifacts may still be in country," Major Collins said.

"Boat..." Boone said, absently.

"What boat?" Pyke asked.

"The *Liquid Asset*." Boone described Price's boat in detail. "He loaded everything into it. Emily said it was heading south from Caulker, on the lagoon side. Maybe..." He looked up. "He has a place on Caye Chapel."

Pyke smiled. "That compound is currently being raided by an elite police force, the GSU. Major Collins here helped vet the members we sent, to be sure we didn't have any of Price's insiders on the team. If the boat is there, we will find it." She took out a notepad. "Now, Mr. Fischer... I will be needing a statement. Let's start at the beginning, shall we?"

Boone swayed on his feet and Manuel quickly caught him. Boone collected himself. "Can... can I do this later? Right now, all I can think about is Emily... and I'm not even sure I'm going to be able to do *that* for much longer, since I'm about to pass out." He managed to hold Pyke's eyes. "I'll be able to give a much clearer statement when I'm rested, and I've got Emily by my side."

Pyke tucked the notebook back into her jacket and retrieved a card, handing it to Boone. "Very well. Please call me tomorrow."

"Right, let's get this head over to the Central Bank," Major Collins said.

Dr. Goldson began rewrapping the head while Manuel took Boone by the arm. "I'll take Mr. Fischer back to the waiting room and then join you." He ushered Boone back up the hall. "You must sleep."

"I don't think I'll have any choice in another minute or two," Boone mumbled. He looked around at the rooms of the hospital that they passed. "I don't know how we're gonna pay for this... we're not citizens of Belize..."

"I'm working on something, don't you worry," Manuel said as he passed him off to Ras, who settled Boone into a chair.

Boone was asleep the moment the seat cushion took his weight.

The first thing Emily became aware of was a steady, electronic beeping. Next, light leaked in through her lashes as her eyes slowly began to blink. Fluorescent light. *Hospital?* She glanced to the side. A tube ran into her arm, ending in a patch of gauze and tape. Slowly, she raised her head.

*Boone.* The lanky divemaster was folded into a chair in the corner of the room, sleeping soundly. Pale blue hospital scrubs hung loosely from his thin frame. She tried to speak his name, but her mouth felt like it was stuffed with cotton. Emily managed to work up enough moisture to speak in a harsh whisper. "Boone..."

He jerked with a sudden intake of breath, sitting bolt upright, confusion on his face for a brief moment before his eyes locked on her and he rose from the chair in a rush.

"Emily! Oh, thank God! I..." She watched his Adam's apple dip in a swallow. He took a deep breath, taking hold of the hand that wasn't currently hosting a tube. "How are you feeling?"

Emily just looked at him for a moment before answering. "Like I'm too full of drugs to answer that question truthfully," she murmured. "How 'bout you?"

"Better, now." He smiled at her, reaching down to shift a lock of hair from her face.

She squinted at him. "Did you… get a medical degree… while I was out?"

Boone tilted his head quizzically before looking down at the clothes the hospital had provided him with. He laughed. "Oh… no, no… my clothes were shot, is all."

"I'm sure there's some… some joke about playing doctor I should make, if my brain didn't feel like it was stuffed with… marshmallow fluff." Then she laughed softly as the image of Boone's recovery in Saba entered her mind.

"What?"

"Now I'm having a little… *reverse* déjà vu…"

Boone smiled, reaching up to brush away a tear. "Yeah, we gotta find a way to go on dates that don't end in the hospital."

"For the record… a snakebite beats a machete wound, in my book."

"No argument from me."

"Although, I can't really be *too* mad at Mother Nature… with that croc and that jaguar, I'd say the score is two to one, helping over hurting." She winced. "Which isn't to say this doesn't hurt." She looked down at her leg, swathed in bandages. "How bad is it?"

"The doc said you should make a full recovery. You were very lucky. Thank God we ran into that Mennonite boy with the horse and buggy."

Emily squinted at him. "Um… I think we better ask them to turn down the dosage on whatever they're giving me—I just heard you say something about a horse and buggy…"

"Tell you later. I should go let them know you're awake."

"Wait!" Emily reached out and grabbed hold of Boone's scrubs. "Just… just stay for a bit more, yeah?"

Boone nodded and reached down to stroke her face with his fingertips. Emily closed her eyes, enjoying the simple sensation. After a while, she felt his touch lift away and she drifted off to sleep.

A week later, Emily was well enough to leave the hospital and the pair were ready to return to Caye Caulker. The danger having passed, Dr. Hernández explained how lucky she was that necrosis hadn't set in, as many fer-de-lance bites resulted in tissue damage when treatment was delayed. He advised them to avoid the unpressurized cabin of the puddle jumpers that flew to the offshore islands and instead take a boat. When they called Ras Brook to let him know they were coming, he insisted on picking them up.

"We can just take the ferry, Ras," Boone had said.

"No, no... you have to let me take you. Dere's a special reason I gotta do it, seen?"

"Okay then... thank you, Ras."

"Dere's a restaurant on da nort'west coast of Belize City, near da Mexican embassy—da Calypso Bar. It open at eleven and it has a pier. Wait for me dere."

It was only half a mile from Karl Heusner Memorial Hospital to the bar, but Emily was supposed to minimize her walking for another week, the doctors having provided her with a padded boot and crutches to help her keep the weight off of the foot. They grabbed a cab and were there in minutes. The gate to the restaurant was shut so they hung out at the coffee shop in the adjacent Ramada until eleven.

"I miss the Caye Caulker Bakery," Emily said, scarfing down a second croissant as they crossed over to the Calypso Bar.

"I'll shower you in pineapple Danishes, I promise you."

"Sounds sticky. Yum and ick."

"Gate's open," Boone said as they approached the restaurant. "And there's Ras out on the pier."

"And Manuel!" Emily said.

"Boonemily!" Ras called as the pair reached the pier. A flurry of hugs, handshakes, and back-patting was exchanged as everyone reunited.

"Where's your boat, Ras?" Boone asked, looking for his friend's small fishing boat.

"Didn't bring my boat. Brought your boat."

Boone frowned. "What are you…?" Then he saw it. The *Alhambra*, tied up at the end of the pier.

"Is that Welk's… or Cavelli's… dive boat?" Emily asked.

"No, it is *your* dive boat," Manuel Rojas said. "It was actually in Price's name… but now it's in yours." He pulled out an envelope and handed it to Boone. "Price bought it at a police auction in Honduras. But now… ironically… all of *his* possessions from Caye Chapel are being sold at a police auction."

"Did they find the artifacts?" Boone asked.

"No. Nor did they find his yacht. Also…" He hesitated.

"I don't like the look on your face," Emily remarked.

"The military searched the jungle around Lamanai. They found three mercenaries, one dead and two injured... but there was no sign of Oliver Price."

"Well, that makes sense, since he'd be cat-poo..." Emily trailed off, looking at Manuel's expression.

"They found the jaguar," Boone said.

"Yes... beside the body of the dead mercenary, the one you said Price accidentally shot. The jaguar had a stab wound in its eye from a large knife. But there was a lot of blood in the vicinity, so they are bringing in a tracking specialist and dogs to try to find Mr. Price's body. It's assumed he bled out somewhere in the jungle."

"What about that fake archaeologist guy?" Emily asked.

"No one knows, but James Cavelli is on all travel watch lists and INTERPOL is looking for him."

"Sorry to interrupt me brudders and sistah, but I don't really have a permit to use dis dock. Let's hop aboard and head home."

Boone stepped into the dive boat, then reached back to grab Em's crutches before helping her across. "This boat... how exactly is it ours? I mean... well, for one thing, I can't afford to dock this... or pay for insurance."

"Actually... yes you can," Manuel said.

During the hour-long voyage, Manuel explained that the Belizean government and various archaeological institutes—including his own in Mexico—were well aware of the magnitude of Boone and Emily's discovery. The jade head of Kinich Ahau was still the largest jade object ever found in the Mayan world, at just under ten pounds, but the new head of Ix Chel was close, only two ounces lighter. Actually, with the serpent crest, it was a little taller.

In addition, the cavern they had documented was soon to be explored, in the hopes that still more objects might be uncovered. A team was already being assembled and a Belizean Coast Guard vessel was stationed there in the interim.

The various organizations and the Belizean government were also aware of the hardships that Boone and Emily had suffered through, as well as their financial situation. As a result, their hospital bills had been covered and a "finder's fee" had been agreed upon, supplemented by sales of Oliver Price's Caye Chapel possessions. All told, Boone and Emily's bank accounts were to be bolstered by $150,000, split however they liked.

"Crikey, that'd buy a lotta pineapple Danishes…" Emily breathed when Manuel quoted the number. She was sitting on the starboard bench, enjoying the ocean spray, the oversized sunglasses that Boone had picked up for her during her convalescence covered in droplets.

"And Ignacio said to tell you he's eternally sorry for letting you go," Ras shouted back from the cockpit wheel. Although there was a second station atop the flybridge, it wasn't currently functional—the electrical system would need rewiring. "Apparently he was threatened with having his business license revoked. But now dat Price's men have been purged from Babylon, he say you can have your jobs back any time you like."

"Yeah, bit early to be thinking of that," Boone said. "Lazybones here needs more rest."

"Y'know what would be a good way to test my leg's recovery?" Emily said, dipping her sunglasses down to peer at Boone. "Kicking you in the bollocks with my giant boot."

Caye Caulker came into view over their shoulder as Ras took them toward the lagoon side. Boone dropped down on the bench beside her and draped his arm around her "So... should we rename the boat?"

"Isn't that bad luck?"

"Well... *keeping* the name of a dive boat that was a front operation for drug runners might be bad luck," Boone suggested. "We would have to make sure to purge all mentions of its name in the Ledger of the Deep, so we don't anger Neptune."

Emily nodded sagely. "Definitely don't want him miffed at us."

"We'd have to get rid of anything with its name on it. And there's a renaming ceremony we can do. I was part of one in Curaçao back before I met you."

"You ever want to go back there?"

"I want to go everywhere. But yeah, someday, let's go back to the ABC Islands."

"Honestly, right now the only place I want to go is to bed." When Boone gave her a smoldering look and a smirk, she shouldered him roughly. "Sleep bed, not the other kind."

The *Alhambra* slowed as Ras brought her in toward the pier at Go Slow Diving. Boone noticed Ras putting away his phone.

"You calling to make sure it's okay to dock here?" Boone asked.

"No, mon, I already do dat. I was calling to let someone else know you're here."

"Who?"

"Oh, he be here shortly. Get da lines, would you?"

As Ras snugged the boat up to the pier, Boone stepped across and secured the lines before lifting Emily from the gunwale and setting her beside him.

"And here he comes," Ras said from the boat.

Boone looked up toward the shore. Coming down Pasero Street was one of the workers from the animal sanctuary, a small brown dog on a leash. Emily squealed and rushed for the shore as fast as her crutches would allow. The dog's ears perked up at the high-pitched sound of glee and its tail began to wag furiously. The worker waved. Stooping, she released the leash and the dog was off like a shot, sand flying as it scampered toward them as fast as its paws could carry it. Girl and dog met at considerable speed and Emily sat down hard in the sand as she received a vigorous licking.

"Ooooooo! Who's a good boy? Who? Is it you? I think it is!"

The potlicker pup whined in barely contained joy. Spying Boone, he jumped off of Emily with a gazelle-like bound and leaped up at Boone, balancing on his hind legs and pressing his forepaws on Boone's waist.

Boone gave the dog a thorough ear scratch, which the dog rewarded with a lengthy tongue bath aimed at his face. "Well, Em… you've had a few weeks to think of one. What's his name?"

Emily remained on the ground and scooted over to them to join in the lovefest. "Well, when I was a little scamp, my best mate lived just off a particular tube stop in South London." She was interrupted as the potlicker switched tongue-targets back to her and she dissolved in a gale of delighted laughter.

Boone sat beside them and waited, watching the scene with contentment. Finally, the dog curled up in Emily's lap, raising shining eyes to Boone.

"Meet Brixton," Emily said proudly. "Brix, for short."

Boone leaned across and kissed her. "I love it."

Keep reading for The Afterword, but first:
If you enjoyed this book, please take a moment to visit
Amazon and provide a short review; every reader's voice
is extremely important for the life of a book or series.

Boone and Emily return in

# Deep Devil

Available on Amazon

If you'd like advance notice of their next
adventures, head on over to

## W W W . D E E P N O V E L S . C O M
or
## W W W . N I C K S U L L I V A N . N E T

where you can sign up for my mailing list. If you're like
me, you hate spam, so rest assured I'll email rarely.

And check out other authors who set their tales on the
water, near the water, or under the tropical sun at

## W W W . T R O P I C A L A U T H O R S . C O M

# AFTERWORD

Way back in the days of yesteryear, my first full dive trip was to Bonaire. My second... Belize. On Bonaire we stayed at a resort, but on Belize we "roughed it" and that trip has a very special place in my heart. When I was on Caye Caulker that first time, it was still largely undeveloped. We stayed at a little hotel that had about eight rooms, chemical toilets, and no air conditioning. Many guests learned to just sleep outside in hammocks. I think it was called The Tides, but it's long gone. I loved Caulker. The sandy roads were home to bicycles and golf carts and a single pickup truck. Potlicker pups were everywhere. (On a side note, Grand Turk has stray dogs of a similar breed, though they call them "potcakes"). We dived with Belize Diving Services and heard about a cave nearby, and that a diver had died in there... this was long before the new owners came along and found out just how big the cave complex truly was.

I had a lot of fun with this book! I ended up with a whole host of things from my trips to Caulker and Ambergris that I didn't use, but was happy to find places to "slot in" many of my favorite memories. Just a few in no particular order: The first time we visited San Pedro we stayed in the venerable Spindrift Hotel... and yes, the owner did throw a *quinceañera* for her daughter and invited all the guests to it. We had a blast. And yes, there was a little shack you could visit to get a jug of orange juice filled by a fisherman who had a big, manual squeezer. And I am the proud owner of three beautiful ziricote carvings—two blacktips and a hammerhead. One of my dive buddies went with a manatee and I still see it when I drop by to visit.

The Jaguar's Temple Club is a real place, and we took many a photo in its gaping maw—but you wouldn't catch me dead going night-club dancing. I'm like Boone in that respect; another area where fictional Boone and actual Nick agree. Elvi's has the best key lime pie I've ever tasted, and it really was my favorite restaurant that I've ever been to on a dive trip. Cozumel had some close seconds... but that's another book.

On our trip to Half Moon Caye, we met a caretaker there who deftly macheted coconuts for the divers during a surface interval. Unlike my fictional Esteban, who just has some scars, this fellow was actually missing a thumb. Oh, and speaking of hand injuries... that kid with the duct tape? Yep. He's real. In the real world, he didn't get on the wrong boat—he was on ours—but he'd gotten chomped by a nurse shark during a previous day's feeding, and his dad didn't want to take him to the local clinic.

Back on Caye Caulker, there was a guy who cooked us some kingfish on a grill made from half of an oil drum. We ate dinner on his porch, complete with Christmas tree lights on the banister, and a pile of music CDs he encouraged us to choose from to accompany our meal. Behind us, his kids played in the house. And the I and I Reggae Bar is extremely cool. We were there in the off-season so it was a pretty sedate place to swing and chill, though I hear it can get pretty crazy some nights.

As I did in the afterword of *Deep Cut*, I want to point out where truth took a back seat to fiction. First off: cave diving. What Boone and Emily did? Don't do that. Cave diving is probably one of the most dangerous (and exhilarating) pastimes you can undertake, and I oversimplified it greatly. Caye Caulker has one of the largest underwater cave systems in the world, and I originally planned to have them make their discoveries deep in an extensive cave system, but then decided my *Deep* books probably shouldn't be six hundred pages long as we followed every super-necessary safety step. I basically designed a dead-end swim-through that ended in a ceilinged cenote.

The Mennonites of Belize: I have family who are Mennonite, and one thing I've learned is that they are a group that is incredibly diverse, with multiple diasporas and varying groups of elders over time leading to drastically different rules among "colonies," although even that term can't really be applied to many groups. I chose the settlement of Shipyard primarily due to its proximity to Lamanai, its farms lying just to the west of the fringing jungle. The Mennonites there are fairly middle-of-the-road in terms of the level of strictures—although I must be honest—I was pleased to discover that this group does use horse-and-buggy for personal transportation.

Tiny chacmool statuettes intended as "souvenirs" to temple visitors? I made that up. But Christians throughout history were certainly offered a chance to buy mementos from a pilgrimage, so who's to say missionaries to the New World might not have given someone the idea? The jade head of Kinich Ahau is very real... and Altun Ha is believed to have been a center for jade production. But it didn't have a lot of jungle around it, so I put

Manuel out at Lamanai. Incidentally, "lamanai"? Thanks to a translation error by a Franciscan monk, the name vacillates between "drowned insect" and "submerged crocodile". Guess which one was more fun for this book?

Two areas of research that I didn't really get to use: Sir Richard Branson did indeed mount an expedition to the bottom of The Great Blue Hole with Fabien Cousteau. In fact, one of my beta readers is buds with one of the chase-sub pilots! But this expedition occurred *after* the time frame of my book. And the other: Software billionaire John McAfee. You may have heard of him. His neighbor on San Pedro was mysteriously murdered and McAfee fled the country when the police came looking for him. Y'know what? Just Google him. And watch the 2018 documentary *Gringo*, available on various streaming services. I decided to relegate this person to a quick mention from Dr. Rojas... but a few inspirations made their way into Oliver Price's storyline, namely the extremely generous donations to local police, and a propensity to hire muscle from certain neighborhoods in Belize City. And the Gang Suppression Unit that raids Oliver Price's Caye Chapel property? Yeah, they raided McAfee's.

Belize is a fascinating country, and it came as no surprise that I'm not the only one intrigued by it. As many of you know, I narrate the audiobooks for best-selling author Wayne Stinnett. Guess where his latest book is set? I promise you, this was a complete coincidence, but when we learned both books were set there, we each put a little "Easter Egg" into our books. Boone and Emily may run into "Stretch" again someday, but this time they were "like two ships passing..."

A quick apology to my readers for the length of time it took to write this book. I began it right after *Deep Cut* was released, but then I had to move to a new place and that threw me for a loop. On the plus side, I'm looking right at the water now... here's hoping the inspiration hits! As I type this, the COVID-19 lockdowns are beginning, so I'll have no excuses. The next book is already percolating.

Another project that took some of my focus last year was the creation of the site "Tropical Authors." We all know that there are plenty of broad categories of fiction—thrillers, action adventure, romance, mystery—that people gravitate to. But if you're reading this book, there's a good chance you're one of the many readers who gravitate toward a *sub*-category of fiction, one where the *setting* is just as important as the genre. Drop by the website and you may discover some new writers to enjoy while you wait for me to "get off my duff" (as Emily would say) and deliver my next. Head over to www.tropicalauthors.com.

We'll be adding more soon, a few at a time, but as I type this afterword we have... let's see... Steven Becker, Chip Bell, David Berens, Kimberli Bindschatel, John Cunningham, Cap Daniels, Evan Graver, Jack Hardin, Nicholas Harvey, Christine Kling, Dawn Lee McKenna, Paul Mila, Chris Niles, Tricia O'Malley, Michael Reisig, Don Rich, Ed Robinson, and Wayne Stinnett. Come on by!

Thank you to all of my beta readers: Lynn Costenaro, Melanie Marks, Chris Sorensen, John Brady, Kevin Carolan, Alan and Joan Zale, Rick Iossi, Mike Ramsey, Dana Vihlen, Patrick Newman, Drew Mutch, Jason Hebert, Deg Priest, and James Cleveland. Many of you have extraordinary backgrounds in diving, boating, and writing and you all kept me accurate and helped me to plump up a few plot points (and "cut the brush back" on some others).

Here's a fun beta reader story. In *Deep Cut*, beta readers John Brady and Chris Sorensen both thought I needed a threatening scene with the Servant earlier in the book. Remember that birdwatcher who died horribly? Named "Chris Brady"? Yeah, that's how I thank people. And once again, John Brady had a scene to suggest in this book. Hey John, did you know "Juan" is the Spanish name for "John"? Thanks for the suggestion, annnnd... you're dead again.

A big thank you to Shayne Rutherford of Wicked Good Book Covers for yet another beautiful cover, Marsha Zinberg of The Write Touch for her on-point editing (you were right in *Cut*, I should have capitalized the "T" in "The Servant"), Colleen Sheehan of Ampersand Book Interiors for her excellent formatting, Kristie Dale Sanders for her interior artwork, and Gretchen Tannert Douglas and Forest Olivier for their keen-eyed proofreading skills. A deep bow to Karl Cleveland for his bang-up job on my DeepNovels.com website. Sorry we didn't get to Palau this year. Pandemics suck.

A huge thank you to Clive Cussler, who passed away on February 24, 2020. No one did more for sea-based thrillers, and I'm sure many of the Tropical Authors grew up on his books. In fact, now that I think of it, the first audiobook I remember listening to was one of his books. As many of you know, I came to writing from my narrating of over five hundred titles. And I came to narrating from my love of audiobooks. There was a show on NPR in a few markets, The Radio Reader with Dick Estell. He would read a half-hour chunk of a book every weekday, and I have a memory of listening to *Vixen 03* in the car with my mother in the parking lot of my elementary school. Thanks, Clive!

And finally, thank you to my readers (and my listeners, you audiobook fans). Your encouragement has meant the world to me, and I'll do my best to have another "Boonemily Book" in your hot little hands sooner rather than later. I already have the answer to Boone's question at the end of *Deep Cut*: "What island?" Stay tuned.

# ABOUT THE AUTHOR

Born in East Tennessee, Nick Sullivan has spent most of his adult life as an actor in New York City working in television, film, theater, and audiobooks. After narrating hundreds of titles over the last couple decades, he decided to write his own. Nick is an avid scuba diver, and his travels to numerous islands throughout the Caribbean have inspired this series.

For a completely different kind of book, you can find Nick Sullivan's first novel at:
**WWW.ZOMBIEBIGFOOT.COM**

Made in the USA
Middletown, DE
26 March 2024